I0670304

# sana's escape

## BOOK ONE IN THE CASIN VILLAGE SERIES

## KITT LYNN

LUPO PUBLISHING

## CONTENT WARNING

This book contains possibly triggering content.

If you are a survivor and need assistance or support, please
call the National Sexual Assault Hotline at
800-656-HOPE (4673)
https://hotline.rainn.org/

If you are in a dangerous situation and need help or
support, please call the National Domestic Abuse Hotline at
800-799-SAFE (7233)
https://www.thehotline.org/

Please do not struggle in silence. You are not alone.
If you need a more detailed list of the triggers within this
book, please reach out to me at misskittlynn@gmail.com.

I don't want to be the reason for someone to be hurt, upset,
or traumatized.

- Kitt -

# the enchanted lands
## of havre

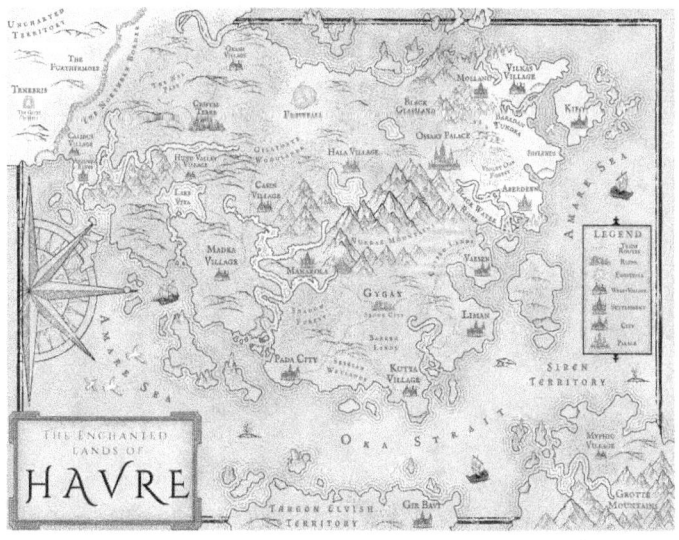

To see a full map of Havre, visit www.kittlynn.com.

*To Louis. My imaginative warrior.*

# the omega origins

IT HAS BEEN SAID THAT HUNDREDS OF YEARS AGO, WEREWOLVES roamed free, dominating the land and all other creatures. Men that easily slipped into their wolf form at will, they were savage and unforgiving. Destroying anything that crossed their paths.

Humans kept their distance from the unhinged animals until a young noblewoman found herself lost in the enchanted forests. A werewolf found her and they fell in love, and she birthed twins. The first Beta and Omega.

The Omega, unable to transform into its wolf, was a gentle creature, fragile and obedient. The perfect mate for the more aggressive Alpha werewolf.

The Beta had more beastly characteristics but could only shift into its wolf when the Moon hung at her fullest. Calm and smart, the child held the perfect balance between human and wolf.

The birth was hard and bloody, and the noblewoman died, her body unable to handle the horrors of birthing beasts. But she left behind a new breed of weres, creating a fragile balance between wolf and man.

The villages grew, bursting with werewolves of all kinds: Alphas, Betas, and Omegas. And soon, the humans realized the wolves finally had a weakness. Their mates, the Omegas.

The humans attacked, slaughtering hundreds of the gentle creatures, pushing werewolves almost to the point of extinction until the fairylands came to their rescue. Fighting the humans and staving them off. Reclaiming Havre as a land of enhancement and magic.

To protect their kind from any further attacks, the Alphas locked their Omegas away in villages fortified with large border walls, shutting them in and keeping them safe.

# CHAPTER ONE

## *the casin gardens*

Sana

———

"SANA!" EMMY WHISPERED FAR TOO LOUDLY, MAKING ME JERK. She pointed in the distance and bounced on the balls of her feet. The movement made her long dark hair swish around her shoulders.

Trying to keep myself hidden, I ducked my head beneath the hedge of pink rose bushes and rushed to her— if she didn't settle down, she was going to get us caught.

"I think he's here!" she squealed. She clapped her hands and motioned to the front of the packhouse again. It was hard to believe the sweet omega was almost an adult. Her soft, child-like energy always made me smile, but not today.

Moving slowly, I peeked over the bushes. A young alpha with tan skin and shaggy dark hair stepped out of a carriage. His father, the Hund Valley Pack alpha, quickly followed. I had met the older alpha, Rollen, when he visited

3

a few years ago, but I had yet to meet his son—my soon-to-be mate, Rin. Our bonding had been arranged practically since birth, but we weren't allowed to meet beforehand. It was "*bad luck.*" I resisted the urge to roll my eyes every time someone reminded me of that fact.

Emmy stared longingly at the Hund Valley wolves, letting out a dreamy sigh. She had no idea the realities of mating a future pack alpha. Their egos and tempers were agony to tolerate, and after spending the last twenty-three years putting up with my father, I wasn't eager to mate one.

"Is that him?" Emmy whispered.

I tucked a strand of my blonde hair behind my ear. "Maybe."

It was him.

*I could feel it.*

But I had convinced Emmy to sneak out to the gardens so we could spend our last day together in the sun. Not to stare at the massive alpha stealing me away from my home.

"I don't know what he looks like," I said honestly, slumping back down and plucking the pink petals off the rose bush next to me.

My dress bunched up a bit from the movement, and I let it stay that way. Nothing enraged my father more than when I wore *revealing* clothing. He insisted my exposed cleavage was risking our alliance with Hund Valley—which only made me want to walk around the market completely bare. If the thought of someone seeing my upper thigh was enough to lessen my worth, then Hund Valley's good opinion was as valuable as my trashy reputation.

"Should we move closer? Get a better look?" Emmy cooed, nuzzling my cheek. *Oh, my heart. I prayed I was doing the right thing.*

"Emmy," I scolded her, leaning away. "Mother would kill me if she knew I was this close."

She craned her neck up, looking over the bushes again. I squished a petal between my fingers, folding it to create dark little creases, then tossed it to the ground. I reached for another flower when movement on the other side of the garden grabbed my attention.

My heart warmed as Rainer pulled a grand mare by a lead across the grounds. The wind whipped the beta's light brown hair into his eyes, carrying his comforting scent toward me. He wasn't a lover—even though everyone thought we were fucking. He was simply my friend. My only true friend, and tonight, he was going to be my savior.

Rainer strolled along, allowing the filly to move at her own pace. Sweat glistened over his muscular chest and abs. I could easily admit he was handsome—all the kitchen staff admired him every chance they got, but I couldn't see past the goofy pup that used to squeal at the top of his lungs when I chased him through the brambles.

Emmy shifted next to me, practically standing to stare at the Hund Valley wolves. I pulled at the hem of her dress, desperate to make her sit. If anyone saw her, we'd both be in big trouble.

"Emmy," I whispered harshly, motioning for her to sit.

She huffed and plopped next to me in the soft grass. "What's wrong?" she pouted. "Why aren't you excited?"

The sweet omega was dangerously innocent sometimes. I reminded myself that she was still a pup. And while I wanted to tell her how unfair this arrangement was, I didn't have the heart to destroy her lovely fantasies. She still believed in love.

"Please, Sana," she whispered, pushing into my side. "Tell me what's wrong."

I pushed out a heavy sigh, brushing a few crumbled petals off the front of my dress. "I just don't want to do this." I shouldn't have even said that much, but I couldn't help myself. My wolf squirmed, uneasy within me. She was growing more restless lately, and it was getting very hard to control her. It was *always* hard to control her.

"Why not?" Emmy asked, her voice way too fucking loud.

"Sana? Omega Emmy?"

My sister flinched at the deep voice and trembled. I cut her a glare. I knew my father's guards would eventually find us missing, but I had hoped we'd have until sunset before we were found.

Emmy let out a delicate whimper and mouthed a quick *"sorry."*

Defeated, I rolled my eyes and stood up. "Lieutenant Andrus," I huffed at the pissy guard.

"Sana!" he barked, his voice practically echoing through the quiet garden. "Where is—"

Emmy slowly stood up next to me, and he narrowed his eyes at her. His pointed features were particularly tight today. It made me want to rip his throat out for looking at Emmy with so much anger. Omegas were much more sensitive than other wolves and needed kindness and understanding more than discipline, despite what my father and his belt insisted.

Andrus let out an angry groan, then motioned for us to follow. He spun toward the packhouse, marching as if expecting us to fall into formation behind him. He looked like shit. His usually slicked-back hair was unkempt, and his face was sweaty. I wanted to laugh out loud at the thought of him running all over the grounds trying to find us.

He was such an ass. He deserved the headache.

We entered the packhouse through the side door, ensuring I wouldn't run into my soon-to-be mate. Andrus, as always, walked through the hallways like he owned the fucking place. I hated how my father favored him. It only emboldened Andrus to act like the rules of conduct didn't apply to him. He always bordered on disrespectful when speaking to me, and was way too familiar with Emmy.

Andrus reached the parlor and flung the door open. His gray eyes narrowed at me, then they moved to focus past me.

I glanced over my shoulder, expecting to see Emmy, but she was still standing at the other end of the hallway. She stared down a long corridor with her hands clasped under her chin. The dreamy look in her eyes was noticeable even from here.

Andrus cleared his throat roughly, and Emmy jumped about a foot in the air.

She raced past me into the room. Andrus's gaze lingered on my sister as she edged past him and he inhaled deeply. It set my wolf on edge. Feeling the need to provoke that asshole, I strolled in slowly, purposefully taking my time. Andrus pressed his lips into a thin line as I passed, and I smiled wide.

The moment I entered the room, Andrus pushed the door shut with a sharp snap. His wolf was clearly begging to break free, and it took everything in me not to smirk. I loved watching weak-willed alphas struggle to control their beasts. It calmed me to know other alphas fought with their wolves too, and it wasn't just me. But, this time, I was too annoyed to laugh.

"I get it," I huffed, plopping down into an overstuffed

chair. "We fucked up, but there's no need to stand inside the room. We'll stay put."

"You'll forgive me if I don't believe you," he gritted out.

I flashed my teeth at his tone, and he turned toward me, meeting my glare head-on. My wolf bristled at his challenge, longing for him to act on his anger. I reminded her that neither one of us could win a fight against a trained guard. But that didn't stop me from narrowing my eyes a bit more at the asshole. After a few moments, Andrus looked away, staring at the wall again. *Pathetic*.

"Andrus!" I snapped, struggling to stay calm and polite. "My sister and I don't have much time together. I want time *alone* with her before I depart for Hund Valley tomorrow. Leave."

He hooked his thumbs into his belt, looking at me with so much misplaced superiority. "Your father ordered me to watch you. I let my guard down, and you both disappeared. The Pack Alpha would have my head if he knew, and I will *not* be fool enough to let either one of you out of my sight again."

"I don't give a shit what my father ordered. I want to be alone with my sister. Get out." I stood, pushing myself to full height and squaring my shoulders. I was done with his shit. I was required to listen to my father, but not his fucking guards.

"You should be kept as far away from your sister as possible," Andrus snarled, stepping toward me. "It's a blessing that you'll be gone soon."

"What the fuck does that mean?" My wolf edged forward, licking her fangs.

"Your wicked attitude and loose tongue are a horrible example for Emmy." Andrus glanced at my sister before returning his small gray eyes to me. "You may be comfortable mouthing off to every alpha who comes your way, but to do it in front of her is reckless. One wrong word to the wrong wolf, and Omega Emmy could be killed in the blink of an eye. You should be teaching her how to hold her tongue, not wield it like a blade!"

"*I'm* a horrible example?" I laughed, pressing my palm to my chest. "Emmy? Did you hear that? I'm a horrible example. All the shit wolves in this packhouse, and *I'm* the fucking problem." I continued to laugh.

My parents were by far the worst alphas to have ever lived, but, to this guard, I was horrible for having a fucking opinion. I would need to thank him later for the best laugh I'd had in years.

"Andrus," I let out a satisfied sigh, "what I do or don't do, say or don't say in front of Emmy is none of your business. Now, fuck off."

He took a careful step toward me, testing me with his every movement, but I held firm, keeping my smile in place. If he thought he could intimidate me into submission, he had another thing coming.

"You think because you're a member of the Pack Alpha's family, you can't be put in your place?" the guard seethed. It was clear he wanted his tone to command the room, but he sounded more whiny than anything else. "Be careful, Sana. One day you'll really piss off the wrong wolf, and there will be no one to save your pampered ass."

"How dare you speak to me like that!" I growled, curling my fists tight.

"S-stop!" Emmy sobbed, trembling under a mountain of pillows on the couch.

Guilt hit me hard, and I rushed to her side. Snuggling

9

her close, I wrapped her up in my arms and rocked her gently. My wolf snarled at me for upsetting her. "I'm so sorry, sweetheart."

Emmy pushed herself into my hair, and I narrowed my eyes at Andrus, daring him to say something. He sucked in a deep breath before moving back to his post by the door.

"Sana! Emmy!" my mother's shrill voice cut through the door like a blade. Andrus jumped to open it like a good dog.

My mother shimmied her way into the room, her slim figure commanding and cold. She wore one of her favorite dresses with matching teal jewelry, and her hair was pulled into a bun so tight, her forehead struggled to move.

"It's getting late," she said flatly, "and you both need your rest for tomorrow. Go to your rooms."

Emmy leaned away from me, glancing out the window before slowly standing. I kept my place on the couch, waiting to hear what my mother actually wanted. It was far too early for bed, and she only forced Emmy to her room when she didn't want to deal with her anymore.

"Sana," the she-alpha said in an overly sweet tone, "walk with me." She turned to the still seething guard. "Andrus, take Emmy to her room."

Emmy shuffled slowly across the parlor, ducking her head as she passed Andrus, then our mother. I wanted to hug the omega, squeeze her, love her, then promise her she wouldn't be suffering these assholes much longer.

Not wanting to give anything away, I fixed my face and swallowed down my emotions. They settled heavy in my gut like a fat stone. I stood and walked toward my mother, my eyes staying on Emmy's back for as long as possible. I couldn't help but wonder if she would be upset when I woke her tonight. *Would she want to leave with me?*

She didn't know it yet, but we were escaping this hell-hole. By this time tomorrow, we would be on the other side of the mountains. Far away from Casin, Hund Valley, and everything in between.

# CHAPTER TWO

## *the parlor*

Sana

---

"I simply do not understand how anyone can crave trouble as much as you do." My mother narrowed her eyes. They were the same deep brown as both my sister's and older brother's. Part of me wished Emmy had blue eyes like me so I wouldn't be forced to think of my sweet sister every time my mother looked at me. I wanted to keep them completely separate. My heart and my torment, in no way related. But it was those brown eyes that had made me bow to my mother's will on more than one occasion.

Mother ran her long fingers over her teal bracelet, spinning it slowly in place. "Would you like to confess your crimes now? Or would you prefer the hard way?"

I kept my mouth shut. Confessing never meant a reprieve, and I had no idea what she thought I had done wrong. So I stared back at her, not saying a word.

"The hard way then," she snipped. She inhaled deeply,

and her upper lip curled. "What the hell have you gotten into today?" I tensed, ready for her to insult me yet again. "You smell awful."

I narrowed my eyes, not in the mood. She was constantly telling me I smelled bad—sharp and bitter. Emmy insisted she was just a jerk and I smelled lovely, but between Mother's harsh words and the whispers I occasionally heard from the guards, it was hard to know if she was telling the truth or not.

"Come." Mother turned and marched off, making her long dress swish.

I knew she meant for me to follow—and I thought briefly of draping myself over the couch to provoke her—but when she couldn't control me, she took it out on Emmy. Swallowing down my growing anxiety, I followed the wicked woman down the hall, through several corridors, and toward the kitchens. She didn't turn to look at me or speak—she just pulled me along, her anger a thread anchoring me to her incredibly straight back. She pulled every inch she could find out of her spine.

Even though supper had already passed, the kitchens were still very busy. The staff of betas were busy prepping the feast for after the ceremony. My eyes moved over the flurry of activity, settling on one of the cooks. Her wiry gray hair stuck out from beneath her bonnet as she mixed a big batch of cinnamon apples with her hands. Glancing up, her eyes fell on my commanding mother, and she jerked, returning to her task with renewed vigor.

"Sana," Mother barked.

Understanding her sharp tone, I quickened my pace, following her down the long stone corridor to the cellar. The flat gray rocks radiated a chill that made the hair on my arms stand up. Mother rested her long fingers on the brass doorknob, then turned to me. Holding her head high, she clenched her jaw, but her eyes didn't feel right. There was a trace of something almost sad within them. *It set me on edge.*

"Just know, your father wanted to do much worse, but I wouldn't allow him," she said, lowering her gaze to the floor. She looked almost submissive, and my wolf snarled. *This was a trick.*

I squared my shoulders, and my wolf whimpered loudly, frightened of what was coming next. I could already tell I wouldn't be able to rely on my beast. While she felt strong today, I couldn't get her to shift on the best of days, and right now, she was just too damn scared.

Mother turned the brass knob and pulled the wooden door open. It creaked loudly as a gust of cold air rushed into the corridor. The dull scent of dirt and oak fanned my hair, followed quickly by the sharp tang of blood.

My nose wasn't what it should be for an alpha. It was something that pained me to admit, but the fact that I could smell blood so clearly meant there had to be a *lot* of it.

My wolf mewled, and I snapped my eyes to my mother. I waited for her to tell me what was waiting at the bottom of the stairs, but she kept her dark eyes fixated on the wall. Whatever was down there, she didn't enjoy it, and my mother enjoyed all manner of punishment.

Shoving down my fear, I stepped inside the cellar. The door pushed shut, the metal latching in place. It echoed off the walls, making the hair on the back of my neck stand on end. I walked slowly down the rough steps. Dirt ground into the soles of my feet, and my face cooled as the temperature dropped.

I reached the bottom step and inhaled deeply, trying to steady myself. The muted scent of sweat and blood filled my lungs. There were a few alphas down here; I couldn't tell who, but only one of them scared me.

I cleared my throat, trying to sound strong, "Father."

Standing on the other side of the room, he stared down a long row of shelves. Casks of wine and massive barrels of whisky blocked my view. But the unmistakable sound of a fist connecting with flesh pricked my ears, and I froze, listening hard.

"Why is it," my father said in his deep, gruff voice, "that you can never just do what you're fucking told?" He turned his head, finally looking at me. He hitched his thumbs into his belt, his big barrel chest making him look twice the size of a normal alpha.

"Since the day you were born," he continued, "you have been determined to ruin this family."

I wanted to cross my arms and shield myself from his red glare, but I kept them at my sides, refusing to fidget or even blink.

"This mating with the Hund Valley wolf is going to happen," he said as if issuing a command. "And I'm getting sick and fucking tired of reminding you of that fact."

A smack of flesh and a pained grunt echoed around me. My wolf sat up, needing to hear the voice again. *It was familiar.*

"You and Rin have been arranged since you were pups, and if you think for one moment I will allow you to embarrass—"

"What is it you want, Father?" I said loudly, hoping he couldn't scent my growing distress.

The muscle in his jaw ticked, and another grunt hit the air. "I just want your loyalty." A wicked smirk pulled at one side of his face, then he slowly took a single step to the side.

My eyes moved down his intimidating form, settling on

an object just behind him. On the floor, near the wall, sat a small brown leather bag with a tuft of bright blue feathers tied to the strap. Ice tipped into my veins, and my heart pounded wildly in my chest. I spent weeks deciding what was necessary to pack in that tiny bag, then I gave it to Rainer for him to hide in the stables. He swore no one would be able to find it.

*How did my father get it?*

Another pained grunt hit the air, and my feet moved. I ran at full speed at my father, toward the sound. I rounded the wooden shelf of wine, then came to an abrupt stop. All the air whooshed out of me, and I jerked as if being punched in the gut.

Rainer hung from the ceiling by a barrel hook. His hands were blue, and his naked body was covered in fresh welts and dark blood—it poured from his mouth, nose, and the deep cuts that littered his pale skin. I jerked to run to the beta, but before I could make it even one step, a big arm wrapped firmly around my waist and jerked me back.

"Let me go!" I screamed. My father ignored me, his vise-like grip staying firmly in place.

Two guards stood on either side of Rainer's limp body, but I couldn't focus on them. All I could see was my friend. He choked, forcing out a spray of blood, then he slowly tipped his head up.

"Rain!" I twisted, trying to free myself. My father's arms tightened around my ribs, making my eyes water. I scratched at his hands and wrists with my nails, cursing my useless beast for not letting me have my claws.

"Fucking the help is one thing," Father snarled in my ear, "but running away with them," he clicked his tongue, "that will *not* do."

I opened my mouth to plead for Rainer's life, but before I could speak, my wolf burst out of me.

Muscle and bone twisted and popped into place, my shift far too fast and painful...*like always*. My black pelt was too smooth for my father to hold on to, and I slipped onto the cool floor with a thump.

I scrambled quickly onto my paws, then launched myself at one of the guards. I aimed for his throat, but his arm blocked me, and I bit down hard, feeling the bone snap. Someone grabbed my scruff and threw me hard into a stack of heavy barrels. My body hit with a crunch, my ribs connecting hard with the lip of a barrel. Something deep in my side snapped, and I yelped loudly.

Before I could stand, my father grabbed me by the scruff and wrapped the other big hand around my snout. I whined and jerked, swiping at him with my heavy claws, but I had no training, and my wolf was too small for such a mighty alpha—even in his human form.

He lifted me easily out of the splintered whiskey-soaked wood, then jerked my neck hard. "Shift!" he barked.

I narrowed my red eyes at him and tried to growl, but the sound was muted with his hand pushing hard into my throat. He shoved my snout down and pushed his face even closer to mine. "Shift," he whispered, baring his long, pointed teeth.

I shivered, pulling black fur back into my skin. My bones ground together, forcing their way back into position. The pain in my side burned, flashing up and down my body. I ignored it, staring hard into my father's eyes. He snarled right back at me, his upper lip curling at my pointed glare.

Jerking the hair at the back of my skull, my father forced my head to turn toward Rain. The beta's eyes were wide and glazed with tears, but he wasn't scared for himself. It was all for me.

"Sana," he whispered, his voice holding no strength. "I'm so sorry."

Not wanting my father to hear the pain in my voice, I mouthed a silent "*me too*."

Rain smiled, and a few tears fell down his blood-soaked face. I should have been the one crying, but I couldn't. It wasn't allowed. Weakness was never allowed.

"End it," my father ordered.

There was no point in begging or screaming.

I kept my eyes locked with Rain's, not focusing on anything else other than the deep honey color. A soft moment of silence settled between us as one of the guards moved. It was private and lovely and horrifically painful.

And then it was over.

Rainer's face contorted, and his mouth hung open in a silent scream. My eyes moved down his body as long claws slipped into his gut and tore all the way down to his groin. His innards pushed against the seam of torn flesh, his abdomen bulging with guts and gushing blood.

I couldn't look away. *The stars help me.* I couldn't blink or scream or move.

My father released me, and I fell forward onto the cold, gritty floor. My fingers brushed a bit of soft fabric, and I balled the tattered remains of my dress up in my fist.

I sat there, staring at my friend. Weak and useless.

Rain's expression was so soft. I could almost believe he was resting. But there was no life in his eyes. His body twisted slightly, and the ropes that held his wrists in place creaked. His hands were an unnatural shade of blue-ish gray, and a bit of blood dripped from two fingers. It caught in the dim light, making the vibrant crimson color shimmer.

It was all I could see. *Red dripping from tight, dead flesh.*

"Sana," my father growled my name, making me snap my eyes to him. He stood just next to Rainer's body, looking the corpse over. He turned his narrowed eyes to me. *More red.* Everything was red. The floor, the walls, the ceiling. It was even splattered over the dusty bottles of wine.

"Go to your room," he commanded.

I stared at him in shock, unable to move and refusing to blink. He almost sounded casual, as if he were disciplining me for sneaking out after curfew.

The heat in my father's angry gaze intensified, and his fists tightened. "Go!" he roared.

My knees shook as I stood, but I locked them in place, forcing my head high and my shoulders back. I dragged my eyes over Rainer's face one last time, then paused, taking a moment to look at the two guards who had beaten and killed my only friend.

I wasn't surprised to see Kade, one of my father's closest advisors. The alpha held his bloody, broken arm loose at his side, refusing to meet my glare. While I didn't really know Kade that well, he was a constant presence in the packhouse. I had known him since I was a pup.

The other guard, Tamen, tipped his chin up, looking almost proud. His arms and chest were spattered with blood, and his pants were soaked almost black with it. Our eyes met, and deep, animalistic rage pulsed in my veins. He might have been the only alpha in this fucking village I hated more than my father.

"You will pay for this," I said as loudly as my failing voice would allow. I glared at each one, then settled on my father. "You will all pay for what you've done."

# CHAPTER THREE
## *the market*

Cyrus

---

"You okay?" I asked Tallis, wrapping my hand around his wrist.

He gave a slight jerk of his head and grunted out something that sounded like "*yes.*"

He was such a shit liar.

Tallis scanned the crowded market, acting as if we were surrounded by a bloodthirsty battalion and not a mix of alphas and betas leisurely shopping. I couldn't help but notice there wasn't a single omega in sight. I seemed to be the only one.

"We'll be fast," I said, trying to soothe my obviously distressed mate. "No one knows. Just hold on to the bag, and it'll be okay." I smoothed my hand over the wide, flat strap across his muscular chest, making sure it covered the juncture of his shoulder and neck. Thankfully, the strap concealed the mark beneath it well.

"Cyrus," Tallis growled, keeping his dark brown eyes on our surroundings, "*I'm* the alpha. I don't need my omega treating me like a fucking pup."

His chin jutted out slightly, and I had to resist the urge to poke the small dimple in the center. Wrapping my arms around his waist, I rested my chin on his chest and looked up at him. He was so tall, a full head taller than most alphas, with long, dark-blond hair and a soft layer of stubble.

"I just like to fuss," I whispered, keeping my tone light. "Maybe we should go to the tavern. Enjoy a pint? It would be nice to pretend to be normal for a change."

He shook his head, still not taking his eyes off the crowd. "No. I can't risk it." He pressed his hand over the strap, making sure it was in place. After several moments of taking in the entire area, he finally looked down at me. Slowly, the corners of his mouth relaxed. I stuck my tongue out and scrunched my nose, and he gifted me a proper smile.

"I'm fine," he said, his tone a little more at ease. He wrapped his arm around my shoulders and gently squeezed me. "I promise I'm fine."

I walked slowly next to Tallis, his footsteps deliberate and forced. In truth, I was just as on edge as he was. Sneaking into villages was so dangerous we never risked it before. But the bustle of an obvious village-wide celebration made it easy to hide amongst the busy crowd. Pack members hung paper lanterns, fixed poles with colorful ribbons, and made last minute purchases at the quickly closing shops.

Tallis guided me sideways toward the blacksmith. He abruptly stopped when a few guards crossed our path. His grip on the strap tightened, and I placed my hand on his impressive biceps, not allowing myself to breathe until the guards were gone.

A sharp scream made my heart squeeze as I spun toward the sound. A handful of squealing pups chased each other, laughing at the top of their lungs. A few elders scolded them from the comfort of a porch, insisting they get their butts back inside. I let out a nervous laugh, trying to urge my heart to calm. Just as I turned back to Tallis, a massive guard in a dark green uniform smacked into my shoulder, making me jerk and stumble.

Tallis instantly reacted, stepping in front of me to shield me from the unknown alpha.

"Watch where you're fucking going!" He bared his teeth at the guard. The chatter around us eased, and a few wolves stopped what they were doing to watch.

A long scar ran across the guard's cheek and the bridge of his nose. He smirked, flashing sharp teeth. "He ran into me." The buttons on his shirt pulled tight as he crossed his arms.

Tallis jerked toward him, and I grabbed my mate's arm, pulling as hard as I could. His big body stayed firmly in place. "Let it go," I begged. "I'm fine; let's just go."

He needed to calm himself before we were recognized.

I pushed as much urgency through our bond as I could, but Tallis remained immobile, glaring hard at the guard. My fear spiked, and I jerked on his arm again.

The guard narrowed his eyes at me, then inhaled deeply. I could tell he was confused by my scent. It was a look I was used to. I didn't look like a typical omega. I was tall, the same size as a beta, and while lean, I had a decent amount of muscle. But my scent and mannerisms always gave me away.

"What the fuck is an omega doing in the market?" the

scarred alpha asked loudly, glaring hard at my mate. The guard gripped my upper arm as if trying to pull me away from Tallis, and panic burst in my chest. "Are you *trying* to tempt someone into stealing him?"

"Don't you *fucking* touch him," Tallis growled, shoving the guard hard. He released me, and I rushed to Tallis's side, praying to the Moon he'd just walk away. "You touch him again, and I'll rip your fucking arm off."

"Get him the fuck out of here!" The guard's temper flared, and I took a step back, a little shocked. Everyone around me seemed to zero in on my face, like my simple presence was offensive. "He has no place out in the open. Do you want him snatched and fucked—"

Before my mind could even register the movement, Tallis's fist connected hard with the alpha's face. The guard's head popped back, and his knees gave out, making him fall ass-backward into the dirt.

Using every ounce of strength in my body, I pulled at Tallis's arm, urging him to run, but he still didn't move. He loomed over the guard with tight fists and an angry glare. My mate was looking for a fight, and, knowing him, he'd do anything to get it.

The scarred guard stood up and spit a bit of blood onto the ground. He popped his neck then widened his stance. "Fucking asshole," he snarled.

A shift in the crowd made me look over my shoulder. Five more guards, all alphas, marched straight for us. Their red eyes glowed bright in the quickly setting sun.

Desperate, I grabbed a handful of Tallis's long blond hair and jerked with all my might. His eyes widened with shock as I forced him to look at me. I quickly tilted my head to the side. "Guards."

Tallis's eyes went wide, and he wrapped his arms

23

around me, holding me protectively. He turned to run, but before we could take a single step, the scarred alpha moved, blocking our path.

My wolf roared within me as my fear grew, but I didn't have time to panic. Not now. I sucked in a deep breath, tensed my shoulders, then sprinted right at the fucker. Aiming low, I shoved my shoulder right into the unsuspecting guard's ribs, making the alpha stumble back.

I didn't stop or look behind me.

Tallis's warm scent and heavy footsteps told me he was just at my back. He could have easily passed me as we raced toward the village gates, but he was shielding my back from any threat. Betas scrambled to get out of our way; some yelled out for us to stop, while others cheered and clapped. I let out a quick laugh and pumped my arms and legs faster, the warm summer air whipping my hair into my eyes.

The lone guard stationed at the gate took a step to the side, letting us run out of the village. I picked up my pace, thankful they weren't going to waste their time trying to catch us for causing minor ruckus. And, honestly, who cared who *left* a village? It was the monsters who tried to enter who were the real problem.

We ran toward the trees as fast as we could—or as fast as *I* could. I broke the tree line first then cut left. Racing through a few miles of trees and hills, I didn't stop until I finally came to a familiar cut of land. I leaned against a mighty pine, holding the stitch in my side and panting hard.

Tallis rested his hands on his knees, then laughed. His deep rumble filled the air, making me smile. His muscular chest rose and fell with a sheen of sweat highlighting the beautiful grooves of his abs. His long hair was wild, falling into his eyes and caressing the scars along the top of his broad shoulders.

*Fuck, he was beautiful.*

I opened my mouth to tell him, but before I could, he slammed into me, pushing his hips forward. His thick member settled against my stomach, and I moaned loudly. I swore, if he were any harder, his cock would cut through his pants.

Channeling his fingers through my hair, Tallis kissed me with a possessive strength that made my spine tingle and balls tight. I loved him like this. *Wild and possessive.* His fingers curled a little tighter, making my scalp sting in the best way.

"Ride my cock," he commanded in his alpha voice. There was no need, but I still loved it.

I nodded weakly at my mate, but he was already ripping my pants down my legs. I was so hard and wet, desperate to have him inside me.

Tallis moved to drop to his knees, but I stopped him. "No." I turned and hugged the nearest tree, pushing my ass out. "I need you. *Now.*"

A teasing glint sparkled in his eyes as he unbuttoned his pants. His member jutted from his hips, straining toward me, thick and proud. Staring over my shoulder at my beautiful alpha, I licked my lips as a drop of precum glistened in the last rays of the setting sun. It took everything in me not to turn around and suck it right off his beautiful cock.

"Is this tight little hole ready for me?" he growled, palming my cheeks and spreading me painfully open.

"Yes," I said, my voice breathy.

"I'll be the judge of that." He leaned down and pushed his tongue deep into my ass, feasting on my slick.

I tipped my head back, falling into the sensation of my

mate's tongue sucking and flicking my rim. His mouth disappeared but was quickly replaced by three long, thick fingers. He pushed into me, and I groaned at the brief burn. He moved my slick in and around my rim, filling the quiet forest with wet, squelching sounds. Once his fingers moved freely, gliding in and out, he stood and lined himself up.

Then he drove into me.

I gasped as his cock breached me, sinking inch by inch into my desperate body. We had been together for years, but fucking him was like the first time every time. His dirty praises and powerful body drove me wild, and nothing tasted sweeter than his cum.

"Fuck, Cy," Tallis growled. "This little hole sucks me up so good."

I nodded, the base of my spine already tingling with my building orgasm.

Circling his big arm around my waist, Tallis grabbed my cock, stroking me in time with his hips. He set a brutal pace, fucking me just the way I liked: hard and deep, jerking my body with each savage thrust.

He squeezed the head of my cock, then slammed right into my prostate. Heat shot up my spine as I tried to hold off from coming, but it was pointless. He knew exactly how to touch me. His knot, pressed right up against my rim, started to expand. I clenched around him as he pressed harder, trying to force it in.

"Let me knot you," he snarled against my shoulder.

I shook my head but couldn't form any words. I was sitting on the edge of my orgasm, my balls tight and my cock pulsing in his hand. He pressed his hips harder to my hips, his knot nudging its way into me.

"Let me fucking knot you," he growled, grabbing a fistful of my hair and pulling me flush with his chest.

Knotting me wasn't smart. We were exposed, and being stuck together in such an intimate way could be deadly if we were being followed.

"I...ugh...Tallis!"

He pegged my prostate especially hard, then sank his fangs deep into my shoulder. Cum burst from my cock, splattering across the tree and ground. Tallis snapped his hips forward, popping his knot past my rim, sealing us together. My pained gasp was muted over his guttural roar as he came long and hard inside me.

My knees gave out, and Tallis wrapped both arms around me, holding me up. He rolled his hips forward, milking every drop of his orgasm. Cum and slick pushed out around his thick knot and down the back of my legs. It was warm and sticky, making me wish we were near a stream.

"Fuck," he whispered against the back of my neck. "Fuck. Cyrus. *Fuck.*"

"I told you not to knot me, you asshole," I mumbled. I wanted to sound angry, but I just sounded drunk. My balls still tingled with lingering pleasure, and my legs were numb. In truth, I felt too damn good to be mad.

"I'm sorry," he whispered, kissing his mating bite just beneath my ear. His cock pulsed inside me, and I hissed.

"No, you're not." I laid my head back on his shoulder, pressing our cheeks together. His breath fanned over my skin, making goosebumps rise over my neck and down my chest. "If someone were to find us right now, we'd both be dead."

He nuzzled against the crook of my neck, scenting and kissing me. "To die balls deep in your ass would be such a way to go."

I snorted. "What am I going to do with you?" I reached

27

back, cupping the back of his head to hold him to me. "I can't believe you hit that guard. What were you thinking?"

"He touched you." He pressed his big hands flat against my chest, holding me a little tighter. It felt so safe and wonderful. My big, protective alpha.

I smoothed my hands over his. "I still need to have my dagger fixed, but we can't go back to that village."

"That's okay," he said, trying to sound like it didn't matter.

But it did.

As an omega, I couldn't shift into my wolf, which made me more vulnerable than others out here. The wildlands were filled with rogue alphas that would gut a wolf for a well-made shirt, or even out of simple boredom. Tallis couldn't be by my side at all times, and I didn't want him to be. I was strong and could hold my own in a fight, but not against an alpha in his wolf form. I needed to be able to protect myself. I needed my dagger.

"We'll figure out how to fix your blade without going back to the village," he said, kissing my shoulder. "There's nothing for us in Casin anyways."

# CHAPTER FOUR

## *sana's room*

Sana

---

I HAD NO MEMORY OF LEAVING THE CELLAR, WALKING THROUGH the packhouse, or sitting down on my bed. I couldn't even remember who dressed me in the oversized shirt that was hanging off my shoulders.

The sound of running water from the washroom made me tense. I hoped it wasn't my mother. I couldn't stand to see her bitter, pointed face right now. I didn't have the strength.

Trying to steady myself, I gripped the thick pink quilt beneath me. My wolf whimpered hard, begging me to hide, but I was too exhausted and numb. Unwilling to give up, my beast clawed at the inside of my chest, urging my feet to move. I squeezed my eyes shut, wishing just once our desires could be in sync.

The washroom door swung open, and my brother's big body emerged. I instantly released a long breath. Davon was shirtless, and his dark hair—the same chestnut color as Emmy's—was wet with sweat, hanging into his eyes. He looked like he had just come from the sparring grounds.

He crossed the room, holding out the damp cloth. "You reek of drink," Davon said.

I turned my head slightly and sniffed my hair that fell over my shoulder. The sharp scent of whiskey burned my nose.

"Did you just scent yourself?" Davon shook his head in disbelief. "The stink is flooding the room. There is something wrong with your wolf."

"There's nothing fucking wrong with my wolf, and don't you ever say it again," I snarled, hating the fact that my fangs wouldn't engage. My wolf was too busy wallowing to act like a real fucking alpha right now.

Davon held out the rag again, but I turned away from it. I would sit with Rainer's blood on my skin until it soaked through to my bones.

Annoyed with my defiance, my brother grabbed my chin, then set about scrubbing my face. I swiped at him with a clawed hand, catching his cheek. He grabbed my wrists and jerked me to my feet. I snarled, prepared to take whatever shit he had to offer.

"You're lucky you're pampered, San," he snarled, shoving me back down onto my bed. "You could never make it out there by yourself. Your wolf's got no real fight."

My beast whimpered with me, suddenly wounded and sad. I ripped the rag from my brother's hand and threw it onto the floor. It hit with a wet smack. "Like you'd fucking know," I bit back with just as much vitriol. "You're just as soft as I am, or has Father not reminded you of that today?"

Davon took a slow step back, the muscles in his jaw flexing. It wasn't fair of me to attack him, but the need to destroy something, to make someone feel as shitty as I did, pushed hard on my shoulders.

"Is there something you need, Davon?" I tipped my head back, issuing a very clear challenge. "Because if you're done, get out. I don't need you or your assessment of my wolf."

He crossed his arms over his bare chest, taking his time to look over my face. His gaze fell to my hands, and he pushed a heavy sigh from his nose.

"I'm sorry about Rainer," he said. "He was a good beta. A good friend."

"Get out," I whispered, turning away from him.

"I understand why you want to run away."

I balled up my fists, wishing I had the strength to beat him senseless. Even though I was an alpha, I was small compared to most, and my lack of muscle made me a joke among my kind. Not that anyone mocked me to my face. Fear of my father's wrath was very real. But it didn't stop me from feeling their judgment every time I entered a room.

"There's no escaping your duty," Davon continued, "and I've met the Hund Valley wolves. Rin seems like a good alpha. You could do worse."

I jerked at his words. "Don't you dare lecture me on duty. You've been allowed freedoms I've only dreamed of. I'm nothing more than a prized pig put on display and traded to the highest bidder."

"This alliance will strengthen Casin. The weapons and gold Hund Valley is providing in this trade…" He shook his head as if it was ridiculous I couldn't see how wonderful it all was. "Our little village has far too many enemies at our door. Hund Valley will keep us armed, and, in turn, we can continue to keep all of Havre safe. You owe it to our people—"

"I don't owe anyone a single fucking thing," I snapped. "I—"

The unmistakable sound of my mother's footsteps echoing down the hallway cut me off. The soft placement of her toes followed by the forceful smack of her heel wasn't normal, but it was a welcome warning of her presence.

Davon grabbed the wet cloth off the floor then pushed it into my hand. "Collect yourself before she sees."

"Sees what?" I asked, not understanding.

"Your tears," he said pointedly.

Confused, I took the rag from him, then touched my face. He was right. My cheeks were wet, but I couldn't remember crying. I quickly scrubbed. The rough fabric was cold, scratching at my skin. When I pulled it back, the amount of red that had soaked through the once white cloth made my heart race. There was also blood under my nails and dried in the creases of my palms. The splatter of red continued under my sleeves, but I didn't push them up to look.

The door creaked open, and I turned to the noise. The second my mother's face appeared, Davon cast his eyes to the floor, and I quickly followed suit.

"Are we feeling better?" she asked in an overly light tone.

Her maid, Mallin, slipped in behind her. The elderly beta set a tray with a small teacup on it next to me. She smiled sweetly before backing away. I never really spoke to the beta; she worked for my mother, but I always felt bad for her. It must have been hell to spend so much time with someone so horrible.

Mallin bowed low to me then to my mother as she

slowly backed out of the room. Her loose gray bun bobbed as she scuffled backward, finally disappearing out the door.

Leaning forward, I scented the steam drifting off the teacup. The slight earthy scent contrasted wildly with the overly sweet taste, but just the sight of it made my wolf instantly calm. Mother always forced it down my throat when she felt I was being unruly—which was frequent. Pretty much every night. It helped settle my nerves, so I rarely fought it, but today I wanted to push it onto the floor.

"Are you finally ready to stop all this nonsense and act like an adult?"

"Act like an adult?" I whispered with complete disgust at her ridiculous choice of words.

The way her long fingers curled around her narrow hips made her look ready to scold me for sneaking sweets before dinner. It was as if she had no idea I'd just seen my oldest and dearest friend murdered. But she knew. She always knew the horrid things my father did.

"You are twenty-three years old," she snipped in a tight, overly formal tone. She was holding back, but I wanted her to lash out. I wanted an excuse to hit the wretched woman and make her feel just as awful as I did. "It's high time you start acting your age. Your duty is to mate that Hund Valley wolf and provide him pups. And I will be damned if I let you ruin our pack by running off with the fucking stable boy." She didn't yell, but she didn't need to. She was the kind of alpha who didn't tolerate any tests of her authority.

If she wasn't such a hateful creature, I might have admired her.

"Now," she sighed hard, crossing the room to my wardrobe, "I know you probably aren't in the mood, but Alpha Rollen has requested to meet with you tonight. He wants to bless your bonding tomorrow. Apparently, his pack is big on prayer."

She pulled out a purple dress, admiring the detail along the high collar and long sleeves. "Davon, leave." She placed the dress on the bed next to me. "Sana needs to get ready."

He gave our mother a quick bow, then left without a word. I wanted to mock him for acting like a frightened mouse in her presence, but I was no different. Any time she dismissed us, we always ran as if our lives depended on it.

Mother picked up the paddle hairbrush off my vanity, stalking toward me like the predator she was. She pressed her palm to the top of my head, then jerked the brush through the tangled, bloody mess. I stayed completely silent, not giving her the satisfaction of knowing it hurt.

"Drink your tea," she commanded, ripping through several knots.

Gripping the edge of the tray, I slowly pulled it to me. The delicate blue and white china tinkled as it moved. I stared at two cream-colored petals shaped like withered hearts that floated on the surface. They swayed with the liquid like leaves on a pond. It all looked so delicate and proper in my still bloody hand.

*I wanted to throw the fucking cup across the room.*

As if sensing my desire, my mother raised a perfectly manicured brow, silently challenging me to do it. Her voice dropped dangerously low as she asked, "How do you want your night to end, Sana?"

My wolf whimpered at her dominant glare, urging me to cower and submit. My beast's treacherous urge enraged me to no end. She was supposed to be my rock, the vicious driving force inside me, but right now—despite the rage pulsing in my veins—my beast was lapping her wounds like a fucking omega, and my worthless body trembled right along with her. I hated how much control my wolf had over my human form.

Slowly, I picked up the teacup, and my fingers trembled as I brought it to my lips. The sweet liquid spread across my tongue, instantly calming me. I liked the familiar, slightly bitter taste it left on the back of my tongue. I took another sip, and warmth bloomed from my chest, spreading outward like a fog. It made it so damn hard to hang on to my rage.

Mother smiled, nodding with approval.

I relaxed my hand, letting the teacup fall. It landed on the plush carpet with a soft thud, the sweet brown liquid turning the pale blue carpet a deep color.

I tipped my chin up. "Oops."

"You know," she grabbed a thick chunk of my hair and jerked my head to the side, "I think Hund Valley will be very good for you." She pushed the paddle brush into my scalp then jerked down. Pain rippled across my skull, and I struggled not to tear up. "I think they'll teach you to appreciate the things you have, and what you've been given."

Without thinking, I gripped her arm, stopping her from placing the brush back on my head.

"What have I been given?" I whispered harshly, struggling not to scream. "A forced mating to a stranger? The death of the only friend I've ever had? What—" My words caught in my throat, tears burning the backs of my eyes.

Her upper lip curled in disgust at my display of emotion. "Cry as much as you need to, but do it now." She pulled her arm free, tossing the brush next to me. "I expect you to be downstairs, sweet and smiling, in twenty minutes. And before you get any ideas, you'll have a guard at your door all night."

Her eyes burrowed into mine, waiting for me to react.

But I couldn't. If I moved even a single muscle, I would have burst into tears, and I'd rather die than cry in front of her.

"Now," she snapped, satisfied when I didn't speak, "wash the blood out of your hair and cover up your chest. You aren't a fucking harlot." She grabbed a small glass bottle off my vanity, dropping it onto the bed next to me. "And put on some perfume. Your scent is unbearable today."

---

I squished my breasts together, making my cleavage press up and out in my far-too-tight dress. The black material was sleek and soft, and I knew it would enrage my father to no end. It was so tight, I wasn't even sure if I'd be able to sit properly. The purple dress my mother had picked still lay draped over the edge of my bed. The beading sparkled in the setting sun, casting flecks of light onto the ceiling. I always hated purple.

Taking one last look in the mirror, I ran my hands over the sides of my chest, down my tapered waist, and over my hips. Rainer's blood still streaked my usually blonde hair, making it a rusty, reddish color. If I was going to be forced to spend the evening with my father, I would spend every moment making sure he remembered what he did to Rainer.

I smiled at what would probably be my last act of defiance. After tomorrow, I'd never have to return to Casin ever again.

Unable to put it off any longer, I left my room. My feet carried me quickly through the halls, down the stairs, toward the lavish sitting room. But before I could reach the door, my father's booming voice made me stop. His grating, exaggerated laugh made my skin crawl. He was a good three doors down, but his voice boomed as if standing right next to me.

I took a deep breath and forced my feet to move. *Why did it feel as if I were marching toward my own death?*

"Sana really has grown into her own, Hector," the deep voice of whom I assumed was the Hund Valley Pack Alpha drifted toward me. "She's lovely."

"She's just like her mother," my father said loudly. "A bit of a bitch, but beautiful."

They both laughed.

My heart quickened, and my gut churned. Needing a moment, I ducked into the nearest room, trying like hell to calm down. Now wasn't the time to fall apart. I glanced around my father's study, trying to control my thundering heart. But there was no helping it. *I just wanted to run.*

I pressed my forehead to the wall; the sitting room was just on the other side. The sound of ice clinking in glasses pushed through the thin barrier, followed by the alpha's loud voices.

"Sana will provide several pups," my father assured. "Our family has been blessed with excellent breeding and even better young."

"I am impressed by the size of your family," Alpha Rollen said. "It's unusual for female alphas to birth so many with an alpha mate."

"Three is a lot," my father snorted. "Too many!" His roaring laugh vibrated through the wall, pushing into my fingertips.

"You know," Rollen's voice dropped, forcing me to press my ear to the wall, "it's always the omega offspring packs want for arranged bondings, but your Sana," the ice in a glass clinked, "I think she's almost better than an omega."

"I'm just happy you're smart enough to see past that shortcoming."

I jerked back as if the wall had burned me. My father loathed omegas. He claimed them to be useless, or at least that was what he always told Emmy.

"I know most prefer omegas," my father continued, "and I understand why, but a Casin female alpha really is better than any other kind of wolf. Sana is strong, well trained, and fertile. She will provide your son with more offspring than he'll know what to do with."

My stomach clenched, and bile rose in my throat.

I knew what this arrangement was for, but to hear my father promise something so crass made me want to vomit.

I turned to the window next to me, watching the orange sky slip darker and darker. It was still hot outside, the heat of the summer days not burning off until well after dark. My gaze lingered on the tall evergreens in the distance. By this time tomorrow, I'd be on my way to Hund Valley, never to see my fucking parents ever again. *Or Emmy.*

My sweet Emmy.

A brown filly cantered in the distance. Her dark form was almost impossible to see against the shadows of the trees, but her sleek coat gave off a lovely sheen. She was alone, still wearing her bridle. I stared at her. She was the same horse Rainer was leading through the garden only a few hours ago. It looked like she had been abandoned to roam the garden by herself.

I pressed my hand to the window pane, watching her nibble at the grass. My eyes drifted from the horse in the distance to the blood still caked under my nails.

My father's booming laugh hammered inside my head, and I balled up my fists tight, pressing them into the glass. I wanted to break the fucking window and slice up my face with the shards. I wanted to be so ugly, no alpha would ever want me.

But I was powerless—destined for whatever future my father desired.

I glared at the sweet horse. Her tail flicked, and her coat rippled as if something had spooked her. Then she ran, bolting like a beautiful wild beast into the trees.

I wanted to follow her.

"Where the hell is that girl?" my father asked loudly, his words growing slurred from too much drink. "She's probably still brushing her hair. You know how women are."

Rollen laughed as a door pulled open.

When my father spoke again, his voice was just outside the study, his close proximity making my skin crawl.

"Kade!" my father snarled in a harsh whisper. "Go get Sana and drag her ass down here now! Then stay on her ass for the rest of the evening. The last thing I need is for her to wander off."

Kade responded with a quick "yes, sir," then his heavy feet disappeared down the hallway.

I held my breath, staring at the shadow of my father's feet just under the door. Everything in my life had led to this horrible moment. If I left this study, I'd never escape. I'd trade my father's prison for my mate's and would live the rest of my life bowing to the commands of another fucking alpha.

I turned to the window, staring at where the filly had just disappeared.

And I smiled.

*It was now or never.*

Turning to my father's cluttered desk, I grabbed his favorite pen then scribbled out a quick note. I leaned back, satisfied at the rage and panic it would cause come morning.

> *I hope Hund Valley kills you all. I'm just*
> *sorry I can't. -Sana*

I wasn't sure how I'd survive in the wildlands without Rainer, but I'd either figure it out or die trying. Either way, the unknown was better than what I'd be forced to endure here.

I'd still have to come back for Emmy. *And I would.*

If the wild didn't kill me, I'd be back. And then I'd exact my revenge.

For Rainer.

# CHAPTER FIVE

## *the market*

Sana

---

THE TIGHT BLACK DRESS WAS SO FUCKING SNUG AROUND MY HIPS, it made it impossible to run. I shuffled forward as quickly as I could, then stumbled for the fifth time in the last five minutes. My wolf snarled, wishing I'd just rip the damn dress off and allow her to burst out of me. The intense need to get the hell out of the village as fast as possible almost had me giving in to her, but I stayed in my human form. Shifted wolves weren't allowed inside the village unless under attack, and I couldn't risk the attention.

A few loud voices drew my attention, and I edged away from them, into the cover of the trees. Two alphas stumbled out of what I assumed was the tavern. I suddenly felt exposed, my white skin practically glowing in the moon-light, but I had no idea where to go.

I had lived my whole life in this fucking village and had never been inside the town square before. I was allowed to go to the temple and the gardens behind the packhouse. That was it.

Movement caught my eye, and I turned toward an older beta in the distance, pinning up her laundry. Lines of sheets, blankets, and towels fluttered in the evening breeze. I waited, not moving until she collected her empty basket and went back inside. Racing toward a dusty gray shawl, I jerked it down and draped it over my head and shoulders. It was still damp, but the chill felt good on my flushed skin.

I grabbed a handful of my dress and pulled it above my knees. Then I walked as fast as I could without running around the back of several shops and through alleyways. A few betas glanced my way. One stern-looking alpha barked out that curfew was soon, but no one stopped me. I shimmied down an empty passageway between two buildings and crouched behind a barrel. Peeking over the edge, I scanned the area.

The shops were closing up, the last of the pack heading home for the evening. The storefronts and lantern posts were all decorated, covered in brightly colored ribbons and flowers.

Our little village hadn't had much of a reason to celebrate lately. The northern orcs and griffins that lived high in the mountains had ventured closer and closer to our borders. Casin's guards were the strongest in all of Havre and always bested the beasts, but that didn't help the somber atmosphere that settled after each attack.

A twist of guilt settled in my gut as I wondered what might happen to my pack when I was found missing, but I pushed it away. I couldn't think like that. Not with freedom so close.

Slowly, I stood up and edged around the barrel, trying to look as normal and unhurried as possible. The village gates were a straight shot, the spiky metal tips beckoning to me. If I was anyone else, I'd hold my head high and run through the market, but it was too risky. Any one of these wolves could work at the packhouse, and if they recognized me...

I let out a slow breath, forcing myself to walk slowly.

Several large figures in green guard uniforms moved toward me. I turned my head and pulled at the edge of the shawl to hide my face. Max, a fierce alpha and one of my family guards, spoke to his friends, laughing about a scuffle that left him with a deep bruise on his cheek. Max was a brawler in every sense of the word, covered in thick scars— one even running across his cheek and nose—so it didn't surprise me that he was in town picking fights with so many visitors around. The alphas in Casin loved to prove how much stronger they were than everyone else.

The guards strutted past me, heading for the tavern. It wasn't until his deep voice disappeared that I allowed myself to breathe. Prickling fear rose along my spine, and I moved my feet faster, needing to get the fuck out of here. I stared at the tips of the gate as if it were a lifeline, willing it to be closer. Picking up my pace, I hiked up my dress a bit, rushing past shops and merchants.

No one was looking at me. I knew that. But an awareness in the air skated across my skin, making me feel as if I needed to shift. Did Max recognize me? Was someone following me? Was I about to be captured?

My shoulder bumped into an enormous alpha, and my wolf yipped, jerking hard within me.

*I ran.* It was stupid, but I couldn't help it. I needed to get out of here *now*.

A few betas turned their heads as I raced past them. My dress shifted, falling down my legs and growing snug across my hips. I forced myself to slow down at the gate, expecting the guards to stop me. Keeping my head down, I marched forward with my heart pounding in my throat.

A young guard narrowed his eyes at my face, dragging them down my body. Confusion twisted between his brows as he took in my odd clothing—an elegant, tight black dress and a worn gray shawl.

A loud laugh ripped through the air, making the guard snap his attention behind me.

I rushed past him straight out the gate.

The land outside of the border walls was thick with trees and mountains, vast and terrifying. Not sure where the hell to go, I picked a tree in the distance and ran toward it as fast as my body would allow. The hot summer air whipped into my face as I made my way to the tree line. I tried a few times to shift into my wolf, but my bones wouldn't budge. I needed to stop and concentrate to let my wolf out, but I couldn't risk it. I was too desperate to get as far away from Casin as possible.

So I ran.

I ran until my thighs ached and my lungs burned.

I ran until darkness settled over the forest and the Moon shone high in the sky.

I ran until I simply couldn't take another step.

Leaning against a rough pine tree, I gulped down painful bursts of air. I couldn't hear anything other than the rush of my own blood in my ears, and it was so dark under the thick canopy of the trees, I couldn't see anything.

I needed to find shelter, but I wasn't even sure where I was.

The sound of a stream, or maybe even a river, hit my ears, and I turned toward it. My throat was too dry to think. Once I got some water in me, I'd decide what to do next.

Pushing myself away from the tree, I took a single step, but as my foot connected with a mess of leaves and branches, the ground suddenly gave away, and I fell. My arms flailed as my body hurled into the black pit. A blinding crunch stabbed through my side and hip, ripping the air out of my lungs.

Clutching my spinning head, I tried to breathe and think, but I couldn't. Rainer was dead, I had abandoned Emmy, and now I was going to die in the bottom of a fucking hole in the middle of the woods.

Slowly, I rolled onto my back, then froze as a flash of pain ripped up my leg and through my body. Sweat bloomed across my forehead and side, and I gagged hard into the dirt. Not sure what else to do, I sagged into the soft ground beneath me, defeated.

Then I cried.

For the first time in my life, I sobbed loud and free, not caring who heard me. Hot tears covered my face as my chest heaved and my throat burned.

I prayed to the Moon to end my suffering once and for all.

# CHAPTER SIX
## *the next morning*

Tallis

---

A snore jerked from Cyrus's throat, waking me. The sun streaked into the entrance of our little cave, illuminating his features. I couldn't help but admire him. His sun-kissed skin, pulled over lean muscle, was so soft. He had perfect lips for sucking cock, and his dark hair fell into his eyes, touching the top of his angular nose. I loved the bump in the center where it had been broken more than once.

The corner of my mouth lifted, then stopped as my mind clouded with the memory of how that fucking guard had looked at him. *Touched him.*

"What's wrong?" Cyrus asked, his throat raspy with sleep.

"Nothing." I placed a quick kiss on his lips, then sat up. "Hungry?"

He ran his hand down the length of my back. "Yes, please."

He was a skilled hunter, but he could always tell when my urge to care for him hit. My alpha instincts were in overdrive today, making me want to dote on him. "Stay and sleep." I smoothed my palm over his knee, squeezing slightly. "I'll bring back some breakfast before we head out."

"We can probably stay a few more days," he said, bending his knee so I could caress down the inside of his thigh. He smelled so fucking good. His scent was delicate and sweet, like dew-covered moss. My mouth watered.

"Get that look off your face." He glared. "You destroyed my ass yesterday, and while I love that big alpha cock, I'm not quite ready for more."

Guilt twisted my gut. "I'm sorry. I got lost in the moment and didn't prepare you properly."

"You got lost in the moment and knotted me after I told you no." Our bond burned with his displeasure, but it faltered just as fast. He always forgave me too quickly and far too often. "I do love it when you wreck me," he caressed my arm, "but not with a village full of pissed-off guards on our heels."

Feeling like complete shit, I moved over his prone body, cupping his cheek. "You're right." I kissed his soft lips, bumping my nose against his. "You're always right, and I'm a complete fucking asshole."

"Yeah, but you're my fucking asshole." His mouth curved into a soft smile.

I ran my thumb down the side of his face. He was so kind and caring and far too good for a whelp like me. "Why do you stay with me?"

Anger flashed in his eyes, and he grabbed my face, holding me above him. "I will not answer this question again, Tallis. You are mine, and I am yours. Where you go, I

47

go. Just don't wreck my ass unless I ask for it. Or..." he bit his bottom lip, his dark eyes sparkling, "if I deserve it."

Leaning up, he nipped at my bottom lip, pulling it slightly before letting it pop back into place. I crashed my mouth to his, forcibly kissing my omega. He moaned against my tongue and wrapped his legs around my hips. Our cocks pressed against one another, mine thick and dripping, his a bit smaller but just as hard.

"I need to suck you off," I whispered, knowing his ass was still too sore. That and I wanted to make him feel good after my barbaric behavior.

"Please," he moaned, tugging at the roots of my hair.

The sharp scent of more than one foreign wolf hit my nose, and I jerked up.

"What..." Cyrus started to ask, but I held up a hand, indicating he needed to be quiet. He tensed, staying completely frozen in place.

"Alphas," I whispered.

His eyes widened. "Do you think they're from Casin?"

"Only one way to find out." I moved off him. "Stay here," I commanded, but I knew he wouldn't listen. Whenever there was a threat, Cyrus always rushed in head first right at my side.

Settling at the mouth of the cave, I leaned forward and looked down. We were a good thirty feet up, which was both good and bad. The likelihood of someone stumbling upon us was very slim. If by some chance they did climb up here, there was no quick escape, but it was a risk we were used to taking. You couldn't be too picky about where you laid your head when you wandered the wildlands.

About a mile off, the sight of a few bare-chested alphas appeared between the trees. As they moved closer, I could see a thin green stripe down the sides of their slacks. They were Casin guards.

"Are they looking for us?" Cyrus whispered, sitting down next to me.

"No," I said confidently, sending him reassurances through our bond. But I didn't actually know.

It had been a while since a village went so far as to track us through the wildlands, but maybe I punched the wrong fucker yesterday. Maybe he was the pack alpha's son or a high-ranking official. Either way, the guards below were edging a little close for my comfort.

Cyrus inched forward to look over the ledge, and I gripped his shoulder, pulling him back. Mimicking my position, he sat quietly next to me, leaning against the wall.

We stayed there, watching the guards stalk through the trees. One of the guards had an ugly bruise on one arm. The injury was so deep, it was practically black on his tan skin, and the way he held it told me he might have broken it recently. Alphas healed quickly compared to others, but a snapped bone always took a bit more time and care. No matter how strong the wolf.

"Tamen," the bruised alpha said, motioning to a smaller, pale guard. "Let's circle around the gully, then head north." He spoke quietly, but the forest was calm this morning, making him easy for my alpha ears to hear. Cyrus leaned in a bit, trying to pick up what they were saying.

The pale guard raked his nails through his short brown hair, looking all around him. "She couldn't have gotten far." He shook his head. "She's not strong enough or smart enough to survive out here by herself."

The bruised alpha tensed, glaring down at the obviously lower-ranked wolf. "Sana might not have the training we do, but she's not simple." His voice rose, and Cyrus leaned back as if the alpha's anger had physically pushed him away. "She made it out of the packhouse, past the guards, and out of the village without anyone noticing. Assuming she's stupid is exactly how she got this far."

"Yes, sir," the pale alpha said in a quick, official tone, but the tick in his jaw spoke volumes. He was pissed.

"Karis, Max, Breck!" the bruised alpha called the other guards over.

The bond with my mate thrummed with his unease as more alphas came into view. I placed my hand on his shoulder, rubbing slow circles over his collarbone with my thumb. He let out a more controlled breath, but he was still on edge. In truth, so was I.

The scarred alpha I had punched in the market walked toward the two guards, followed by two more. I couldn't help but wonder what the fuck this female, Sana, had done that they were looking for her so far east of the village. Usually, once a rogue was beyond the borders, villages just let them go.

"Cut back to the gully, then head north," the bruised alpha commanded. "Remember to be gentle. Alpha Hector wants her unharmed."

The guards nodded, then they all set off.

Cyrus and I sat in the same spot, waiting quietly as the hours passed. The sun rose to midday, making the air thick with an insufferable heat. The stone against my back warmed as the day wore on, but I remained still. Slipping back into the cool cave meant we might miss the guards if they returned, and crawling down to the forest floor was just stupid. So we stayed put.

Evening shadows settled across the land, and the sun dipped toward the tree line. It had probably been safe for a few hours now, but I couldn't risk my mate's life with simple impatience. I readied myself to wait until well after dark when Cyrus' stomach gave a loud rumble.

He placed his hand over his toned abs, then mouthed "*sorry.*"

My urge to tend to him pulled hard at my wolf. I rocked forward onto my knees and placed a hand on his leg. "It's not smart to risk going on a proper hunt, but how about fish?"

His eyes widened with excitement, and he nodded quickly. Cyrus loved fish. Especially mako with its fleshy, pink meat.

Without a word, we both made our way down the rock-face. Cyrus moved slowly. He didn't make a sound, but I saw his face wince with pain more than once. The moment his feet touched the ground, I gripped his arm, turning him away from me.

"What—" He jerked as I moved to spread his ass cheeks.

"I need to see how badly I hurt you."

He spun hard, pulling out of my grasp. "I'm fine, Tallis." He took a step back, anger making his nose scrunch. "I'm an omega, and I can handle my mate's needs just fine."

I hesitated, knowing full well that while omegas were built for an alpha's pleasure, they still needed rest and comfort afterwards. Two things Cyrus rarely got living out here.

"Can we please go eat?" he snipped.

My wolf bristled, not pleased with his tone. "Cyrus," I growled his name. I didn't mean to, but his refusal to obey me was more than I could handle right now.

"No," he sliced his hands through the air, "I told you I'm fine, and I meant it. Let it go." He walked off, a slight limp in his step.

It took everything in me not to race after him, pick him up, and carry his stubborn ass to the stream. But not wanting to make things worse, I walked slowly behind him, my fingers flexing the whole way.

---

"If I had any self-control, I'd save some of this, but it's just too damn good." Cyrus smiled, popping another big bite of mako into his mouth. His cheeks bulged as he ate, a look of pure euphoria in his dark eyes. No one liked to eat more than my mate, and nothing made me happier than to feed him.

"Get your fill," I said, handing him another fillet. "Fish isn't good dried, so there's no sense saving it. We'll track down some proper game tomorrow."

"Fish is good no matter what," Cyrus said around a very big bite. He tossed the bones and fins of the last mako into the stream, then washed his hands. "Where are we heading next?"

"I was thinking Stone City or the Faelands. No one will look twice at my brand." I resisted the urge to touch the mark burned into my skin. Reaching out, Cyrus traced it with the edge of his thumb. Its awkward position at the juncture of my neck and shoulder was sensitive to touch and made goosebumps flash down my back.

"And even if they do," he said, "it was done so poorly and in the wrong spot. I honestly doubt anyone will notice."

I placed my hand over his, squeezing his wrist with affection.

"Is the ocean that way?" he asked. "I'd love to see the Amara Sea."

"No," I shook my head, "Stone City is in the middle of a desert."

His smile dimmed a bit, but he didn't protest. "Well, I've never seen a desert either."

Standing up, Cyrus brushed the dirt off his beautiful, bare ass. We had clothes in case we needed to enter a city, but there really wasn't much of a reason to be dressed outside of a village. Alphas wandered freely in the wild-lands, often traveling in wolf form, and clothes only made shifting more difficult.

"Do you smell that?" Cyrus asked, turning with the wind.

"Yes." I stood, scenting the breeze. The stench of dried blood had been in the air since we arrived at the stream, but a fresh waft had finally caught Cyrus' omega nose. It wasn't wild game or a mountain creature. In fact, it had the distinct scent of a female-were.

Cyrus turned to me, concern twisting between his brows. "Should we check it out?"

"No," I said quickly.

"But what if someone is hurt?" He looked at me with his big brown eyes. I hated it when he looked at me like that. I almost always caved.

"It's not our problem, Cy. It's probably one of those Casin-fucks." I grabbed the satchel off the ground, slinging it over my shoulder. "We can stay in the cave tonight, then head out first thing in the morning."

Cyrus tilted his head to the side and let out a long breath through his nose. I knew what he was going to do before he even moved. Holding his head high, he turned and marched toward the metallic odor.

"Cyrus," I said, my tone sharp. "This is *not* our problem. We are going back to the cave *now*."

He kept walking, practically daring me to use my alpha voice on him. I cursed under my breath then rushed after him. My beast snarled and snapped at my mate's disobedience, and I clenched my fists to calm myself. Cyrus was normally good about not provoking me, but sometimes the omega got a wild hair up his ass, and it took everything in me not to remind him of his place.

*Or maybe he's just punishing me for being too rough with him yesterday.*

The thought immediately cooled my temper.

"Oh, my stars," Cyrus gasped as he stared into a deep pit. "Tallis!" he yelled over his shoulder. "Help!"

I rushed to his side, ready to fight if needed.

A blonde female lay unconscious at the bottom of the deep hole. Her left leg was bent at an awkward angle, the bone pushing out midway between her knee and ankle. The ridiculous black dress that clung to her curvy figure was twisted around her thighs, binding her legs together. She was toned, free of any blemishes, and her dress appeared to be finely made.

The hairs on the back of my neck stood up, and my wolf inched forward.

Everything about this felt wrong.

I scanned the area, turning every which way to see if any movement caught my eye. There was no scent of any other wolves or mountain creatures in the area, but that didn't mean someone wasn't looking for her. It was clear she belonged to someone. A pack for sure, but maybe rogues.

Or those guards...

"Cyrus," I whispered, turning back to my mate. "Cyrus!" I yelled down at him.

He was at the bottom of the fucking pit, ghosting his

hands over the female's broken limb. Blood, mixed with clumps of dirt, clung to the protruding bone. A wheezy breath left the she-wolf, but she still didn't move. She might be alive for now, but who knew for how much longer.

"The leg is obviously broken, but I'm not sure what else," Cyrus said, his big, expressive eyes holding so much pain for her. "Help me get her out."

"Absolutely not," I growled. "She's not our fucking problem. Get your ass back up here *now*!"

He instinctively bowed his head at my tone but didn't let up. "Tallis," he hissed, appalled at my words. He always felt way too damn much for those he didn't know. "I can't just leave her."

"For all we know, she's a Casin guard."

He gave me a pointed look. It was clear she wasn't, but that didn't change my stance.

"I'm serious, Cy." I jumped down next to him, prepared to haul him up by his nape if I had to. "We can't risk taking her with us. I mean, look at her." I motioned to her mangled body. My gaze drew up her curvy form to her face. Her cheeks were round and pale, and her skin smooth. She looked so soft. So young. Something warm pulled within my chest, urging me to touch her. Care for her. Help her.

She was lost and broken. Two things Cyrus and I knew *very* well.

I sighed hard, and my shoulders slumped.

A small apologetic smile lifted one side of Cyrus's mouth, and he whispered, "Thank you."

# CHAPTER SEVEN
## back to the cave

Cyrus

---

TALLIS CAREFULLY HOISTED THE SHE-WOLF OVER HIS SHOULDER and gripped her hips hard, his fingertips pushing into her plush flesh. I tensed as he began climbing, terrified he'd fall and hurt them both. He paused with every shift of his feet, making sure she was in place. I held my breath, not moving until they reached the ledge.

Tallis looked down at me, and our bond flared with his annoyance, but he didn't say a word.

It was important to let him control most of our decisions—he was the alpha, after all—but I wasn't going to budge on this. This poor girl clearly didn't belong out here. Her hands were smooth and free of all indications of work, and her arms and legs held not a single scar—except for the broken leg. She was a sheltered wolf, and I couldn't live with myself if we left her out here to die.

"How are we going to get her up there?" I asked Tallis, eyeing the steep climb to our cave.

He cut me a glare. "I don't know, Cyrus," he grumbled. "How the fuck do we get her up there?"

"Stop being an ass." I glared right back.

He let out a soft growl, then adjusted the female on his shoulder. His hard expression fell, and he jerked his chin upward, indicating I should climb.

I moved as quickly as I could, pulling myself onto the ledge of our home. Tallis was right behind me, moving with incredible ease. *He's so strong.*

Reaching down, I grabbed the she-wolf's tiny waist, hauling her up. She was thin, about half my weight, but her hips and chest were full. It was the kind of figure frequently sketched on the front of steamy books.

"She's short," Tallis said, looking over the length of her body. I was sure she'd be an inch or so taller than me once standing.

"Everyone is short compared to you." I laughed. Even compared to other alphas—I had never seen an alpha taller than Tallis. "What do you think? Is she a beta?"

"Maybe," he said, inhaling the air around her. He pulled a face and pushed out a forceful breath.

"Yeah," I agreed. "She smells off. Sour." It had to be the sweat and grime clinging to her skin, but there was something beneath the harsh odor I couldn't quite place. It was subtle and pleasant. Almost sweet. It pleased my omega nature, making me want to push my nose into her hair and inhale deeply. I hated that it was so muted.

"She's definitely not an omega." Tallis sniffed her again. "I can't really tell, though."

I brushed the tangled hair out of her face. She was pretty. A pointed nose, heart-shaped face, and long, dark lashes. She looked so sweet and soft, covered in mud and blood. My heart broke a little bit for her.

"Are you okay?" Tallis asked, caressing my back.

I forced a smile. "Yup."

"She'll be okay," he whispered, squeezing my neck with gentle affection. "We'll help her."

I leaned into his touch, so thankful to have him in my life. Tallis was big, mean, and said the most inappropriate things, but more than any of that, he was a softy. Determined to help anyone weaker or smaller than him—which was pretty much everyone.

"Okay, omega. Now what?" Tallis looked down at the female, ready for me to give him his orders.

"She's wheezing," I said, "so I'm thinking she probably has a few broken ribs, but we need to set her leg first."

"Do you know how to do that?"

"It's been a while," I said honestly. "And only with pups." I grimaced.

He nodded, giving her leg a wary look. "Just tell me what to do."

I opened the satchel, pulling out a pair of Tallis's pants. "I need to see her chest. Make sure her ribs aren't poking through before we set the leg. I don't want to make one injury worse trying to fix the other. Can you tell how bad her ribs are?"

Tallis leaned over the she-wolf, scenting her breastbone. "She's hurt deep." He cocked his head to the side as if thinking. "She's got to be a beta. Right? She's too big to be an omega."

"Everyone says I'm too big to be an omega," I reminded him, still rummaging through the satchel.

He smiled wide, nodding. "That you are."

I huffed then dropped the bag. "I can't find my dagger to cut her dress off. Do you have that old flaying knife still?"

Not bothering to answer, Tallis wedged his fingers into the fabric at her cleavage and jerked his hands apart, easily ripping the dress straight down the center. The she-wolf's breasts spilled out, revealing a tapered waist and a complete lack of undergarments. My face warmed as I forced myself to look at her face.

"She's got big tits," Tallis said, and I rolled my eyes. He was never good at keeping his opinion to himself.

Being gentle, Tallis lifted her arm away from her side to reveal a large, puffy bruise. It was an angry black color against her pale skin, the outline of a few ribs very clear.

"What do you smell?" I asked, leaning forward to get a better look.

"I can scent a crack in her bones, but it might just be the leg." He ran his nose over her chest. Jerking back, he coughed hard. "*Fuck*. She smells awful."

"Internal bleeding?" I sniffed the air just above her breastbone, again smelling nothing but the sharp stench of sweat and blood, and something acidic? No. Maybe rotten.

"No," he coughed, pulling back with a pinched expression. "It's not a wound, it's...weird. Bitter. Female alphas don't always perfume with a sweet scent, but..." He curled his lip in disgust. "There's something wrong with her."

My wolf whimpered at the thought. She looked so weak and sad, crumpled on the floor of the cave. *I had to fix her.*

"Well, there's no sense putting this off," I sighed hard, hoping I didn't hurt the poor girl. It really had been an eternity since I had set a bone, but it wasn't like I could ask a healer to make a house call.

I instructed Tallis to sit at her ankles, then I encircled the pants under her knee, lifting it. My nerves flared hard, and my mate sent me silent assurances, reminding me I could do this. I appreciated his confidence, but I wasn't sure I felt the same. I had helped Tallis reset his nose and even my own a few times, popped shoulders back into place, and had done a few rough stitches, but this leg was something I had never faced before. Even in the infirmary, wounds like this weren't my specialty.

"I'm ready." Tallis nodded, gripping her ankle with both hands.

"Alright." I took a deep breath. "On the count of three."

# CHAPTER EIGHT

## *where am i?*

Sana

---

I JOLTED UPRIGHT AS A SCREAM BURST OUT OF ME, THE FORCE OF IT burning my throat and shredding my lungs.

*Someone was ripping my leg off!*

Sharp pain shot up my leg, making my skin flash hot and sweaty. I tried to move away from the pain, but my ribs squeezed, making it impossible to breathe. The intense pressure in my shin increased, and my tongue pushed out as I gagged, but my stomach was empty, making my gut roll on nothing.

I thrashed, and firm hands pinned down my shoulders.

The unmistakable voice of an alpha barked out, "Hold her still!"

My leg was bent in the air with some kind of fabric wrapped around my knee. One of the hands on my chest disappeared while the hand around my ankle tightened, then my leg was pulled in opposite directions.

My voice scraped across my throat as I screamed again, clawing at the cold stone beneath me. My wolf tried to push forward to fight, but nothing would move. My body locked up, and my beast fell into a full-on panic. She whimpered and wailed, spinning in tight circles in my mind.

The pain hit a crescendo as someone pushed roughly on my shin, then my bone popped. I flung my arms out and tried to swipe at anything within reach, but my vision was blurry and filled with little white bursts of light. I couldn't see anything.

*I was going to pass out.*

"Done!"

The pressure on my leg eased, and my ankle was placed carefully on the cold ground. My whole body pulsed with too much sensation. Pain, fear, heat, nausea, relief. It all beat inside my temples in time with my heart.

I tried to move again, but warm hands settled on my knees, keeping my legs still.

"It's okay," a soft male voice whispered from some-where above me. A gentle hand cupped my cheek, making me realize I was drenched in sweat. "We're all done. You're safe. It's okay."

My chest heaved as the pain in my body slowly faded to something more tolerable. I still couldn't move, but at least I didn't feel as if I were being ripped in two.

The soft voice whispered again in my ear, "I'm going to sit you up a bit, so you can drink some water."

Hands hooked under my arms and pulled me up, making me grunt. I settled against a firm chest, but I was too exhausted to move to see their face. A canister of water was pressed to my lips, and I tried shoving it away, but I didn't have the strength. So instead I drank. If they were going to kill me, poison would be a very unusual weapon of choice given that I was already on death's door.

I took a few careful sips, fighting the urge to gulp. My stomach was already clenching on the small amount of liquid, and the last thing I needed was to get sick. After another quick sip, I turned my head, breathing deeply through my nose, but I couldn't smell anything. My sense of smell was always weak at best, but right now it was as if I had a face full of linen. I couldn't even smell the blood that trickled slowly down my leg.

"What's your name?" the soft voice asked.

Trying not to move too much, I looked up at the male holding me. The throb in my leg and ribs demanded all my attention, making it hard to see his features, but after a moment, he came into focus. The soft-spoken wolf had dark hair that fell into dark, sparkling eyes, tan skin, and a soft slip of something lovely drifted from him. He was clearly an omega. And it instantly soothed me.

"You're safe here," he whispered. His sympathetic smile made his handsome face look sweet and young. He reminded me of Rainer.

*Rainer.*

My nose itched as the urge to cry flared up. I squeezed my eyes shut, sucking in a painful breath. Grief and pain pushed heavy at my breastbone, begging to break free. Unable to fight it any longer, I let my weaker emotions take hold, and a few hot tears fell down the sides of my face. *I hated how pathetic I was.*

"Sana," an alpha said softly as if testing the sound of my name.

I snapped my eyes open as wide as they would go. "How do you know my name?" I gritted out, trying to push myself away from the wolf holding me. He shushed me, gently touching my shoulders. I easily fell back against him, too exhausted to fight.

"It's okay," the omega whispered. "We're not going to hurt you. My name is Cyrus, and this is Tallis."

All too quickly, defeat settled over me like a fog. After everything I had done, everything I had fucked up, I was now being held captive by two rogues. I should have been fighting and running, trying to escape so they wouldn't violate me, but I just didn't care anymore.

I had fought my entire life. I was controlled, beat, starved, and tormented.

*And I just couldn't do it anymore.*

"Where are you from?" The omega pressed his hand to the base of my throat. The gentle pressure felt good, steadying my heart.

"How do you know my name?" I whispered, my voice rough from screaming.

"Casin guards," the alpha said from the shadows. He leaned forward, and a bit of light illuminated the side of his face. Blond hair caressed his shoulders, his sharp jaw was covered in stubble, and there was a small dimple in the center of his chin. It was too dark to see the color of his eyes, but his expression made me uneasy. It was filled with pity, and I hated it.

"Why are Casin guards looking for you?" he asked, his tone soft as if speaking to a frightened pup.

I looked past the alpha at the rough rock wall behind him. I was in a cave. It was spacious and chilly despite the thick summer heat outside. Cool air brushed over my skin, and my nipples went hard. Looking down, I was horrified to see my dress was ripped down the center. The black fabric hung open, exposing every inch of me.

My arms shook as I gripped the frayed material, trying to pull it closed, but it was no use. The dress was shredded, and my arms were too weak to hold it together. The tattered remains fell loose at my sides, and I let them. If these wolves were going to violate me, a thin piece of fabric wasn't going to stop them.

"Tallis," the omega said, pointing at something on the ground.

The alpha moved toward me, his big body blocking out the light from the entrance. My abs flexed as I tried to prepare myself for what was coming next. My wolf sat up, looking at the alpha with gentle interest. I wanted to rip her to pieces for not feeling my fear.

After all these years of my wolf always feeling or doing the complete opposite of what I needed, was it too much to ask that she help me just once? My beast should be on high alert, protecting me, guiding me to be strong and smart, but instead she was acting as if these wolves were fascinating puzzles.

*I was broken in every sense of the word.*

The omega, Cyrus, pulled at the black fabric of my dress, slipping it off my shoulders. I didn't fight him. There was no point. I would simply have to endure this. I closed my eyes and clenched my jaw, determined not to beg.

Shock washed over me as a shirt was pulled over my head, then tugged down to cover my chest and hips. The alpha, Tallis, situated the fabric under my bottom, being careful not to move me too much. It confused me, and I stared at the big wolf, watching as his eyes pulled in the corners, his obvious sympathy growing with each passing second.

It made my skin itch.

Cyrus swooped his hands under my hair, pulling it free

from the collar and smoothing it over my shoulders. Their pointed kindness made me even more nervous.

"What do you want?" I whispered, watching the alpha's expression carefully. He leaned back, giving me a bit of space. It didn't make me feel any better.

"We just want to help," Cyrus said, picking a few leaves from my hair.

"Don't," my ribs pinched, and I sucked in a breath through gritted teeth, "don't fucking lie to me."

"He's not lying," Tallis said softly, his gentle tone pissing me off.

I wished like hell my wolf would give me strength and challenge the alpha—prove to him that I wasn't as pathetic as he clearly thought—but my beast remained too interested by their presence to show any kind of anger or caution. "Fucking bitch," I mumbled to myself.

The alpha tensed. "What the fuck did you say?"

"Whatever your game is, I have no intention of playing it," I said with a bit more strength. The urge to run burned within me, but my body wouldn't obey, and I remained limp against the omega.

"I'm not playing any kind of game here, little wolf." Tallis gave me a pointed look, letting me know his kindness only extended so far.

I pushed out the fiercest growl I could muster, but it sounded more like the mewling of a sick pup.

Tallis smiled wide, an amused chuckle pushing from his chest. "Do you know what, little one? You want to go?" He held a hand out, motioning to the entrance of the cave. "Be my guest."

I stared at him, not believing he'd just let me go.

"Stand up on that shit leg and be on your way. But I'm

warning you," his teeth flashed as he laughed, "that first step is a big one."

"Tallis," Cyrus hissed. "Stop it. She needs to rest, and you aren't helping." His tone was shocking. I had never heard an omega speak to an alpha with any kind of bite in their tone. Nor did I think an alpha would allow it. But Tallis didn't snarl or correct him. He simply smiled wider.

"Why are those guards looking for you?" Cyrus whispered, rubbing the sides of my arms. I leaned into him, trying to scent him, but I couldn't smell anything. "Did you do something?"

"I didn't do anything." I clenched my teeth tight. The memory of Rainer's lifeless body flashed in my mind, and my eyes burned red.

"Told you she wasn't an omega." Tallis smirked.

My wolf snarled at his assessment. I hated that my first instinct was to be offended, but I couldn't help it. My wolf wanted to be seen as strong and commanding.

"No. I'm *not* an omega." I tipped my chin up, unable to move anything else. "I'm an alpha." Cyrus's eyes went wide, and his mate snorted as if I had made a joke. "Is something funny?" I snarled at the blond asshole.

He raised one eyebrow and gave me a lazy smirk. "You fell into a hole and shattered half the bones in your body. A real alpha would have sensed something like that in their surroundings and easily dodged it. Not to mention, you don't smell like an alpha. At least not one I've ever scented. And you're short," he added as if that settled the matter.

"I am not short!" I yelled, and pain squeezed my ribs so hard, I gagged. I coughed hard, then snarled, "I may be closer in size to a beta," I whispered, trying like hell not to throw up, "but I still tower over any omega."

"You're *real* fucking short," he mocked.

Cyrus groaned, squeezing my arms as if trying to calm me. It just pissed me off more.

"And I do *not* smell," I said loudly, not caring how much it hurt.

The alpha laughed and clicked his tongue.

I jerked forward, desperately wanting to claw the smug look off his fucking face. I barely sat up before I crumpled, falling limp onto my stomach. My body burned with an intense agony, making it impossible to breathe. I was so dizzy, and despite the cool air around me, my body was drenched with sweat.

Pressing my forehead to the cold rock, my fingers trembled as I tried and failed to sit up. I was exhausted and thirsty, and I missed my sister.

Was Emmy okay?

Did she believe I had abandoned her?

*Did she hate me?*

I had to go back for her, but right now, I wasn't even sure I'd live.

Slowly, I turned my head and rested my cheek on the cold stone. I opened my eyes and jerked at the sight of Tallis a mere inch from my face.

My wolf jumped within me, panic and distress making her slam into every corner of my mind. I tried to calm her, but she was out of control, shoving my claws forward and punching out my fangs. My head spun, and my heart beat faster. Then, without any ability to stop myself, instinct made me jump to my feet and run.

My broken leg quickly buckled, and I fell toward the mouth of the cave, but my body didn't stop. Tumbling across the smooth stone, I slid, hitting the ledge of the cave. I was several stories up, and there was nothing I could do to stop myself from falling.

But just before I fell over the ledge, hard hands grabbed my shirt and jerked me back inside the cave. Tallis looked down at me, his face twisted with rage and relief.

Uncontrollable panic flooded my veins, and I closed my eyes.

*I was trapped.*

# CHAPTER NINE
## the mouth of the cave

Tallis

---

"WHAT THE FUCK WERE YOU THINKING?" I ROARED, FIGHTING THE urge to beat the she-alpha's ass raw. *If I hadn't gotten to her in time...*

She didn't say anything, but her chin quivered slightly, making my wolf whimper. My instinct to protect and care for anyone smaller or weaker made me want to tuck the poor she-wolf into Cyrus's nest and protect her from the horrible world below.

Letting out a long sigh, I pressed Sana to my chest, then settled back on my feet. She was so damn tiny. Well, at least her arms were. They were like little twigs that looked so fucking easy to snap. Her ass, on the other hand...

I scented her hair, then pulled back. Sharp emotions pulsed off her in waves, making her already bitter scent almost unbearable. The stench enveloped her like a poisonous cloud, consuming whatever her natural scent might be. But I couldn't let her go. She was too scared.

Cyrus rushed to my side. "Are you okay?" Panic made his voice pitch higher.

"I'm good," I assured.

He pressed his hand to my chest, and my thundering heart eased a bit at his touch. I nodded at him, feeling his comfort and love thrum through our bond.

Once he was sure I was good, he turned his attention to Sana. Her eyes were closed, and she was breathing in slow, deliberate breaths. She was so fucking pale, and a sheen of sweat covered her face, making her blood-streaked hair stick to her forehead.

My wolf inched forward, wanting to ease her distress but not entirely sure how. She wasn't an omega, so gentle touch alone probably wouldn't do it.

"Fuck," Cyrus whispered, looking at her leg. The bone was bulging out of her skin again. A slow trickle of blood pushed from the open wound, dripping down the sides of her calf and onto the ground. Her blood tap, tap, tapped as it hit rock. I listened to the sound, trying to figure out what the hell we were going to do. "Why did she run?" he whispered more to himself, but I couldn't help but answer.

"I don't know." An uneasy grit settled in my gut.

Slowly, Sana's lashes lifted, revealing dark blue eyes. She looked dazed. Almost drunk. Her pain had to be unbearable.

"Careful there, doll," I said, tightening my hold on her as she tried to move. "You fucked up your leg real good again."

"Just...please," she whispered, emotion making her voice crack, "tell me what you want. Stop fucking with me

71

and just do whatever the hell you're going to do. I can't take not knowing."

Cyrus's anger flared in our bond, and his jaw went tight. He was usually calm and far too understanding, but when his patience ran out, he was an impossible force. "What the hell happened to you that you simply can't believe someone might want to help you? Why on earth would you do this to yourself? You could have died!"

She pressed her cheek to my chest, her strength quickly fading, and she whispered, "Stop pretending you have any honor and just do what you're going to do."

Confusion and anger pulled Cyrus's brows together. "I'm not pretending. I just want to help you. Why is that so hard to believe?"

"I don't know you!" Her voice scraped across her throat, her cheeks flushing a deep red. Her ability to rage while in so much pain was admirable. She was short and weak for her status, but I'd be damned if she didn't have grit. It made me respect her a bit.

"For all I know, you're going to, to..." She inhaled a sharp breath, her eyes glowing red. Her beast was restless, making her whole body shake. "Just let me fucking go!" She growled high in her throat, baring her teeth at my mate. I smiled, knowing she had no idea who she was up against.

Cyrus leaned in, returning her hard glare. Sana's eyes pulsed red and blue, and her claws grew ever so slightly, but my mate didn't even flinch.

*Fuck, I loved him.*

"Where the fuck are you gonna go on one leg?" Cyrus pushed out an angry breath, trying to calm himself. "I refuse to let you just wander off and die in the dirt like a fucking animal."

Sana sagged against me, not having the strength to do anything other than listen to my enraged mate.

"You don't trust us, and I get that," Cyrus said, a little more in control, "but out here, the only thing that matters is surviving. And if you don't have the strength to fight, you don't have the strength to run. You have to be smarter, or you'll die long before your bones knit."

Her eyes narrowed, and her voice came out a low growl. I understood her anger—it was hell being challenged by an omega, but when Cyrus was right, he was right. "It's the *reason* for your kindness that concerns me," she whispered. "Should a pig thank the farmer for fattening him up?" She swallowed hard. "Do you expect me to really just lie down and let you do whatever the fuck you want because you're being nice?"

I liked her.

She was a bit of an ass, and I still hated that Cyrus made her our problem, but, in truth, we needed something new to distract us. Things had been hard out here lately, and there was nothing like someone else's suffering to make you forget your own.

"All we want," Cyrus said in a low, deliberate voice, "is to help you. We know what it's like to be injured and scared. But if you are determined to make it on your own, just say the word. Tallis will carry you down, and you can be on your way. Otherwise, we need to set your leg."

She curled her fingers inward, pressing a weak fist to my chest. When she finally spoke, she sounded so defeated, her voice pitching into a whine, "Why do you care?"

"He can't help it," I said, smirking at the still riled omega. "My mate has a thing for wounded rabbits."

Cyrus crossed his arms and glared at me, not amused with my choice of words.

"What?" She tipped her chin up, narrowing her blue eyes at me. She was cute when angry. Not as cute as Cyrus, but still adorable.

"We're helping you because Cyrus can't leave a wounded rabbit in a snare. It breaks his heart." I smiled softly at my mate, and his cheeks blushed. "He has nursed more meals back to health than he's killed. Waste of a snack if you ask me."

"You aren't helping," Cyrus gritted out.

"So what's it gonna be, doll?" I asked Sana. My eyes pulled to her pretty mouth. Despite the dark circles around her eyes and her pale, sweaty skin, her lips were still puffy and red. She looked like the kind of girl made to suck cock. "Do you want to be on your way or suffer my mate fussing over you for a few days while you heal?"

She looked down at her leg, and her teeth gnashed together. "I guess I don't have a choice." Her voice was flat and her fists tight.

Deep voices carried through the forest below, and I snapped my head around. The trees rustled, and twigs snapped as two alphas came out of the brush. Sana's scent flooded with pure terror, burning the back of my throat as she shook violently in my arms.

She recognized those voices and was in full-on distress.

Cyrus instantly sprang into action.

Being as gentle as he could, he pulled her out of my arms and heaved her up, carrying her deep into the cave. Crouching down, I watched the wolves below. Using my senses, I swept the area for signs of anyone else. There were a few more wolves not far from here, but these two alphas were the only threat. *For now.*

I instantly recognized both of them. They were the Casin guards searching for Sana earlier.

"We've checked here, Tamen," a younger alpha with shaggy black hair said. He looked bored, kicking at a few rocks.

"I know." The other wolf, Tamen, sniffed the air, glaring into the distance. "I just feel like I can smell her."

"How? She has no real alpha scent."

Tamen kept his eyes on the trees, concentrating very hard. "She does. It's just...weird. And you have to be close to catch it."

The shaggy wolf grabbed Tamen's shoulder, forcing him to turn. "How fucking close have you been to her?" His tone bordered between curious and shocked.

Tamen smirked, flashing his pointed teeth. There was something violent in his smug expression that made me want to rip his throat out.

I didn't know Sana, but she was broken. A possessiveness washed over me for the girl, and my instincts urged me to shield her from whatever these assholes wanted. Even if she was an alpha, my beast didn't care. She needed protecting.

I shoved down a groan.

Cyrus was definitely rubbing off on me.

## CHAPTER TEN

# *some time later*

Sana

---

I WOKE UP CONFUSED AND ALONE. VAGUE MEMORIES DRIFTED IN and out of my mind: restless sleep, cold water pressed to my lips, my leg being cleaned and bound, and someone begging me to eat. Even flashes of that big blond alpha holding and caressing me flitted through my mind, making me question my sanity.

*Was that a dream?*

Moving slowly, I pushed myself up, and a deep ache pinched inside my chest. I rubbed my eyes hard, then blinked several times. Every muscle in my face was stiff, and my skin itched with a thin layer of sweat.

Looking around the cave, I tried to figure out if the rogues had abandoned me. A few of their belongings were scattered around the edges of the cave, and a plush nest made of moss and leaves was settled in one corner. It looked like they planned to return. I hoped.

Just outside the cave, the lush green treetops swayed. The rustle of their leaves was almost calming, but unfortunately my body's needs wouldn't allow me to enjoy it. I needed to use the washroom. *Bad*.

Trying to distract my bladder, I examined my leg. Strips of black fabric were wound tight around two sticks to hold my bone in place. It appeared to be my dress. I smoothed my hand down the cotton shirt that swallowed me up, thankful to the omega, Cyrus, for having his mate put it on me. They *seemed* to be kind rogues.

I shifted uncomfortably, my bladder so full it was sore. I couldn't wait for someone to return. I wiggled my toes, wincing at the sharp stabbing sensation that shot up to my knee. But there was no helping it. It was either try to find somewhere to go, or soil myself where I sat.

Slowly, and using the wall to steady myself, I forced myself onto one foot, keeping the other one carefully off the ground. I looked around for a cup or bowl, but there was only a damn water canister. My bladder squeezed, and I let out a long sigh.

I picked it up and removed the stopper. The opening was very small. This was *not* going to be easy.

Keeping my wounded leg outstretched, I tried like hell to squat on one foot. My butt hovered in the air as I placed the canister between my legs. It was awkward, and I kept jerking, unable to keep my balance.

I closed my eyes and tried to go, but nothing happened.

Leaning my whole side against the wall, I concentrated hard, forcing my abs to relax.

Still nothing.

"Come on!" I yelled. The intense urge to pee, but not being able to, had me on the verge of tears.

A deep voice, followed by heavy movement, made me

jerk, then topple over. Trying not to hurt my leg, I forced myself to fall sideways, smacking my arm onto the hard stone.

"Tallis! She's awake!" Cyrus gasped. He dropped an armful of brush and moss as he rushed to me. "Sana, what are you doing? You're going to hurt yourself."

"I need to pee!" I yelled, not caring how unrefined I sounded. "Please! To the Moon and the stars and all that is holy, I need to pee!"

"Okay, just take it easy. You've been out for almost a full week," Cyrus said, hooking my arm over his shoulder and helping me to my feet. I leaned into him, noticing his gentle scent for the first time. He smelled soft and clean like a spring breeze with an edge of sweetness that all omegas carried. If my bladder hadn't been consuming all my senses, his soft perfume probably would have calmed me.

"Tallis, help me get her down the rock wall," he said as he guided me to the cave's entrance.

I glanced up at the enormous blond alpha, trying to convey as much gratitude as I could with my eyes. He hooked an arm under my knees and the other at my back, picking me up easily. Cyrus adjusted my clothes, making sure my bottom was covered.

My wolf roused, still sleepy and weak but liking their attention. I kept my face blank of all emotion. I hated how starved my beast was for affection, even from strangers.

Tallis moved us to the ledge, then without hesitation, he jumped. The quick drop and jerky landing made my stomach flip and my bladder clench. Biting my bottom lip hard, I prayed I wouldn't lose control of my faculties while he was holding me.

He walked quickly toward the sound of a stream. The increased sound of water trickling over rocks, pebbles, and brush made me squeeze my knees together so tight, my thighs shook.

"You okay?" Cyrus asked, keeping pace next to us. "How do you feel?"

"I really have to go," I whined, unable to hold it for even a second longer. "Please, I'm so sorry."

"That's okay." Tallis set me on my feet, then he and Cyrus walked off to give me some privacy.

Bunching up the oversized shirt, I tried to squat while bearing weight on only one leg, but with nothing to hold on to, I immediately fell. Both my leg and ribs blazed in agony. I groaned in defeat. There was simply no way I could stand. Lying on my side, I closed my eyes, and prepared myself to just go. There was no helping it.

Firm hands gripped my upper arms and pulled me up. My eyes went wide at the sight of Tallis steadying himself just behind me. He crouched down, easing me into a deep squat.

"Don't think about me being here," he whispered in my ear.

His warm breath fanned over my neck, making the apex of my thighs tingle for a completely different reason. My body's inability to react appropriately in any situation mortified me. I should have been used to it by now, but honestly, it still made me want to scream.

"Just...go," Tallis said.

Trying not to think about how humiliating it was, I widened my stance, let my weight settle into Tallis's arms, and I peed.

I peed forever.

It was euphoric.

Goosebumps danced across my legs and up my sides, and I sighed with relief. Tallis jerked a bit as he adjusted his feet, and I tried not to think about any splatter hitting him. But even if it did, I couldn't stop.

Once every drop left my body, I rubbed my fingers together, looking around. I needed to clean myself, but I was too embarrassed to ask for some leaves or moss, so instead I just turned my head toward the sound of the stream, resolved to simply wash the ick away.

"Done?" Tallis asked. His deep voice, so close to my ear, vibrated down my spine, making my nipples shamefully hard.

I whispered "*yes*," then gasped as he scooped me up again.

My face burned at what I had just done in front of the alpha, but I refused to look down or hide behind my hair. If I was going to survive in the wild, I'd have to shake off what little decorum I had. A lingering drip of pee rolled from between my legs down my backside, and the heat in my cheeks crawled down my chest. Tallis's nose twitched, and I pressed my lips together, praying he couldn't scent that something so silly brought me so much embarrassment.

Perhaps if he and his mate weren't so breathtakingly handsome, I wouldn't have cared.

I grimaced at the thought, reminding myself that, while they had been kind to me, I didn't know these wolves. For all I knew, they were nursing me back to health so they could force me to bear their young, or trade me to a pack of orcs for supplies. Rogues weren't exactly known for their charity.

"Do you feel better?" Cyrus asked, pulling me from my thoughts. He smiled sweetly, waiting for me to answer. His soft demeanor was a welcome balm to my soul. He was very fit for an omega—lean, wiry muscle covered by tan skin. He looked so sweet and strong at the same time.

I cleared my throat roughly. "I do feel better. Thank you."

I forced myself to look at Tallis, determined to make eye contact. The tall alpha kept his dark eyes to the front, walking rather quickly. His gait was enormous, forcing Cyrus to hustle to keep pace. I tipped my chin up, hoping I sounded commanding and strong. "I'd like to walk, please."

Tallis's eyes widened a bit at my request, and he looked at his mate as if asking for permission.

"I don't know if that's a good idea." Cyrus cast a nervous glance at my leg. "Your wound—"

"I'm an alpha," I reminded him as politely as I could. I didn't want to sound offended or annoyed, but I was both. Alphas healed quickly. A broken bone would only take a day or two to knit at most, and while the ache in my bones was still deep, it was healed. *It had to be.*

"Please, put me down," I repeated, tired of these rogues acting as if I were made of glass.

With a quick smile, Tallis obeyed, setting me on my feet. I wobbled as I carefully placed some weight onto my bad leg. Pain shot up my knee and hip, beating a path through my whole body.

"I...uh..." I licked my lips, trying to stay calm. "I think the bandage is too tight."

Cyrus hesitated, cutting a quick look at Tallis. "I don't think it's heal—"

"Of course it's healed," I snapped. My voice shook with fear, but I cleared my throat, holding my head high. "You said I've been out for a week. That's more than enough time. The bandage is just too tight. Please." I swallowed hard, whispering, "Please, remove it."

Cyrus pushed out a heavy sigh, then knelt in front of

me. Tallis stayed close to my side, his big hand hovering at the small of my back, steadying me.

The omega took his time, slowly untying the strips of fabric, exposing more and more of my battered skin. My calf itched as the breeze moved over my wound. Streaks of black and blue ran from my knee to my puffy ankle.

Cyrus placed a hand just under the jagged cut, examining my leg. Warmth radiated from his palm, making me a little dizzy. My wolf inched forward, watching the omega carefully.

I forced my eyes away from his face and stared at my wound. It was puckered, shiny, and appeared to be just barely holding together. *My first scar.* It should have brought me pride—all fierce alphas had scars—but its still fragile appearance scared me. *Why hadn't it healed?*

"It does look a little better today," he said, nodding in approval.

"Better?" I whispered, unable to believe what he was saying. "*This* looks better?"

Tallis grimaced and turned away from me, staring into the trees around us. I knew what he was thinking. *I was a pathetic excuse for an alpha.*

Just like the whispers that followed me up and down the corridors of my home, these two rogues thought I was less than them as well. I was an alpha with a shit sense of smell, no control over my wolf, and now it appeared I couldn't heal myself either.

Without a word, Tallis picked me up. I didn't protest or fight, letting him carry me to the stream. He settled me on a large flat rock on the edge, easing my legs into the freezing water. I hissed as the cold rushed over my fragile skin. It made my joints ache, but somehow still felt good.

After I was settled, they both moved away from me,

turning their backs, once again giving me privacy to wash. I stared at them, trying not to think about the cold water lapping over the lip of the rock. The soft waves sloshed, and goosebumps flashed up my sides. It was calming—the cold anchoring me to this moment.

Tallis smoothed his hand down Cyrus's broad back, then back up to his nape. He squeezed his mate's neck, the touch possessive but somehow still sweet. Cyrus leaned in, resting his head on the alpha's big shoulder. They stayed like that, touching gently while they waited for me to finish.

*It must be so lovely to have someone love you.*

The only people who ever loved me were Rainer, who was dead, and Emmy, whom I abandoned. If my leg refused to heal, there was no way I could save her, and even if it did heal, I wasn't sure if I'd be able to actually save her. Shame burned through me, and I scowled at myself for ever thinking I was bold enough to break back into the pack-house and steal her away. I was so fucking stupid.

*Emmy must hate me.*

Even as the awful thought burrowed through my mind, I knew it wasn't true, but I couldn't help but think it. Emmy was small, fragile, and still living in that horrible house. How could I leave her? What was I thinking?

A deep sadness squeezed my chest, and I gripped the wet hem of my shirt, trying to control my emotions. My nose itched, and I sniffled.

"Sana?" Cyrus's soft voice made me look up. "Are you okay?"

His dark eyes held so much worry for me, and I swallowed hard to keep from bursting into tears. In all my time on this earth, I had cried maybe a handful of times, but lately it seemed I couldn't stop the urge. A part of me wanted to lean into it. *If I was broken, I might as well let my cracks show.*

"I'm okay." I cleared my throat, needing to distract myself from the pain radiating through my body and the tears burning the back of my eyes. "How long have you two been mated?"

Cyrus smiled up at his mate, his brown eyes sparkling. He looked so young despite the dark scruff along his jaw. "Five years. Tallis was passing through my village, got drunk, and picked a fight." The corner of Tallis's lips twitched as if remembering the moment fondly. "He ended up with a blade between his ribs. Two guards dragged his angry ass all the way to the infirmary."

"I won that fight." Tallis bumped his shoulder into Cyrus's. "Those assholes made me leave before I could enjoy my victory drink."

Cyrus rolled his eyes. "He acted like an animal, tearing up the cots and snarling at everyone. But there was something about him that pulled me to him. And the second I touched his arm, he went quiet."

A slow, sexy smile spread across Tallis's face, and he brushed his fingers through Cyrus's hair. They looked at each other as if the rest of the world didn't exist. It seemed almost too intimate to watch.

"I didn't believe in fated mates until that moment," Tallis said. "But this little healer stole my heart instantly."

I raised my brows in surprise. "You're a healer? Like not just growing herbs for the infirmary, but you *worked* as a healer?" I shifted a little closer to the pair. My feet were growing numb, but it dulled the pain, so I kept them in the water.

"Of course." Cyrus smiled sweetly. "In Hala, omegas don't work to heal alphas, but we can be helpful in calming an alpha quickly when we have to. Do omegas not work as healers in your village?"

"Absolutely not," I said quickly. "Omegas aren't allowed to work." Cyrus's smile fell a bit. "I don't mean to upset you, but this isn't Hala. Here in the mountains, the orcs and griffins seek omegas out. Having a mess of them congregating in the marketplace or the infirmary would attract monsters to the village. We keep omegas inside to keep them safe."

"We aren't weak," Cyrus said softly, offense clear in his big eyes.

"I don't want to be the asshole here," I said, trying to keep my tone light, "but there's no way you have the ability to fight off the monsters that live out here."

Tallis stiffened, taking a few controlled steps toward me.

"*I* live out here," Cyrus snipped. "*I* have fought off many monsters."

I pressed my lips together. I was fucking up what I was trying to say. "I don't mean to imply you're weak. But the fact is omegas can't protect themselves. You don't have the same strength—"

Tallis growled, crossing his arms over his big chest. "Doesn't really surprise me that someone from Casin would think that."

I glared, refusing to back down from his cutting tone.

"That's why your village is dying out. The whole fucking place is just alphas mating with alphas. You're lucky to get one heir with those kinds of pairings."

I bared my teeth, pleased when my fangs easily pushed forward. "We need warriors to protect our borders. Mating an omega or beta means the possibility of weaker pups, and more pack members who can't fight. My father encourages alpha pairs to keep us strong."

Tallis looked down at me with barely contained disgust, as if I were the one who controlled our pack's customs. "You cage your omegas," he snarled, "and you use betas like they're fucking property."

"We do *not* cage our omegas," I said as loudly as I could, but I was still so tired. "Just this last winter, orcs broke through our gates and almost made it past the market. We were able to fight them off, but a few almost made it to the pack cabins. Do you honestly believe omegas should be allowed to wander wherever the hell they want with those monsters at our door?"

"But you don't deny using betas," Tallis said, his features pointed. Cyrus turned to his mate, his expression hard to read. He didn't look upset, but something like sadness pulled at the corners of his eyes.

"I don't mean any offense," I said, fighting the urge to touch Cyrus. The need to caress him and make sure he was okay was hard to ignore. "Betas are very important to all villages. We wouldn't exist without them. They're just weaker than—"

"Let me ask you this," Tallis barked.

It made my hackles rise. I wanted to grab Cyrus and force him behind me—shield him from his mate's growing anger.

"Do betas teach your pups? Train them? Care for them? Care for you?" He lowered his voice, his fangs growing sharp. "Have you ever used a beta during your heat?"

I clenched my jaw, refusing to answer. I held a deep respect for betas. The servants in the packhouse put up with an unimaginable amount of shit from my demanding mother and barbaric father. Betas were proud, determined, and honorable, and what Tallis was insinuating was disgusting.

When I didn't answer, Tallis closed the space between us, standing so close I could touch him. "If you've ever *used*," he let the word ooze from his mouth like poison, "one beta—"

"I don't understand why the fuck you're yelling at me about this!"

"I've loved a few betas in my time," Tallis snarled. I didn't miss the way Cyrus's gaze dropped, and he took a step back. "They don't deserve to be treated like shit by assholes like you."

"I've never used a beta!" I yelled, shocked when my voice came out loud and strong.

Tallis's eyes widened at my outburst, then he quickly collected himself. "You're full of shit," he spat. "A pretty doll like you would never suffer a heat by yourself."

"Tallis," Cyrus whispered, giving his mate a disapproving look. But he still looked so sad. I cursed my nose, wishing I could scent him. "This isn't appropriate. We don't know—"

"I have only had one lover, and I never *used* him." I balled up my fists to keep them from shaking. "I have always been grateful to the betas in my life. My best friend was a beta."

"Oh, well," Tallis let out a mocking laugh, "if your best friend was a beta, then clearly you're not prejudiced. But tell me, doll," he flashed a shitty smirk, looking as if he had bested me, "why *was* he your best friend? What did you do to end your friendship?"

"My father fucking gutted him!" I roared. Pain shot up and down my body like a lightning bolt, but I was too enraged to care. "My piece of shit father strung Rainer from a hook, murdered him right in front of me, then told me to put on a pretty dress so I could be a gracious host. All because I didn't want to be forced to marry a stranger!" I panted hard, shocked when Tallis's expression fell, his anger completely gone. The pity and shock that poured out of his brown eyes was worse than his rage, and I wished he'd yell at me instead.

"Sana," Cyrus whispered, rushing to my side and placing his hand on my forearm. He squeezed gently, and my thundering heart instantly slowed. "I'm so sorry."

I took a deep breath, letting him calm me. A slip of his comforting scent tingled my nose, pushing some of the tension from my shoulders. I inhaled deeply, trying to pull in as much as I could. It was rare for me to be able to scent others without pressing my nose to their skin.

"Is your father an advisor to your pack alpha?" Tallis asked, watching my expression carefully. The muscle in my jaw ticked, and he shook his head. "Your father *is* the pack alpha, isn't he?"

I dropped my gaze, watching the water slosh gently against the side of the rock. It was rhythmic and quiet.

"I knew you were someone important," Tallis said. "No one sends a fleet of guards to look for a merchant's daughter." He turned to Cyrus, speaking as if I wasn't sitting right next to him. "I told you not to pull her out of that pit."

Cyrus glared, meeting Tallis's hard expression head-on. I could only assume they were communicating through their bond.

Unable to take the silence, I asked, "What are you going to do with me?" They would probably get a handsome reward if they returned me. My wolf whimpered at the thought, wanting to stay with the wolves. For some reason, she trusted them. It should have brought me comfort, but she was too unpredictable to be trusted.

Tallis broke eye contact with his mate, taking a few steps back. He looked ready to crack a boulder in two.

Taking a calming breath, Cyrus stared at where my legs disappeared into the water. "First we need to feed you. You haven't eaten properly in days, then we can work on putting more weight on that leg. I think the bone is good, but I'm concerned about how long it's taking for your muscles to heal."

He was purposefully not answering, and I snarled, sick of their games.

A twig snapped in the distance, and my muscles tensed. My wolf was suddenly alert, begging me to run and fight. Trying to ignore my intense instincts but completely failing, I stood and jerked, hobbling toward the shore. Cyrus yelled at me to stop, both he and Tallis reaching for me. A warm hand touched my arm, and my wolf slammed hard within me. My fangs punched out, and my claws instantly engaged.

"S, stop!" I begged my beast, but it was too late. Both my legs jerked, and I fell forward. I flung my hands out to protect my face, but just before I hit the ground, Tallis grabbed me around the waist and crushed me to his chest.

"What the fuck?" he snapped, his dark eyes darting all over my face.

I panted hard, trying to pull my beast back. She was still spiraling inside me, begging to break free, but it was so fucking hard to control her right now.

"There's something seriously wrong with her," Cyrus said to his mate.

His hand pressed to my forehead, and my lungs filled

with an intense mix of both wolves. It was sweet, soft, and earthy. I inhaled again, and the knot in my chest eased a bit.

Tallis lifted me up, pressing me against his chest.

I wanted to shove him away and fight my own battles, but how do you win a war with your own body?

Reaching up, Cyrus caressed my arm, and Tallis splayed his hand across my back, holding me as if I was something valuable and worthy. I sagged against his big chest, feeling safe.

And for the first time in my life, my wolf agreed.

# CHAPTER ELEVEN

*fishing*

Sana

---

"Careful there, doll," Tallis warned.

"I got it," I said, trying not to sound too annoyed but failing miserably.

"Not too much weight," Cyrus reminded me as I waded in a little deeper.

I pressed the toes of my wounded leg into the pebbles and silt, trying to be as careful as possible. A decent-sized trout circled my ankle, and I jerked toward it, splashing the water and falling over.

Tallis's booming laugh hit my ears, and my face warmed. "It's not fucking funny, asshole," I snarled. "It's really fucking hard to do this on one leg."

Cyrus popped Tallis in the arm before wading out to me. "Fishing isn't for everyone," he said sweetly, reaching for my arm. He pulled me up, resting his hand on my back to help steady me.

I didn't know why I was fishing anyway; my appetite was weak at best, and I just wanted to sleep. Feeling a little overwhelmed as my temples pulsed, I rested my head against Cyrus's shoulder, trying to breathe deeply through my mouth. The last few days, nausea kept hitting me out of nowhere in waves.

Tallis smiled as he watched Cyrus hold me upright, but it didn't look as mocking as before, his eyes pulling downward in the corners. *More pity.* "Are you two going to be okay if I step into the tree line?" he asked, adjusting his belt buckle. "I've got to piss."

"We're okay." Cyrus nodded, smoothing his hand down my back. My skin prickled with far too much sensation, his touch both soothing and uncomfortable at the same time.

I stared at the big alpha's back, not speaking until he disappeared behind a fat spruce. "Thank you." I cleared my throat, leaning away from the omega. "Thank you for everything."

Cyrus smiled sweetly, caressing my upper arms. I needed him to stop touching me. Even my shirt felt like sandpaper against my skin, but it also felt so good to my wolf, making my heart settle and stomach ease.

"You've improved so much in the last few days," Cyrus said, glancing at my leg. "But you need to eat more. And..." he hesitated for a moment, "I've noticed you're not sleeping well either. Is it the pain?"

I shrugged, not sure what it was. Cyrus had made me a lovely pallet on the cave floor, but every time I lay down, my skin felt as if ants were crawling just under the surface. It itched and burned, making me restless.

"I'm fine," I said, not wanting the omega to worry. "Once I'm a little steadier, I'll be on my way."

His smile dimmed and he crossed his arms. "Where will you go?"

"I haven't decided yet." I cast a look at the mountains in the distance and the endless row of trees between me and the snow-white peaks. It would be hard to care for Emmy in such exposed lands, but I had no other choice. "I'll figure it out," I said, hobbling toward the shore. My back hurt, and sweat flashed down my sides. I just needed to sit for a moment.

"Why don't you just stay with us?" Cyrus asked, following me.

I plopped onto the nearest rock, just next to a filleted fish Tallis had caught earlier. Cyrus reached for a chunk of the silvery white flesh, handing it to me. I pushed my lips up into a smile, then popped it into my mouth. It sat on my tongue, my mouth watering as if I might be sick.

Lately, nothing tasted good. And I glanced at my leg, wondering if there could be a deep infection that Cyrus couldn't see or Tallis couldn't scent. Feeling Cyrus's eyes on me, I forced myself to chew, then swallow. It slid down my throat, a fat lump sitting heavy in my gut.

"I don't think Tallis would like me staying with you," I said, glancing into the trees. "He doesn't like me very much."

"Trust me." Cyrus smiled wide. "He does."

I furrowed my brow, giving the omega a pointed look. He pushed out a small laugh, understanding what I meant.

"Tallis hates anyone touching me," he said. "And I mean *anyone*. Even an innocent touch."

"Of course," I said, understanding. "Any alpha would. You don't fucking touch someone else's mate."

"Yeah." He leaned forward. "But he doesn't mind when you do."

I paused, thinking about it. The alpha didn't seem all that bothered when Cyrus would hug or caress me. It was probably because of my weakened state. After all, a dying alpha couldn't steal an omega.

"I'm sure he's just being polite," I said. "He probably doesn't want to upset you."

"Tallis is shit at hiding his feelings. If something bothers him, everyone in a five-mile radius knows it."

I snorted, my ribs pinching at the sound. "Yeah, he definitely seems to just do or say whatever pops into his mind."

"And when he gets protective over me, it doesn't matter where we are or what we're doing. He uses his fists, then asks questions later. But with you..." he paused as if thinking, then shook his head, "there's no possessive rage or territorial alpha shit. He likes you."

"I just wish he'd stop saying such crass things," I whispered, glaring at the trees.

Cyrus nodded in understanding. "He tends to speak his mind, but he's got a good heart."

"He's still an ass," I mumbled.

"I've been called worse," Tallis's booming voice cut over the sound of the stream as he walked toward us.

I crossed my arms, looking the alpha right in the eyes. He smiled lazily at me, pushing his shoulders back and stretching. "Cyrus thinks you like me," I said, watching Tallis's reaction carefully.

"I do," he said, giving me a quick nod. My mouth hung open, unable to hide my shock. "You've got grit." He pointed to my leg. "Any wolf able to push through something like that deserves my respect."

I closed my mouth, unsure how to respond to his compliment. I was convinced he thought me weak and pathetic, something to pity and not to take seriously.

Tallis's expression shifted, going playful. "But you still smell like shit," he shot.

I glared hard as he tipped his head back, laughing loudly. Unable to help myself, I finally smiled at the big idiot. He was an ass, but at least he was harmless.

"Here." Cyrus handed me another piece of fish, popping a large chunk into his own mouth. "Eat up. We need to get you better."

I stared at it. The cool meat warmed in my palm and heat flashed up and down my sides. My stomach churned hard, and I fell to my hands and knees, gagging hard into the ice-cold water.

# CHAPTER TWELVE

## walking home

Cyrus

---

SANA'S HANDS TREMBLED UNCONTROLLABLY AS SHE PRESSED HER forehead to Tallis's chest. I had only ever seen one other alpha display symptoms like this, and it scared me for her.

That first night, after Sana passed out, I took the opportunity to sniff the crook of her neck. She smelled sharp and acidic. It wasn't natural, and I had wondered if she had been poisoned or bewitched. But now, watching her shake and pant, it was clear what she was going through. *Withdrawals.*

My healer training urged me to question her about what she had eaten, if she took any unknown herbs, the state of her wolf, and a plethora of other things that might be causing her symptoms. But now wasn't the time. She needed rest.

"What's wrong?" Sana asked, looking right at me. Her voice was strained.

I hadn't realized I was staring. "Nothing." I smiled, trying not to worry her. She narrowed her eyes, the she-alpha clearly not in the mood to be brushed off. I cleared my throat, hoping I wouldn't offend her. "I was just trying to figure out what's wrong with you."

Her vibrant blue eyes widened. "There's *nothing* wrong with me," she whispered, trying to look fierce, but the dark circles under her eyes just made her look tired. "I'm sick and tired of being told my wolf is wrong or broken or—"

"Quiet," Tallis ordered, coming to an abrupt stop. Every muscle in his big body went still, his eyes scanning every leaf and pebble. He held Sana a little tighter, cradling her against his chest.

Facing the same way as him, I scented the air. My nose wasn't able to pick up the subtleties an alpha could, but there was a slight stench of sweat in the air. *Someone was here.*

Tallis hunched his shoulders and slumped a bit as if trying to make himself smaller, a laughable attempt. He gave a soft click of his tongue, indicating I should follow, then he set off.

Sana wrapped her arms tight around his neck as he rushed toward a familiar cut of land. We had slept in the jagged formation of rocks and shallow caves when we first arrived in the area. It was too exposed to stay there, but right now, it was a suitable hiding place.

Tallis raced across the flat stone, easily hopping over the fractured cracks that led deep into the earth. He jumped over a particularly wide gap, then stopped. He jerked his head to a wedge at the base of a massive boulder, and I immediately ran to it. I slipped my legs down the narrow opening, pushing myself inside. The space was long but tight.

Rolling onto my side, I looked up. From this angle, all I could see was Tallis's feet. He crouched and pressed Sana in after me, followed by his big body. He had to force himself inside, the rock scraping over his thighs, chest, and arms. Once he was settled, he wrapped an arm around me with Sana sandwiched between us. It was a tight fit.

Sana looked up at me, her brow twisted with confusion. "What's happening?" she whispered.

Before I could answer, a thick waft of a foreign alpha hit my nose. Sana's eyes dilated and flashed with deep anger, but her hands curled into tight fists. I wasn't sure if she was ready to fight or struggling to control her wolf. I wished like hell I could smell her natural scent to know for sure.

Footsteps quickly approached, slapping against the smooth stone. Sana tensed and shook uncontrollably between us, but to her credit, she didn't make a sound. Tallis gently squeezed her upper arms, pressing his chest into her back and forcing her closer to me. He liked to tease me for caring too much, but his fierce determination to protect those who couldn't fight was one of the things I loved most about him.

He was just as soft as me, if not softer.

A deep voice groaned, and an alpha whined, "It's clear she isn't here, Tamen. We need to head west. Maybe even north. Hell, at this point we're probably just looking for a body."

The thick scent of three, maybe four alphas hit my nose. I looked at my mate, not sure.

Tallis held up three fingers, answering my unspoken question.

"I'm telling you, I can fucking feel her," another male whispered.

I recognized the voice. Tamen. He was one of the Casin

wolves who had been searching for Sana that first week, but we hadn't scented them in a few days. I was hoping they had given up.

"You're full of shit. You can't sense anything about the damn girl, and you know it." A she-alpha moved into view. Her legs were long and toned, a few deep scars lining her knees. She huffed then growled, "Alpha Hector is going to skin us alive when he returns from Hund Valley, but there's no helping it. She's gone."

Sana stiffened at the female's words, and deep lines settled between her brows as she glanced over her shoulder, trying to see the Casin wolves. Tallis shook his head, indicating she needed to stay still.

Leaning down, I nuzzled my nose into Sana's hair, hoping to settle her. Her scent bloomed, a trace of something sweet cutting through the strange bitter scent. I glanced at Tallis, and he smiled softly at me. He could smell it too.

"If you want to cut north then fucking go. But she's here." Tamen sucked in a long breath, the sound almost sharp. "I can feel it."

Sana closed her eyes. Her fists were so tightly balled up between us, I half-expected blood to seep out between her fingers. Her legs jerked, and fear beat hard in my chest. She was struggling with her wolf again.

Tallis gave me a panicked look as I grabbed her tight fists, trying to ease her. Her eyes snapped open. They were bright red, pulsing repeatedly between a violent crimson color and dark blue. She opened her mouth, and her fangs punched out, making her grimace.

*Fuck.*

Sana jerked again, this time so hard, Tallis jerked with her. My mate grabbed her hip, trying to hold her still, but it was no use. A muffled yip slipped from Sana's throat as she struggled. Tallis's eyes went wide, and the footsteps grew closer.

"Did you hear that?" Tamen asked. The air went dead silent, and my heart thundered so damn hard, I was sure they could hear it. "Over here."

I looked up to see Tamen's feet just next to us. If he crouched down, he'd see us, and there was no escape. My wolf yowled and cowered, terrified of being caught.

Sana arched her back, the veins in her neck straining as she struggled to stay in control. She needed a distraction, and I thought seriously of kicking her wounded leg to refocus her wolf, but she'd probably scream.

Not sure what to do, I looked at my mate, my mouth open in complete panic.

Taking one look at my face, Tallis gripped Sana's arm, jerked the collar of her shirt down, then sank his fangs deep into her shoulder. She gasped and tensed, then the tension left her body as she sagged against the ground.

Letting out a slow breath of relief, I pushed my gratitude to my mate through our bond.

"Do you smell that?" the female alpha asked, stepping up next to Tamen. They both turned with the wind, their backs to us. "Blood."

My eyes widened, and Tallis closed his lips around Sana's bite mark. He sucked deep to keep any blood from hitting the air. My bond with him pulsed as his mind settled, and he closed his eyes.

Sana's eyes fluttered, and I pressed my forehead to hers. "It's okay," I whispered as softly as I could, trying to push my comforting presence into her. She gave me a small nod, her eyes hooded as if drugged. She looked like she might fall asleep at any moment, and a part of me prayed she would. She needed the rest.

We stayed like that for a while, Tallis's fangs buried in Sana's skin while I touched and caressed her. I pulled my fingers through her long, thick hair, keeping my eyes on the Casin guards' feet. They paced and argued before finally moving away from us.

After a few more minutes, Tallis slowly withdrew his teeth, then lapped at Sana's torn flesh. I brushed her hair out of the way, tilting her head to expose the full length of her neck and shoulder, so Tallis could clean the bite more thoroughly. A soft hum left Sana's throat, and she closed her eyes while we tended to her.

Whispering so softly I almost didn't hear him, Tallis leaned into Sana's ear. "I think they're gone." He didn't seem angry with her, which made me feel a bit better. This wasn't her fault.

As if coming out of a trance, Sana blinked a few times, then whispered, "I'm sorry." She pulled in a deep breath. "My wolf was just...she gets...distressed sometimes, and I can't..." She stopped talking, clearly not wanting to admit she had no control over her beast.

An alpha disconnected with their wolf was dangerous. They were violent, unhinged, and unpredictable. If it weren't for the guards who were clearly trying to drag her back home, I would have assumed she was banished from her village for being a threat.

"Have you always struggled to control your wolf, doll?" Tallis asked Sana, his voice hushed.

She looked over her shoulder, glaring at my mate. Their faces were so close, I couldn't help but wonder what they might look like if they kissed. Fierce, strong, powerful. They were beautiful alphas.

I jerked at the thought and pulled my hands away from Sana's hair, tucking them under my arms.

"Why do you keep calling me '*doll*'?" she asked.

Tallis's mouth curved into a smile, and he looked past me as if remembering something. "My sister had a porcelain doll that looked like you. Big blue eyes, yellow hair with ringlets, smooth white skin. It was a pretty doll."

Sana softened between us, the corner of her full lips pulling upward at his compliment.

"But it had this big, ugly crack that ran down its face, and right over one of its arms." He glanced down at her leg, cocking an eyebrow with a teasing smirk. "You look exactly like it."

Sana snarled and jabbed her elbow back into his ribs. He pressed his lips together, his chest shaking with silent laughter.

"I am *not* broken," she hissed, but she didn't really seem offended. She looked like she was fighting off the urge to smile.

"Just a little cracked." His smirk grew.

I reached over Sana and smacked his biceps. He was trying to distract her from the alphas still lurking in the trees around us, but if he wasn't careful, he'd work her up too much, and she'd shift into her wolf, killing both of us.

"You're a dick," she shot.

Tallis's mouth dropped open, feigning offense. I couldn't help but smile at the lug. "I am the definition of proper," he said. "Some would even say I'm posh."

"I'm sure," Sana snorted softly.

"It's true," Tallis continued, his eyes becoming comically wide. It was so nice to see him goofy again. It had been a hard year, and I missed him like this. "I'm a proper fucking gentleman. I have never told a lie or spilled a drink."

She raised her brows. "Does spilling drinks mean you're a rogue?"

"Absolutely. Only a bastard would waste a good drink." His expression went deadly serious. "I down my brew with a pinky in the air, and I've never even looked at a bar wench with an improper thought."

It was a bald-faced lie, and I struggled not to laugh out loud.

"Ridiculous." Sana shook her head, the corners of her lips lifting.

Tallis winked at her. I swore he could charm the slacks off a temple priest.

The smile that brightened Sana's pretty face slipped, and she cleared her throat. "My father," she licked her lips, fidgeting a bit before continuing, "my father will stop at nothing to bring me home. Running away really fucked him. He won't be happy until I'm caught or dead."

"Sana." I cupped her cheeks, forcing her to look at me. My wolf pawed at my chest, wanting me to touch her more. I quickly released her, threading my fingers together to keep from touching her again. "I promise you, we won't let them find you."

Her face contorted with confusion. "I know I keep asking, but," she sighed hard, "why do you care? I'm no one to you."

I didn't know what to say that would make her happy. I had told her a dozen times we just wanted to help, but she was so guarded—jaded—she just couldn't believe it. "We know what it's like to be lost out here with nowhere to go."

She nodded, letting out a soft sigh. "I have to go back."

Disappointment and fear twisted inside me at the thought of her leaving.

"Why the fuck would you go through all this just to go back home?" Tallis growled. I pressed a finger to my lips, reminding him to keep quiet. He glared at me, then lowered his voice. "Why risk everything just to willingly crawl back into your cage?"

She glanced at him over her shoulder. "I need to go back for my little sister. I was planning to escape with my friend...Rainer." She hesitated before saying his name, the word holding a lot of emotion. "We had planned everything so well. I was going to bring Emmy with us. I know it's stupid to think I could have managed an omega out here..." She shook her head in frustration. "After my father killed Rainer, I panicked and ran. I left her."

Tallis rolled forward a bit, pressing her snug to my chest. His alpha instincts were driving him hard to protect and soothe the wounded she-wolf.

"She's an omega?" he asked, our eyes meeting briefly.

"Yes," she whispered, "and I have to go back and get her. My parents are cruel, and she's so small and fragile. She's the only thing in this world that loves me anymore, and I abandoned her."

My heart twisted, and so did my bond with Tallis.

Neither one of us wanted to see her go.

# CHAPTER THIRTEEN

*squished*

Sana

---

ALL THE PAIN, FEAR, AND PANIC SEEPED OUT OF ME, SOAKING INTO the cool stone. The bite on my shoulder tingled as Tallis's warm, flat tongue lapped, making my cheeks flush and my pulse quicken. I stared at Cyrus, praying to the Moon. Neither one of them could sense how much I needed them in that moment.

It was pathetic and shameful, but I was an alpha with no control, and they were grounding me. Something I had never had before.

Tallis went quiet after I spoke of Emmy. He was clearly upset about something, and I wondered if it was the bite or the fact that I put his mate in so much danger, but Cyrus didn't seem bothered in the least by his mate's demeanor. The omega chatted softly with a sweet smile on his face, distracting me as the hours ticked by. He asked an endless barrage of questions, urging me to talk about my Emmy and the silly things we did back home. I talked about our adventures in the gardens, the ridiculous books she tried to get me to read, and how she snuck into bed with me almost every single night. Emmy was sensitive and cried easily. It annoyed everyone else, but I liked it. I felt useful, protecting her from her gentle emotions and our parents' hateful comments. It was the only time I ever felt strong.

It was almost dark by the time Tallis allowed us to head back to the tiny cave. I was thankful to stretch, but my wolf whimpered. She wanted to stay crushed between the two wolves forever. It was unusually safe.

Tallis carried me, and I allowed myself to relax against him. His big arms and broad chest were comforting, something I never thought I'd find in another alpha. Once we were back in the cave, Cyrus settled next to me, looking at my leg. I expected him to touch me, but sadly he didn't, making my wolf whimper.

"The first thing we need to do," he said, "is figure out why your leg isn't healing the way it should. This kind of wound should heal easily for an alpha. The fact that you're still having problems bearing weight is a little concerning."

I dropped my gaze, feeling like a complete failure. *What kind of alpha couldn't heal themselves?*

Tallis set a chunk of luminite next to his mate, casting a lovely dim light around the whole cave. The crystal shimmered, giving the illusion of a fire dancing on the walls.

I looked up at him to thank him for everything he had done for me, but before I could speak, our eyes met, and all thought fell from my head. His light brown eyes held mine, making the bite on my shoulder tingle. It felt good and tender beneath my shirt, and I had to fight like hell to keep from touching it.

Warm hands ghosted over my shin, and I turned back to Cyrus. The heat radiating from his hand made goosebumps flash up and down my leg. I shook my head, feeling suddenly hot and far too dizzy.

"It looks okay," Cyrus's voice had a pleasant lift to it. "The bruising has already improved since this morning." He palmed the bottom of my foot, and I hissed. The pain wasn't unbearable, but I wouldn't be racing over the hillside anytime soon.

"Do you take any medicine or herbs on a regular basis? Anything that looks...odd?" Cyrus asked. I shook my head as he jumped into a series of unusual questions. He asked about my eating habits, the kinds of lotions I used, my stress level, which made Tallis laugh, and even about my last heat.

"I'm sorry." I held up my hands, not thrilled to discuss my cycle with anyone outside my family's personal healer. "Why do you need to know this?"

Cyrus gave me a bashful smile. It made him look very young, and very cute. "I apologize. I'm a healer." He paused. "I *was* a healer. It's habit. I don't mean to pry, but it really would help to know."

I didn't have a good reason not to tell him, especially if he could fix me. Maybe he could fix my wolf. But it was so personal. I cut a nervous glance at Tallis. "I'm not in the mood for your opinion on this," I snipped.

I expected the normally vocal alpha to crack a joke or try to rile me up, but he simply nodded, moving to the entrance of the cave. He gave Cyrus an odd look before turning his back to us.

Cyrus bowed his head, his shoulders slumped.

"What's going on?" I asked. Tallis had been far too

quiet, and I hated it. *Who knew I'd miss the jerk's constant jokes?*

"He feels guilty about the bite," Cyrus whispered. His eyes pulled at the corners as he looked at his mate. "He feels bad, like he betrayed me, but he didn't. I didn't feel that way when it happened, and I don't feel that way now. But he still feels bad."

"Oh." I placed my fingers over the bite, caressing it through my shirt. "I didn't think of how intimate that was." *And it was.* And what was even more bizarre was, any time I even thought of another alpha getting their fangs anywhere near me, it would make my wolf snarl and my mind rage. But Tallis's bite had instantly calmed me. How did he know it would do that?

"I'm so sorry, Cyrus. I didn't mean—"

He held up his hand, a sweet smile on his face. "Sana," he laughed softly, "I'm fine. I really am." There was something in his eyes that made me want to believe him, but I still felt like shit. The last thing I wanted was to cause a problem between these two. They had saved me, and to cause a rip in their bond would be a horrible way to give my thanks.

"Stop it," he said. My brows pinched together in confusion, and he pressed his finger between them, easing the lines away. "I swear alphas aren't happy unless you're worrying about something. *I'm fine.*"

My wolf still whimpered with guilt.

"Now," he rested his elbows on his knees and leaned forward, "your last heat?"

My face warmed, and I grimaced. I fucking hated having to admit this, but I had no reason not to. "I don't know," I mumbled. "Over a year. Maybe longer."

He nodded, keeping his face blank of all emotion. "Have you felt any desire since your last heat? Anything that has woken your wolf in that manner? Even a general interest in mating?"

I couldn't look him in the eye, because I had felt that way, and it was shameful.

"Sana," Cyrus whispered. "I promise, it's okay. I'm not asking to be intrusive. I really do just want to help."

"Yes." It was barely a word, more of a breathy sound.

"When?"

I didn't want to answer. The thought of hurting Cyrus was more than I could bear.

"Please," he placed his hand over mine, squeezing gently, "I promise it'll be okay."

Keeping my head down, I licked my lips, then whispered as softly as I could, "When Tallis bit me."

He inhaled sharply, but he didn't react otherwise. "I see." His voice was tight, making me glance up.

Dark hair fell into his eyes, casting shadows across his angular nose. My wolf prowled a little closer, wanting me to touch his face to soothe and comfort him. The intense desire to press my mouth to his and see if he tasted as soft and sweet as he sounded flared up inside me, and I jerked my hands away.

Cyrus didn't react, letting me lean away from him. "You said you had a lover before," he continued, his tone still impressively professional. "Did your wolf respond well to him?"

I paused, having to think about it. "Honestly, I don't remember. He worked in the stables with Rainer. We were both young and had no idea what we were doing. But it wasn't about love. He was just a fun bit of rebellion."

Cyrus cocked his head, not understanding.

"It would have killed my mother if she ever found out," I explained, thankful to be talking about something else. "That whole summer, I snuck out to the stables and let that bashful beta take me in any manner he wanted. Honestly, I was a bit disappointed when my mother never discovered us." Without thinking, I reached out and placed my hand on Cyrus's arm. I needed to feel something comforting right now.

Awareness made my skin tingle, and I turned to the mouth of the cave. I expected to see Tallis glaring at me for touching his mate, but his expression was almost painful. As if having a mind of their own, my fingers circled around Cyrus's wrist.

Tallis's eyes drifted toward the movement. His forehead wrinkled, and his fists slowly tightened. Then, as if coming out of a trance, his eyes flashed to mine. "Don't touch him!"

His alpha tone had me on edge, the need to fight and challenge him building up inside me. I gripped Cyrus's arm tighter. The omega didn't move, just staring at his mate.

I bared my teeth, glaring at Tallis hard. "You had no problem biting me, but me holding Cyrus's hand crosses the line for you?"

The already tense alpha stood up, his head grazing the top of the cave. He stalked toward me, his already enormous body seeming to double in size as he approached. Cyrus's hand trembled in mine, and I released him, letting the omega scoot away.

As Tallis leaned down into my face, his hair swung forward, pushing his rich, masculine scent into my nose. It sent a confusing twist of desire through me, and I snarled, enraged by my body's reaction to the alpha. He smelled like a dirty dream sent to torture me for all my past sins. He was an asshole, hell-bent on pissing me the fuck off while turning me the fuck on.

I growled low in my chest, not in the mood for his shit.

Apparently not in the mood either, Tallis whipped his hand out, grabbing my throat. Then he growled, "What the fuck did you just say to me?"

# CHAPTER FOURTEEN

## *still in the cave*

Tallis

---

"STOP!" CYRUS YELLED, THE LOOK ON HIS FACE MAKING IT CLEAR he thought I was going to attack Sana. I wasn't, but I was too worked up. I wasn't even sure why I was angry, just that I felt like shit, and I needed a moment to figure out what I was going to say.

I opened my mouth to try to calm Cyrus, but Sana cut me off, growling low in her throat, the sound vibrating against my hand.

"Both of you stop it now!" the omega said in a rush of words. He tugged at my arm, trying to pull me away from her.

Sana's throat worked against my palm as she swallowed hard, but she didn't back down. Her eyes flashed red, and she snarled, "You're such an asshole. You have no problem touching me, even biting me, but touching Cyrus's wrist is unforgivable?"

I squeezed the thin column of her throat, loving the way her cheeks blushed pink. She was so pale. Easy to bruise. The thought made my cock plump, and I jerked my hand back.

Deep shock at my body's reaction stole my ability to think for a moment.

"Tallis?" Cyrus asked, deep concern twisting between his brows. "Are you okay?"

Before I could stop it, my sudden lust traveled to him, our bond flooding with desire and confusion. Unable to look him in the eye, I turned back to Sana. "My mate is none of your fucking business. If I don't want you to touch him, you don't fucking touch him. Do you understand?"

"Are you kicking me out?" she asked, completely ignoring my question. I could tell she wanted to look at Cyrus, but she kept her eyes locked on me, refusing to even blink.

I opened my mouth to tell her to leave, to wander the forest on her own, but my wolf roared and raged so violently within me at the thought that I had to take a step back.

"Tallis," Cyrus whispered. It was only my name, but his tone carried the weight of a thousand words. He knew I wanted her. He could feel it. But more than that, he seemed *okay* with it? Maybe not okay, but he wasn't upset.

And I just knew if I threw the she-wolf out on her ass, he'd never speak to me again, especially while she was still hurt. Hell, judging by my wolf's reaction, there was a good chance even he would abandon me.

I just didn't understand what was happening to me.

Sana's scent was off-putting, and she pushed back on every fucking thing I said, but my beast seemed to really like her. When we were in the cave, in that brief moment when I decided to bite her, I just knew it would work. An alpha's bite was rarely soothing to another alpha. It riled us up and made us want to fight, but I just *knew* it was going to calm Sana.

Then the taste of her sweet blood on my tongue...*fuck*.

She tasted so fucking right. So right that it felt like a deep betrayal of my mate's trust.

"Tallis?" Sana's brows pulled together, her voice unusually soft. It was the kind of tone reserved for an omega. "Are you okay?"

Trying to settle myself, I inhaled deeply, and Sana's sharp scent hit me hard, pushing deep into my lungs. But this time, something sweet lingered on the back of my tongue. It reminded me of the first time I met Cyrus. I liked it. *And I desperately wanted more.*

My eyes pulsed red, and I practically ran to the cave's entrance. I sucked in a gulping breath of fresh air, trying to calm the fuck down. Everything was assaulting me: Cyrus's confusion, fear, and worry pulsed in my head. Sana's weird perfume forced its way into my nose. And even my beast was alight with desires a mated alpha should never have toward someone else.

"Tallis," Cyrus said from somewhere behind me. "You're scaring me."

I took another deep breath. In and out. In and out. The smell of oak, elm, and fresh mountain water eased my beast. "I'm okay." My voice was hoarse, but I felt stronger. More in control.

Someone touched my elbow, and I turned, surprised to see Sana. "I'll go," she whispered softly to keep from upsetting Cyrus. He looked almost distraught sitting next to the glowing luminate, his dark eyes watching us carefully. "I don't want to distress Cyrus," she said. "My presence isn't good for him. After he falls asleep—"

"No," I said, loud and firm. The thought of her leaving was too much. I didn't want to keep her, but I couldn't get rid of her either. I just needed some time to figure it all out.

"I thought you wanted me to leave." Her brows pulled together as she examined me with cautious eyes.

I cleared my throat, hoping I sounded firm and sure. "You put Cyrus at risk today." She tipped her chin up, but the slight hunch in her shoulders spoke volumes, and I hated myself for making her feel bad, but I didn't know what else to say. "I don't care how you feel about me letting you touch Cyrus, but he's *my* mate. So if I tell you to keep your hands off him, you don't fucking touch him. Got it?"

I didn't know what I was doing anymore. Why wasn't I kicking her out?

*I was a fucking mess.*

Sana narrowed her eyes, her back going impossibly straight. There was something about the she-alpha not wanting to back down from me that made my wolf purr.

"Cyrus's safety is the only thing that matters to me," I said, crossing my arms. "I'll do whatever I have to to keep him safe, and I really don't give a shit if you understand it or not."

Sana's jaw clenched before she finally spoke. "Understood."

A slow breath pushed out of me, and I turned toward my mate.

Cyrus still sat next to the glowing crystal, his hands in his lap. He was trying so damn hard not to react, but our bond was a flood of relief and gratitude, love and happiness, everything in between. I moved to him, needing to touch him. To remind my beast that he was okay. Settling behind my mate, I tugged him to me, holding his back flush to my chest.

"Please don't fight," Cyrus begged, motioning for Sana to come sit down. She hesitated before finally coming to sit across from us. He cupped my cheek, looking at me from over his shoulder. "I know you bit her to protect us, and I'm *happy* you did it." I pulled back to look deep into his eyes. He smiled sweetly, placing a quick kiss on my cheek. "Stop feeling guilty, you big jerk."

I squeezed him a bit tighter, knowing damn well I didn't deserve his forgiveness.

I glanced up at Sana, her head bowed to give us a bit of privacy. Her hand rested on her shoulder, her thumb moving in slow circles around what I assumed was the bite mark I left in her skin. There was something about the way she touched it that both thrilled and shamed me.

"Now," Cyrus let out a long sigh, "I don't want any more fighting. Not tonight. It's been a long day, and we all need some rest."

Sana quickly nodded before finally looking up. Our eyes met, and she jerked her hand away from her shoulder, settling both her hands under her bottom.

"You're right," she said, smiling sweetly at Cyrus. "But I need to say thank you first." She bowed her head, placing one hand over her heart. Knowing the kind of posh lifestyle she came from, it didn't escape me that she didn't bow to many wolves in her life. "I really am grateful for your kindness." She forced a small smile, her gaze lingering on my hands splayed across Cyrus's chest. "I didn't know rogues could be so nice."

Cyrus laughed, smoothing his hands over mine. "We aren't rogues. We choose to live out here."

Sana balked. "Why on earth would you want to live in the wildlands?"

"I wanted to see the world," my mate said.

I wasn't sure if Sana bought it or not, but she leaned forward, her expression curious. "I guess I understand that desire. Is there somewhere in particular you want to go?"

"I want to see the ocean," he said, a renewed energy flowing through him. I watched his face brighten as he continued to speak. "I know it's far, but I've never seen the waves outside of paintings, and I just have to know if they really look like frothy clouds. When I was a pup, I was convinced they'd taste like meringue."

Sana laughed with Cyrus, the sound pleasing to my wolf. I smiled with them, unable to help myself.

"I've never seen the ocean either," Sana said to Cyrus with such soft eyes. I should have been livid, but her obvious affection for my mate had my wolf purring. I mentally snarled at myself, so exhausted. *I should have kicked her out.*

"Tallis said we might go to the ocean one day," Cyrus continued, "but we thought we'd try Stone City first. We didn't really have a plan when we left our village. We literally ran—"

"That's enough," I said, making it very clear to my mate that he would not be sharing our story. "It's late, and we need to get some rest."

Sana narrowed her eyes at me, her gratitude instantly replaced with far too much attitude. But true to her word, she didn't challenge me. My wolf whimpered, curious to know what she would have said.

"Something to say?" I asked, giving her a pointed look.

"I've got lots to say," her mouth curved into an almost playful smile, "but I'm not an asshole."

*The balls on this girl.* I leaned in, excited to rib her back. "Did you just call me an asshole? Because you have yet to see just how big a dick I can be, doll."

She tilted her head to the side, narrowing her eyes ever so slightly at me. "Why are all male alphas so obsessed with dicks? I swear, you men think about cock more than omegas do."

I smirked, leaning forward. "It's hard to think about anything else when you've got ten inches—"

"Stop it, both of you," Cyrus snipped. Our bond squeezed with his displeasure, and I let it go. He always hated it when people fought. Even if we were just teasing, he was already on edge, and it probably wasn't helping.

"I'm sorry." I kissed his shoulder.

"Well, you backed down real quick," Sana snorted.

Cyrus gave her a pointed look, and she dropped her gaze. It took every ounce of strength within me not to laugh at how fast she backed down as well.

"Now. If you're both done," my mate gestured to Sana's leg, "I'd like to talk about your wound."

I rested my chin on his shoulder, staying quiet. Sana stared at him, waiting.

"I don't know exactly what the problem is," he said in his professional healer voice. I liked it when he talked like that. It was commanding and sure, but somehow still sweet. "I think there might be something foreign in your system. Your wolf's disjointed reactions, your scent, and your general symptoms are indicators of something affecting you, not something broken within you."

Her features softened. "I'm not disconnected from my wolf? I...I can be fixed?" She sounded scared and hopeful at the same time.

"I think so. I honestly think you might be having withdrawals. I can't tell what it was, but the symptoms all seem to point to the same thing." Cyrus placed a hand on her knee, his thumb moving in small circles. I stared at the movement, unable to decide if I was angry or not.

"But I've eaten nothing that has made me sick." Sana's gaze drifted just next to her feet, thinking.

Cyrus nodded, thinking as well. "Maybe it's something that, when you eat it, it doesn't make you sick, but the absence of it does?" He shook his head, sighing hard. "That doesn't make any sense." He looked up at me, and I shrugged.

All I knew was that Sana smelled like absolute shit when we first found her, and in the last few days, she smelled almost bearable. *Almost.*

Cyrus leaned in, touching Sana's knee again. She looked up, her dark blue eyes filled with so much confusion. I felt bad for the she-wolf. "The one thing I'm sure of is your wolf isn't the problem. Disconnected alphas are vicious and bloodthirsty. They have no control over their rage or instincts, and frequently become wolf-locked. You just seem to be...struggling." He grimaced at his own choice of words but didn't try to smooth it over or make light of it.

Sometimes shit news was just that. Something that made you feel shitty.

Hating how uncomfortable and pained they both looked, I changed the subject. "How's the leg feel? For a moment there, you practically ran on it. Does it hurt?"

She placed a hand on her slender calf, then shook her head. "No. It only hurts when I stand on it."

Cyrus bent his head, looking it over. "I think if you take it slow, putting more weight on it is a good idea. A lot of that stiffness is from disuse, and we don't want it to atrophy."

"We should go hunting," I said, trying to be friendly for my mate, but also for my own selfish reasons. It had been far too long since I'd been on a proper hunt with a pack, and I missed it. But Sana didn't look excited in the least. Her eyes cast downward, her hands folded tight in her lap.

"It could be fun," I said. "You can shift into your wolf and let your beast heal you for a bit. If your bone is in place, shifting will heal you faster."

Sana's fingers slowly curled over the hem of her shirt, and she whispered, "I don't know how to hunt."

"Tussle? I can go easy on you. I've trained with wolves with all levels of experience."

Her jaw tensed, and her fingers squeezed tighter. "No," she said quietly.

I couldn't place the reason for her unease, but it seemed more than fear of hurting herself again. "No, you don't want to do it? Or no, you don't know how?"

She swallowed hard, embarrassment clouding her blue eyes. Her reaction told me everything I needed to know. I knew she was pampered, but how the fuck did the offspring of a pack alpha not know how to brawl?

*If an alpha doesn't hunt, fight, or track, then what the hell are they good for?*

"There's no need for any of that right now. I just want you to walk around for a bit," Cyrus assured her. "You two can act like alphas after you're a bit better."

Sana took a deep breath, then spoke as if she were admitting to treason, "I don't have any useful talents. I can't hunt or fight or...." She shook her head. "I can't do anything a normal alpha can."

I snorted. "And you thought running away by yourself was smart?"

"It's okay," Cyrus said loudly, cutting me a tight glare.

He still was so tense. I needed to make him smile. "What do you know how to do?"

"I'm pretty," she said in a cold, flat tone. "That's all that fucking mattered to my parents."

I touched a strand of her dirty, tangled hair, motioning to her oversized shirt. "Couple more days out here, and you won't even have that anymore."

Sana bared her teeth and smacked my arm hard. I grabbed my biceps and hissed, swaying and moaning as if in horrible pain. Her angry pout lifted. "I hope you fall head first out of the cave," she snipped.

I stopped my exaggerated wailing and turned to my mate. He wanted to be annoyed with me, but a slow-spreading smile brightened his face. "You're an idiot," he said, shaking his head.

I kissed his shoulder again, pleased to feel the tension ease in our bond. "What do you think, Healer Cyrus?" I asked. "Can your mouthy patient start training tomorrow?"

"Training?" Sana's mouth fell open, and she sat a little straighter. "You want to *train* me?"

"If you're going to stay..." I hesitated, not wanting to say *permanently*, but not willing to say something that might make her want to leave. "If you want to learn how to hunt and fight," I said, pleased with my choice of words, "I'm happy to teach you. We can start first thing tomorrow morning."

She rubbed her lips with the tips of her fingers, looking scared to speak for a moment. "You aren't scared I'll hurt you?"

My first reaction was to laugh, but she looked so sad. I tilted my head, not understanding what she meant.

She bit her bottom lip and dropped her gaze to her lap.

"You aren't worried that I'll lose control and shift? Broken wolves shouldn't—"

I placed my hand on her shoulder, squeezing gently. "You're not broken, doll. Just cracked." I smirked. Her lips twitched, fighting that pretty smile. "And if you can actually get the best of me, I'll help you break into that fucking packhouse and steal your sister back."

Even as the words left my throat, I couldn't believe I was saying them.

A brilliant smile spread across Sana's face. "Really?" Her voice was breathy with excitement.

I leaned in, flashing my teeth. "Let's show this omega how a couple of alphas tussle."

# CHAPTER FIFTEEN

*asleep*

Sana

---

*Heat bloomed between my legs, and my skin flashed with desire. Tallis slipped his tongue up my spine, while his big hands gripped my hips, grinding my ass against his thick cock.*

*"Do you like that, my sweet Sana?" Cyrus purred, pinching my nipples. "Do you like our alpha's fat cock pressed up against your perfect ass?"*

*I moaned, unable to find my words. Tallis's potent scent washed over me, soaking into my skin. It was deep and sweet, like freshly split white oak and spring water. I had never smelled anything so wonderful in all my life—until Cyrus leaned forward and kissed me. How was it possible for him to taste so good? His soft scent was just as gentle as his lips, seeping into every pore of my desperate body.*

*"Do you want Tallis inside you?" Cyrus teased. His dark hair fell into his stunning brown eyes.*

*A deep growl pushed from Tallis's chest into my back, making my nipples pebble painfully tight.*

*"Lift your hips, doll." Tallis nipped at my shoulder. "Let's see how many cocks we can fit in this tight little pussy."*

---

An orgasm ripped through me, jerking me awake. I gulped for air, trying like hell not to writhe with the waves of pleasure bursting from my cunt. My vision blurred, and my thighs shook, until finally I was able to breathe. I blinked repeatedly, trying to steady my heart.

*I had never come so hard.*

A few feet from me, Cyrus let out a soft snore from within his nest. Tallis's enormous body remained completely still on the other side of him. The alpha's slow, deep breaths assured me he was still asleep. Thank goodness.

Pulling in a long, calming breath, I froze. My arousal hung in the air, thick and sweet even to my wolf's weak nose. A muted growl pushed from Tallis's chest, and his cock grew thick, tenting his pants. I stared at it, both horrified and intrigued.

"Everything okay?" Cyrus asked, his voice groggy with sleep.

I snapped my eyes to him and nodded.

His gaze drifted slowly down my face, stopping at my mouth. I wanted to crawl to him, squish myself between the alpha and omega, let them nuzzle and touch me. But they weren't mine. My wolf snarled, and I repeated it again.

They weren't mine.

"Any pain this morning?" Cyrus crawled over the lip of

his nest, moving toward the pallet of moss and grass he had made me.

"Actually, it feels good." I moved my foot in a wide circle, then reversed the direction. The ache in my muscles from lack of use made the movement slow, and I was a little worried it was still too wounded to run on. But I didn't want to admit that out loud.

*I wanted to train.*

Cyrus wrapped his long fingers around my ankle and placed the other hand on my calf. Goosebumps danced up my thigh, shooting straight to my nipples. I held my breath, so aware of his mate sleeping not far from us. Cyrus squeezed my shin, testing the pressure all the way down to my foot. His hands felt so fucking good. It took everything in me not to moan out loud.

"I'm impressed, Sana." He nodded in approval. His thumb brushed down the sole of my foot, and I shivered. "The bone feels strong. I think you can definitely put some weight on it, but I still wouldn't recommend running. Not just yet."

"I'll go easy on her," Tallis rasped. He reached for the water canister, then tipped it back. His Adam's apple bobbed as he gulped. Water dripped out of the corner of his mouth, trickling down his neck and over his firm pecs.

An uninvited shiver slipped down my spine, and my dream hit me with full force, Tallis's powerful body behind me and Cyrus's handsome face in front. I dropped my gaze, terrified they could sense my growing desire.

"How long does it normally take for you to heal?" Tallis asked, jerking me from my thoughts. "Does it always take this long?"

"What do you mean?" I asked, my voice husky. I cleared my throat roughly.

"In the past, when you've broken bones, how long does it take before they mend?"

Cyrus released my leg, and I fought the urge to whine. "I've never broken a bone before."

Tallis's eyes went wide and shot to Cyrus before finally settling on my leg.

"What?" I hated the way they both refused to look at me.

"I don't want to force you to talk about anything you aren't comfortable with," Cyrus said, giving me a pit-bull look. "But—"

"How the fuck can an alpha live to be as old as you and not break a single bone? You've got to be what? Twenty-five? Twenty-six?" Tallis stared at me in complete disbelief. "You said your parents were horrible. I took that to mean they beat you."

"It was far too important for me to be pretty," I snapped at the asshole. "So, no, they didn't hit me in any way that might leave a permanent mark. They were creative. They withheld food, locked me in the cellar for days on end, slapped me around, or they'd beat Emmy."

Shock flitted across Tallis's rugged face, then it slipped into a deep, bone-chilling rage. His fists curled tight, and his eyes glowed a violent shade of red. "They fucking beat an *omega*?" His thick scent flooded the small space, and my beast roared within me, his aggression feeding into my own. I scooted away from Cyrus, not wanting to accidentally shift and hurt him.

"Un-fucking-believable," Cyrus cursed, his scent edging sharp with rage. Between him and Tallis, I could barely breathe.

"Come," Tallis ordered. I stiffened at his command, my wolf hating his tone. But I still stood, adrenaline pumping hard in my veins. Tallis smirked as I walked toward him. "Let's see that wolf of yours."

---

"Try again!" Tallis barked, ordering me back onto my feet.

My wolf roared at his alpha command, wanting to rip his throat out. I reminded my beast, yet again, that if she just pushed forward and let me shift, she could maul every inch of the fucker. But it had been hours, and she had yet to consume my human form even once.

"I think it's time for a break," Cyrus said, giving Tallis a weary look.

"She can have a break once she shifts." His stern tone forced the omega to shiver and bare the back of his neck.

"I'm trying!" I roared, pushing my fists into the dirt. "I'm still too weak, and Cyrus said—"

"He said you couldn't run." Tallis gave me the same irritated look he had worn since we started several hours ago. I wanted to punch him in the balls. "Now get up and try again!"

I slowly stood, keeping my fists tight, forcing my claws to push into my palms. They pierced my skin ever so slightly, keeping me grounded. The pain felt good.

"I can't just force my beast forward," I growled, sweat dripping down the side of my face. "She has to want to move."

"Your beast doesn't have to want shit." Tallis snorted as if it were just that simple. He stalked back and forth, glaring at me. His aggressive mannerisms were working my wolf up, sending her into an angry overdrive. "An alpha's beast is constantly trying to push forward. Whether tired, hungry, horny, or wounded, your beast should always be pushing at the corners of your mind. It's your wolf's fucking job to take over in any situation your human form can't handle. And let's face it, these bodies," he motioned down his toned chest and chiseled abs, "are weak as fuck."

Cyrus pressed his lips together to hide a smile.

"Yeah, you look real fucking weak," I shot. The alpha let out a deep chuckle, and I swore it made the air around me pulse.

"Stop fucking stalling, doll." He beat his chest with a fist. "Rush me!"

"Stop calling me doll!" My fangs shot out of my gums so fast, the taste of blood hit the back of my tongue. "I am not a fucking toy!"

Tallis's lips curled into a tight smirk, and his voice dropped. "You look like a toy to me. Tiny waist, big tits, and an even bigger ass." His eyes dragged up and down my body. My hackles rose as blinding rage set in. "You look like a pretty little plaything, desperate for a big, fat cock to—"

My beast ripped out of me.

I was a mess of grinding bone and stretching muscle, but once my wolf was in place, I lunged.

# CHAPTER SIXTEEN

*the gully*

Cyrus

---

SANA'S WOLF BURST OUT OF HER, THE MOVEMENT JERKY AND clumsy, and *incredibly* fast. I winced at the popping sound of bone grinding together. She rolled her back, thick black fur throwing off a lovely sheen. Keeping her wounded hind leg off the ground, she lunged at my mate.

Tallis slipped easily into his dusky brown wolf, graceful and controlled as always. He side-stepped Sana's enraged beast then spun, ready for her next attack. Relief washed over me when she turned her body, landing on her side, and not her bad leg. She scrambled to get her paws under her, then rushed to attack again.

It was clear from her movements that she wasn't used to fighting in her wolf form. Hell, it was clear from her slim arms and legs that she had never fought in any form. Most alphas, male and female, easily maintained muscular, fit builds, but Sana's curves more closely resembled that of a beta, or even an omega. It wasn't natural for a wolf of her status, and it broke my heart a little. She was caged for too long, *but not anymore.*

A gentle growl pulled me from my thoughts. Tallis's brown wolf teased Sana, stepping right in her path. His enormous paws sank into the soft earth from his weight. He lowered his head and raised his butt, wagging his tail, taunting her to attack again. He was having fun, and it surprised me a bit.

Not deterred by his hulking size, Sana pounced. But it wasn't the leap of a powerful, angry beast. It was almost playful, like that of a pup. She landed on his back, and he remained completely still, letting her bite at one of his ears. She growled, and he rolled, gently knocking her off.

Tallis's tongue rolled out as he circled her, and Sana moved with him, bouncing on her front paws. I wanted to warn them not to push her too much, but they were having too much fun.

Sana needed it.

And so did Tallis.

Last night, when my mate's obvious desire for Sana pushed through our bond, I wasn't sure how I felt. But I realized very quickly that it didn't upset me. Just like when he bit her. I felt no anger, jealousy, or shame. It just felt... okay.

There was a reason the Moon brought her to us.

And watching the two of them play only cemented my decision further. *I wanted to keep her.*

But I was sure Tallis would fight me tooth and nail on the matter. He was an alpha through and through. Possessive, territorial, and stubborn as hell. But I'd make him see. Sana was good for him. *For us.*

And even if it was scary and new and different, there

was something about the she-wolf that just felt right, and I knew deep in my bones Sana felt the same. Tallis just needed to open his eyes and see it too.

I sat watching the two alphas play all afternoon. Tallis kept a slow pace, not letting Sana run too fast. He'd stop and let her catch him, then he'd pin her down and race off, starting their little game of cat and mouse all over again. I wanted to remind them that she wasn't supposed to run, but if she was able to bear it, then why stop her?

My stomach growled, and Tallis's pointed ears twitched and perked. Sana tackled him, and he quickly shook her off, but there was still a triumphant bounce in her wolf's step as she walked away.

Tallis shifted easily into his human form, his body graceful and sleek. My sexy mate was all pressed muscle and sweaty skin, stalking toward me with a glint in his eye. "Hungry, omega?" He dropped to a knee right in front of me and ran his hand up my thigh. I smiled, and my eyes fell to his plump cock. He palmed it, giving me a teasing wink.

Sana trotted up next to us, and my mate bent his knee, hiding his heavy erection. Tallis scratched behind her ear, and she leaned into his touch. He rubbed both her ears, channeling his fingers deep into her scruff. "That'll do for now, doll. Shift, and I promise we'll tussle again tomorrow."

Sana whimpered, then her fur slowly receded. Her hips and shoulder blades popped loudly as her human took shape.

Smiling wide, Sana plopped onto the ground next to Tallis and wrapped her slender arm over her chest, hiding her breasts. She only managed to cover her nipples, the delicate curve of her flesh displaying easily beneath her arm. Tallis eyed her chest and licked his lips. I had to agree. She was stunning.

"You shift like shit," Tallis said, squeezing my upper thigh. His hard-on was still growing, and he angled his hips away from Sana, hiding it the best he could from the she-alpha.

"And you talk a lot of shit." She cut him a challenging glare. His smile widened, and he winked at her. She snorted, shaking her head. "Has anyone ever been able to actually challenge you, or does that smile always get you out of trouble?"

"I've never been in trouble a day in my life," he said in a serious tone, pressing a hand to his chest. "I am a pillar of honor and good sent by the stars to irritate pampered porcelain dolls and to fuck sexy, dark-eyed omegas." He raised his brows in a suggestive manner, and I rolled my eyes. Sana laughed. I swore to the Moon it sounded husky.

"How about you two wash in the stream?" I eyed their flushed, sweaty bodies. "We can fish."

They both nodded, reaching for their clothes flung over a nearby branch. I tried like hell to keep from watching Sana dress, but I couldn't help it. She turned, showing her backside as she slipped the oversized shift over her head. The impressive curve of her ass was dusted with dirt and grass, and my wolf whimpered as the black fabric fell over it, hiding her tempting flesh.

I glanced at Tallis, his eyes glued to Sana's ass as well. I smacked his arm, and he cleared his throat roughly. "Let's go." He gripped my nape, gently squeezing.

We made our way to the stream, Tallis and Sana walking just in front of me. There was a slight limp in her step, but for the most part, she moved well. Sana stumbled then, as if not even realizing he was doing it, Tallis rested his hand on the small of her back, helping to steady her.

I stared at their backs.

They were beautiful together. Both with long blond hair —his darker, hers golden—soft skin, and a fierce energy that made my wolf sit up and take notice. A pulsing electricity made me shiver, and I let out a shuddering breath. I wasn't due to have my heat for another few weeks, but I was feeling...off.

"Are you okay?" Tallis asked, stopping in his tracks.

Sana spun, her eyes darting all over my face. "What's wrong? Are you hurt?"

"I'm fine." I smiled, liking both their eyes on me. Feeling a little brave, I pushed my desire and growing need to Tallis through our bond. He cut a quick look at Sana, then sent back a confused twist of emotion. My ridiculous alpha had no idea what he felt.

We walked in comfortable silence toward the sound of rushing water. Tallis seemed tense, staying right at my side.

Sana placed her feet in the stream, then tilted her head back, letting out a soft hum.

"How does it feel?" I asked, reaching for my belt.

"Really good." She moaned, letting the sun warm her face. She looked so relaxed and sweet surrounded by the mountain air. And it thrilled me.

She woke this morning with a healthy glow about her, and for the first time since we found her, I was able to scent her from across the room. She had a lovely woodsy scent with a strong, sweet undertone. Her perfume still lingered in my nose, and I wanted to push my face into her hair to see if any of it remained. It was so pleasant, it made my wolf excited and settled at the same time.

I moved to unbutton my pants, but Tallis grabbed my

hand and jerked me away from the water. "Yell if you need anything," he barked at Sana.

Her wide eyes tracked us, soft rejection making the corners of her lips pull downward. "Okay," she mumbled, her fingers twisting together.

Moving very quickly, Tallis pulled me behind a cluster of trees on the other side of the stream, hiding Sana completely from my view.

"Tallis, wha—"

My back slammed hard against a massive spruce, then Tallis crashed his mouth to mine, devouring me like a wild beast. It took me a moment for my mind and body to catch up with my demanding mate. He dipped his skillful tongue deep into my mouth, and I moaned. He tasted powerful and strong, sweet and smoky. I loved him like this—possessive and wild. My fierce alpha.

"Tallis," I gasped, threading my fingers through his long hair. Kissing and sucking down my throat, he bit down hard, slipping his fangs into my mating bite just beneath my ear. I hissed, pulling his roots hard.

He snarled against my throat, sucking in a long pull of my blood. It instantly had me hard. Slowly, he removed his canines, then looked deep into my eyes. "Cyrus," he whispered, his tone shockingly soft despite the blood dripping from his bottom lip. "I'm so sorry, my omega."

I shook my head, confused by the contradiction between his wounded expression, raging hard-on, and the shame pulsing through our bond. "What's wrong?" I whispered, cupping his cheek.

"I bit her." He closed his eyes and leaned into my touch, guilt flowing off him in waves. "I pushed my fangs into her skin, right in front of you. I'm so sorry, my mate. Please forgive me."

"Tallis." I wanted to laugh, but he was too upset. "I already told you. It didn't bother me. I really am—"

"Don't say you're fine." He looked at me with intense, dark eyes, his mouth set in a hard line. "Don't tell me everything's okay. I can feel you trying to assure me through our bond. Trying to make me believe you liked it, but I *refuse* to be that kind of alpha." His eyes glowed red, his anger taking hold. "I won't allow you to pretend you're okay with it because I acted like a fucking fool and forced you to watch."

I swallowed hard, prepared to enrage my mate to no end, but it was either this or to let him suffer. "It honestly didn't bother me when you bit her. I...I liked it." I held his gaze, letting the meaning of my words push into him.

Slowly, the tension between his brows eased, and his eyes went wide. "You *liked* it?" He took a step back. I wanted to reach for him, hold him to me and promise him it didn't mean anything. But instead I stayed completely still like a complete coward.

"I don't know..." He shook his head, our bond pulsing with a mix of anger and confusion. "What are you saying, Cyrus?" His eyes glowed red, and he closed the space between us. "Are you saying you want to fuck her?" he snarled, his pointed fangs on full display.

An image of Sana naked and panting pressed between me and Tallis flashed before my eyes, and I forced it away as fast as I could, shocked by my own mind.

"No!" I growled, pushing at my mate's broad chest. He stayed completely still, a wall of muscle and rage. "I want her to stay with us. She's..." I struggled, not sure how to tell him what I wanted. "She's a part of our pack."

Tallis's jaw jutted forward, and he pulled in a long breath. "Cyrus, I don't think I can—"

"She's good for you, Tallis. Can you really not see that?"

It was true, but it was also a lie. I *wanted* her, and I wanted Tallis to want her too. *She was ours.*

His tight expression eased, then crumbled as if being punched in the gut. His big brown eyes held so much pain and shame as he whispered, "I don't want her to know what I did."

I jerked at his words, grabbing his hands and squeezing tight. "What happened wasn't your fault." He didn't speak, but he didn't have to. Deep grief and regret poured off him like a torrential storm. "Sana is special. She makes you silly. You tease and provoke her in a playful way that I haven't seen from you since we left home." I cupped both his cheeks, forcing him to look at me. "I miss my carefree mate."

The silence that followed was painful. Tallis's mind swirled with so much emotion, it made me dizzy. Then, finally, his dark eyes softened, and he wrapped his arms around me. "I can't talk about this right now." He pushed his nose into my hair, scenting me long and deep. "I'm sorry, I just can't."

"That's okay." I hugged his middle, squeezing him tight. "I just don't want you to beat yourself up anymore. It didn't bother me that you bit her. That's all that matters right now."

He placed a quick kiss to the top of my head. "Okay."

I let him hold me for a bit, enjoying his woodsy scent and strong arms. The pain and shame my tormented mate had carried for so long broke my heart, and I hated that I couldn't fix him. Nothing I said or did would ever make it better.

"Hey." I rested my chin on his chest and looked up. His long hair fell into his face, hiding both of us in his curtain of blond locks. "I thought you brought me out here for a purpose." I bit my bottom lip, hoping to take his mind off his demons.

"Really?" His eyes widened as his hands roamed up the length of my back. But there was no urgency in his touch. *Not yet.* "Do you really want—"

"So now you're a tease?" I shot, giving him a playful glare. "You bring me out here and kiss me as if it were with your dying breath, and now you're suddenly shy?"

A devilish smirk stole his expression, and his hand flung out, wrapping around my throat. "Do you need me to fuck you?" he whispered, a small smile lifting one side of his face.

I nodded as his fingers traced the edge of my jaw. "Remind me who I belong to," I whispered, pleased when his cock twitched against my thigh.

His eyes flashed, and in one fierce movement, he forced me onto my knees. Excitement and desire pulsed just beneath my skin, my cock already hard and leaking. Tallis towered over me, his massive body projecting so much power.

"I'll remind you who you belong to, little omega." His voice was filled with alpha dominance, and the effect was immediate. Slick dripped from me as I fumbled to pull my pants down. My pulse pounded so hard in my cock, I felt almost frenzied. I needed to be naked *now*.

Moving behind me, Tallis gripped my nape and forced me forward onto my hands, pressing my cheek into the ground. Working the best I could at such an awkward angle, I jerked my pants down my hips, pushing my ass high into the air.

Rough hands parted me painfully wide, followed by a warm, wet tongue swiping up my ass. I moaned, pushing back in a silent plea for him to go deeper. Giving in to my desire, my mate pushed his tongue forward, breaching me. My back ached, and my spine tingled.

"Please, alpha," I moaned, caressing the lush grass beneath me. He flicked his tongue over my rim, sucking and tasting me. My cock grew so heavy between my thighs as he ate me to perfection.

"This is mine," Tallis snarled, pushing three fingers deep inside my slick-soaked body.

I gasped and nodded, my cheek rubbing against the soft earth. The fresh aroma of grass and pollen mixed with his masculine scent and musky sweat. It was bliss.

"Look how wet you are," Tallis hummed, spitting on my hole. He worked his three fingers in deep, pushing spit and slick in and around my rim. The pressure in my balls intensified, but I knew how much better it would feel with his cock inside me.

Looking over my shoulder, I snarled, "Fuck me already." My voice was so raspy, I hardly recognized it. "Give me what I need."

A slowly spreading smile consumed his face, and he caressed my hips, the movement far too gentle for what I knew was coming next. Then, in one quick motion, he jerked my ass back and rutted forward, impaling me in one breathtaking thrust.

I growled deep in my chest. "Oh, fuck!" It burned, then stretched, making me moan loudly. "Ugh! I love your cock," I rasped, pushing back into him.

Raw pleasure ripped through me as he hit my prostate dead on. He pistoned his enormous shaft in and out of me at a brutal pace. I pushed my fingers into the earth, ripping up clumps of grass and little white flowers. My cock swung as he used me, slapping against my stomach, leaving wet streaks in its wake.

"You like that, omega?" Tallis's hips faltered as his knot expanded.

"Don't stop," I panted, meeting each one of his thrusts. "Fuck me harder. Knot me."

Giving me exactly what I wanted, Tallis pounded into me with wild abandon, his thighs slapping hard against the back of my legs. The strength in his big body was both impressive and consuming, making my cock leak long strings of precum onto the forest floor.

Heat sizzled in my veins, and I grabbed my shaft, jerking and squeezing. Deep pleasure swirled, and my fangs slipped forward. A delicate slip of Sana's sweet scent lingered in the air, and my abs tensed, on the edge of the most blissful orgasm.

Tallis roared and rutted forward, popping his knot inside me. My body rocked, and cum erupted from my shaft, coating my fingers and splattering against the ground. His cock pumped and twitched as he filled my ass with his climax. It was painfully tight, but I loved it. I loved him.

With his cock still twitching inside me, Tallis encircled an arm around my middle, pulling me flush to his chest. His heart pounded against my back, beating in tandem with mine.

Unable to help myself, I reached for his hand, bringing his forearm up to my mouth, then I pushed my canines into his skin. He didn't make a sound, letting me claim him with my short omega fangs. I lapped at his torn flesh. Omegas didn't have any ability to mark other wolves the way alphas could, but I still liked staking my claim whenever I could. Even if it would fade in only a few days' time.

"Are you okay?" I asked, realizing how quiet he was.

Tallis was a talker in bed, especially afterward. When he didn't answer, I glanced over my shoulder.

He stared at the ground at the clumps of grass and flowers I destroyed while he took me. Leaning forward, he picked up a small white bud and rubbed it between his thumb and forefinger. A delicate blue dust fell from the center, landing on his thick thigh. Tallis glared at the blue pollen, then sucked in a sharp breath. "Shit."

"What?" I stiffened at his tone.

"I think I know what's wrong with Sana."

# CHAPTER SEVENTEEN

## *at the water's edge*

Sana

I STOOD IN THE WATER FOR A WHILE, JUST STARING AT WHERE Cyrus and Tallis had disappeared. I knew they were close, but it still had me on edge. I didn't like not being able to see them. What if something happened? What if someone attacked Cyrus?

*What if they left me?*

A deep grunt hit my ears, and every muscle in my body tensed. I turned my head, listening hard. Another grunt, followed by a pained growl. Not waiting to hear any more, I rushed to the shore then around the stream as fast as my tender leg would allow. It was sore from so much use, but the sharp pain was gone.

I rounded a cluster of trees, my wolf ready to shift and fight, then I froze.

Tallis's strong, muscular body was draped over Cyrus.

His cut muscles rolled and flexed as he thrust into the omega.

"Did you like that?" Tallis growled, the gravelly sound slipping over my skin with a crackling energy. His long blond hair hung in his eyes as he pumped into his mate. I shouldn't have been watching, but I couldn't help myself. They were...breathtaking.

"Don't stop," Cyrus ordered, his eyes burning with lust. "Fuck me harder. Knot me!"

Tallis instantly obeyed, fucking hard into Cyrus's lean body. The alpha's cut muscles along his back rolled and flexed as he took his mate. Cum leaked from Cyrus's cock, dripping onto the forest floor. The deep urge to taste it made my fingers twitch with a desire to touch myself, circle my clit and ride their wave of pleasure with them.

Tallis let out a vicious roar, and Cyrus clawed at the ground as they came together. My knees almost gave out, and I stumbled back, my hip smacking into a tree. The sweet scent of their combined orgasm hit me so hard, it made my clit ache. I had never seen anything so powerful and sexy before in my life.

I wanted to run to them and squeeze myself between the two, letting their cum drip all over me.

Trying to steady my heart, I gripped the front of my shirt, to give my hands something to do, but also to get the fabric off my painfully sensitive nipples.

Tallis pulled Cyrus flush against his chest, their hard bodies pressed together. Cyrus's impressive length was still hard and shiny, bobbing in front of him. A long string of cum stretched from the swollen crown, dripping on the forest floor. I moved my gaze over his lean body to Tallis. The alpha's hair stuck to his sweaty forehead, his lips wet and his chest heaving. He stared at something white in his hand before rubbing it between his fingers.

As if sensing my presence, Cyrus lifted his head, then turned toward me. I jerked back behind the trees before I could see his eyes. I didn't know if he had seen me, but I prayed he hadn't. Tallis was very territorial with his mate— as any alpha would be. *What would he do if he knew I had watched them mating?*

Whatever Tallis did, it wouldn't be good.

The soft rustle of movement, followed by quiet voices, made me jerk and spin, trying to get back around the steam as quickly as possible. But I forgot to move carefully, and the moment my foot touched the rough ground, my knee buckled. Pain shot up my leg, and I flailed my arms, trying to stay upright, but it was no use. I fell face first into the shallow, cold stream.

"Sana?" Tallis's deep voice boomed just behind me. "What the hell are you doing?"

I slowly turned toward the pair. They both had put their pants back on, making my wolf snarl. She inched closer, wanting to feel and scent them.

Tallis reached for me, but I held out my hand, stopping him. "I'm fine," I said quickly, standing up on my own. "I just fell."

"Are you okay?" Cyrus moved toward me.

His sweet omega scent mixed with Tallis's fresh orgasm was so fucking powerful. I took a step back, the tension between my legs making it hard to walk. "I'm fine," I insisted. "Just a little off balance still."

Tallis raised a brow, his eyes dragging up and down my body. It felt good to have him look at me like that. Too good. "We need to talk," he said. His expression was hard to read, but his voice was unusually soft. Dread slipped down my spine, and I held my breath, waiting for him to tell me to fuck off.

"Can I look at your leg?" the alpha asked. He sounded almost sad. I took a step back, not caring for it. He was easier to handle when he was loud and obnoxious. This version of Tallis had me on edge.

Not giving me a chance to answer, Cyrus guided me back around the steam to the flat rock. He placed his hand just under my elbow, and warmth radiated up and down my body. I quickly sat, and Tallis immediately reached for my ankle. He placed his lips to the puffy scar on my shin, sucking slightly. It was weirdly intimate, and I looked away, scared he'd see the heat warming my face. His tongue lapped my sensitive flesh, then he pricked my skin with his fangs. The pinching sensation made me flinch, but my wolf simpered, loving it.

Cyrus reached for my hand as if trying to comfort me. Between Tallis's firm touch and Cyrus's gentle one, I felt as if I were going to combust. I squirmed, trying to focus on their odd behavior and not the slick gathering between my thighs.

"What's happening?" I asked, knowing I should be worried and not turned on.

Tallis spit a mouthful of my blood into the water. Then, using both his hands, he took big mouthfuls of water so he could swish and spit repeatedly. He nodded at Cyrus, who turned his sad eyes to me.

"You've been poisoned," the omega whispered.

I wanted to laugh, but they both looked so serious. "What on earth makes you think that?"

Cyrus held out his hand, showing me a few small white

flowers. It seemed an odd moment to give me a flower, but I still took it. It seemed rude not to.

"Do you know those flowers?" Tallis asked, his voice edging a little hard. It made me relax a bit. I preferred him hard. He was a stern alpha with a shit sense of humor. His sympathy just made me feel weak and pathetic.

"I'm not sure." I pressed it to my nose, inhaling the blue pollen. It smelled sickly sweet with a very bitter tinge. It was somewhat familiar. "Maybe."

Cyrus's voice dropped into a careful whisper, "Do you eat them? Drink them?"

Thinking hard, I inspected the tiny, white bud. There was something vaguely familiar about it, but I couldn't place it. I had never seen it in the kitchens or at the dinner table.

"Think carefully," Cyrus said.

I plucked one of the heart-shaped petals, holding it up. A puff of blue dust swirled from the center, covering my fingers. "I don't think—" Realization slammed into me. *Tea.* Cream-colored petals floating in delicate blue cups of brown liquid. It was the *fucking* tea.

Pure, unbridled rage sparked along each muscle in my body, making me so tense, my hands shook. A slow rumble built up in my chest, and I could feel Cyrus shiver next to me.

"Tell us," Tallis barked. I stiffened at his alpha command, sending every bit of my own alpha instincts into overdrive.

"Don't fucking order me." I stood, my body tight. Tense. Poised for a fight.

Tallis's eyes went wide at my challenge, and Cyrus instantly moved, placing himself between us. It was a bold move for an omega to place himself between two worked-up alphas, but it spoke volumes as to his trust in both of us. He *knew* I'd never hurt him. Something about that felt so...lovely?

"Please." Cyrus held up his hand, urging Tallis to take a step back. Sensing his mate's growing worry, Tallis reluctantly obeyed, keeping his narrowed eyes on me. I glared right back.

"What does this flower do?" I snarled, trying to stay in control, but it was useless. I was far too fucking angry. Cyrus opened his mouth, then hesitated. "Tell me!"

"It's poison," Tallis said loudly, pulling my attention away from his mate. "It fucks up a wolf real good. And enough of it will kill you."

Cyrus swallowed hard, his mannerisms a bit unsure as he reached for my hand. But he looked me in the eyes, not backing down from my rage. For some reason I liked that. "Who poisoned you?" he whispered.

I crushed the bud in my fists, flinging it into the water. "No one," I snapped. "Tallis," I squared my shoulders, "teach me to hunt. Cyrus is hungry."

Tallis's angry glare immediately lifted, and his nose scrunched up, confusion pulling his brows together. "You want to *hunt*? Right now?"

"I'm done talking about this," I said, pulling off my wet shirt so I could shift. I flung it onto the rocks, not waiting for either to respond. "I want to know how to track and kill something."

"But—"

I cut Cyrus off. "I'm fine. Let's go." I turned from the pair, letting my beast push forward. Rage and purpose pumped in my veins as my wolf form prowled deep into the trees. I needed to quiet my mind, to keep every awful thought from consuming me.

Did my mother poison me on purpose?

Did she know what this flower would do to me?

Was she trying to kill me?

I shove it down, focusing on healing and learning as much as I could. I needed to get Emmy out of Casin. And I was going to kill anyone who stood in my way.

# CHAPTER EIGHTEEN

## *training*

Tallis

---

"THAT'S GOOD," I SAID AS SANA SNARLED AND STOMPED TOWARD her weapon. She had yet to make contact with me, but she was moving faster, getting stronger. "Now, try again. Lunge lower this time. Aim for my middle." I patted my stomach.

She huffed, fanning her hair away from her flushed face. Her blonde locks caught the sun, throwing off golden streaks. "This is stupid," she panted, trying to catch her breath. "Why the fuck would an alpha need to fight with a damn stick? We can shift."

She had been like this for a few days now—restless and fidgety. If we weren't working on tracking or fighting in our wolf forms, she just didn't seem to give a shit.

I took a steadying breath, trying like hell not to snap at her. I was wound so fucking tight lately, and it was only getting worse. "Because there will be times when you can't call on your wolf. Whether it be from injury," I motioned to her leg, "or wolfsbane or elvish shackles, you need to know how to use a weapon. All guards learn to stickfight. When you can't shift, you have to be able to use what's available to you. Even if that means using a *damn stick*."

She groaned, shoving the end of her weapon into the ground. "We should check on Cyrus. I haven't seen him since this morning."

"We haven't seen him all morning because you fucking yelled at him," I reminded her.

She dropped her gaze, not willing to admit she had hurt his feelings. He just wanted to talk to her about how she was poisoned, but she lost her temper, finally yelling at my mate until he snapped and shamed her into apologizing.

My sweet omega just wanted to help her...*and fuck her*. I could feel it in our bond every time I looked at him. The thing that made me feel truly fucking awful was that I wasn't sure if it angered me or not. My desire for Sana was intense at times, but I couldn't do that to Cyrus, and it felt like a deep betrayal that he'd even consider doing it to me.

And he had been trying to talk to me about it for days now, but I had done a better job than Sana at avoiding the determined omega.

I just didn't want to think about it.

I knew I was upsetting Cyrus, but I didn't know what to do. Sana's priority was saving her sister, which was admirable and right. And outside of a few questionable looks at Cyrus, I honestly didn't know if she had any real interest in us, and I couldn't make Cyrus see that. Not yet at least.

"You know," I said, already knowing what I was about to say was going to piss the she-wolf off, "if you had a patient bone in your body, your wolf wouldn't struggle half as much as she does."

"I'm patient," she scoffed. "I've put up with your moody ass all morning long."

I clenched my fists, not caring for her tone. "You were barely able to sit still long enough to catch that jackrabbit yesterday."

She rolled her eyes, and anger burned through me. "A restless hunter goes hungry," I barked. "A patient one feasts for days. And, if I'm honest, I really don't give a shit if you starve or not. Now," I popped my neck and settled into a defensive position, "rush me!"

"Tallis," she whined.

I growled low in my throat, ready to lay into her for being so fucking lazy, but she lunged, catching me off guard. Her movements were so quick. With her weapon in hand, she slipped into a spin, jerking the stick and knocking my feet out from under me. I landed hard on my back, the she-alpha instantly on top of me.

She pressed her weapon to my throat, pushing her body weight into it. A look of pure satisfaction consumed her face. "Got you." She smiled, her hair swinging forward and brushing against my cheeks.

Her sweet scent washed over me. Her natural perfume had grown unbelievably strong the last few days. It was sweet and spicy, with a touch of something floral. It mixed unbelievably well with Cyrus's fresh, clean aroma.

At night, the whole cave smelled like a fresh spring day.

And it was driving me fucking insane.

"Go again," I said, shoving her off me. My stiff cock bunched up as I stood, and I adjusted it quickly, trying like hell not to think about the intense desire tingling at the base of my spine. "Come on," I said, getting into position. "Again."

"I'm done." She released the stick, letting it fall onto the ground. "Let's go check on Cyrus."

"He's fine," I snapped. I didn't mean to sound so angry, but my raging hard-on and distracted wolf were making it so damn hard to concentrate. "He's just tired. Let him nest for a bit, and he'll be fine."

She bit that perfectly plump bottom lip. "But—"

"Stop stalling and get that pampered ass over here!"

Her eyes glowed red as anger flushed her cheeks. I was being a dick. It wasn't her fault my body and beast were going crazy for her, but it still pissed me the fuck off.

"You know," she said, her hands on those curvy hips, "I don't know what's going on between you and Cyrus, but you can stop taking it out on me."

I straightened my back, taking a quick step toward her. Had Cyrus said something to her? "What the fuck does that mean?"

"My nose might be weak and my reflexes shit, but I can still fucking see," she spat. "You two haven't spoken in days. Not since...." her anger faltered for a moment, and the blush in her cheeks traveled down her neck, "...that day with the flowers. I've seen him try to talk to you several times, but you keep avoiding him."

My patience evaporated, and my anger took hold. "You want to talk about avoiding conversations?" I closed the space between us, but she held firm, crossing her arms and popping out a hip. "Cyrus just wants to help you. That's all he's wanted since the moment he found you, and you fucking *yelled* at him for asking a simple question."

A brief flash of regret clouded her eyes, but it just as quickly disappeared. "I'm still trying to work it all out. I don't know who would do something like that to me."

"Work what out?" I pushed out a mocking laugh. "You

keep saying your parents are evil. Like villains from a fairy-tale evil. If they really are that bad, it only makes sense they'd poison you. Don't be stupid, Sana."

Her eyes flashed red, baring her fangs. "It's not that I don't think they're capable," she snarled, bowing up to me. "It just doesn't make any sense. They are hard and controlling, but there is no way they'd risk killing me. I'm too valuable. But either way, it's none of your fucking business."

My eyes widened at her words, tension building between my shoulder blades. "None of my fucking business? None of my fucking business?"

"Yeah!" she roared, baring her pointed fangs.

"I would love for all of this to be none of my fucking business! I didn't ask to pull your ass out of that pit. I wanted to leave you down there, but my mate was dead set on helping you, you ungrateful brat!"

Sana growled high in her throat, her eyes pulsing crimson.

"You have been a massive waste of my time." I shoved past her. "The shit I do for Cyrus."

"Do you know what?" She raced after me, cutting me off. "You don't have to worry about me anymore. I'll go get my shit and leave."

"Then fucking go." The moment the words left my lips, so did all my fight. A heaviness settled in my chest, making my wolf whimper. The urge to grab her and tie her up so she could never leave me was so strong, it physically hurt.

"Fine."

She turned to leave, but I grabbed her arm, jerking her to me.

"What the fuck? Let me go!" She shoved at my chest.

"You're not ready," I blurted out. My mind was a

fucking mess of anger, jealousy, and lust that pounded hard at the base of my cock.

"Make up your fucking mind!" She shoved me hard, and I stumbled. I was so off kilter, I couldn't find my words. "Do you want me to leave or not?" she yelled.

But I didn't know how to answer her, so I settled on the truth: "I just don't want you to get hurt."

Sadness washed over Sana's soft face. I opened my mouth, then closed it. I had no fucking clue what to even say anymore. I wanted her gone. I wanted the rift between me and my mate healed, but I feared we'd never be the same without Sana.

The air between us grew heavy, her big blue eyes holding mine with so many things left to say. Then, with a heavy sigh, Sana turned and left. I watched her, her hair swaying as she moved through the trees. She passed Cyrus, and he turned to her, worry creasing his brow.

He tried to stop her, but she kept walking. "What's wrong?" he called after her.

Not turning to look at either one of us, she yelled, "Your mate is a fucking asshole."

Cyrus stared at the she-wolf, rooted to the same spot until she completely disappeared behind the trees and shrubs. A soft thread of longing slipped through our bond, and it enraged me to no end.

"You don't get to do this to me, Cyrus!" I barked, making him jump.

"What?" He turned to me, his brown eyes filled with so much confusion. But honestly, I didn't really know why I was angry anymore.

"You don't get to tell me you want to be with someone else, then pine after her right in front of me. It's fucking bullshit."

He shook his head, our bond instantly closing. He had been shutting out his feelings for days, leaving me alone with my own damn thoughts. "I'm not...I don't," he stammered.

Rage overtook me, and I flung my hand out, wrapping it around his throat. "You are *mine*, omega," I snarled. He narrowed his eyes, not an ounce of fear in them. "You don't get to lust after pretty little blonde things right in front of me. You are bound to *me*. Now and forever."

"I know!" he yelled, shoving me away. His strength was nothing compared to mine, but I still released him. "What the fuck is wrong with you?" He trembled, but it wasn't from fear. His fists were so tight, his fingers were white. "You have been so aggressive and angry since...since..."

"Since you practically told me you want to fuck Sana?" I finished for him.

He let out a defeated breath, his anger calming for a moment. "That's what you heard?" He shook his head in disbelief. "I tell you that I like you caring for someone else, that I want her to be a part of our family, and you immediately think I want to fuck her."

"Don't do that," I warned, my voice deep and careful. "I'm in your head, Cyrus. You might be able to block me out during the day, but I feel your desires in your sleep. I *know* you want her."

Shame made him bow his head, but I couldn't let up. Since the moment Sana's blood touched my tongue, she was all I could think about. I wanted to stuff her with my cock, fill her with my cum, then watch Cyrus lick her slick off my balls. And I hated him for bringing her to us.

"I understand that you feel a pull to her, something you're dead set on forcing me to talk about." I inhaled deeply, trying to calm down. "But that female," I stabbed a finger at where she had disappeared, "is a pain in the fucking ass."

"So are you," he snipped, tipping his chin up.

"I'm being serious!" I snarled, not caring for his attitude.

"So am I!" He closed the space between us. "I feel a connection to her wolf. But more than that, I feel the connection your wolf has with her. She settles you. You calm her. I *like* seeing you both laugh and fight and train. You're good for each other."

My wolf quickly agreed. He loved everything about Sana. Her scent, her laugh, her sharp comments. *Her tits.*

"You honestly want to see me fuck someone else?" I asked, unable to wrap my mind around it. The possessive ideals I had been raised to believe clashed wildly with the confusing desires pulsing through me. Alphas had one mate and killed anyone willing to even look at them.

"No." He crossed his arms. "I want to see you with *Sana.* She's *ours.* I can feel it."

The wind shifted, carrying something overly sweet on the breeze. It dripped like honey, filling every pore in my body and making my skin hum.

"How often do you think about her?" I asked, my wolf moving within me. He was restless, his body aching to be let loose. "Do you lay awake thinking about me fucking her tight little cunt? Is that what you really want?"

Cyrus opened our bond, hitting me with wave after wave of his lust and desire for me and Sana. It was so intense, I took a step back from the force of it. I had no idea his connection with her was so fierce. But instead of enraging me like it should, it made my cock rock hard, pressing tight against the front of my pants.

I couldn't take it any longer.

In one fierce movement, I grabbed Cyrus by his nape and slammed him to me, claiming his mouth in a searing kiss. My obedient omega moved easily for me, letting me pull him tight to my chest as I devoured his mouth. *He tasted so fucking good.*

My wolf howled, prowling within me, and my cock swelled. I was hard everywhere.

Between Cyrus's soft scent, the sugary perfume dancing in the air, and the debauched thoughts swirling in my head, I felt as if I was slipping into my rut. I just wanted to fuck something hard and fast. I wanted to coat both Cyrus and Sana in my cum, and keep them bound to me forever.

"Alpha," Cyrus moaned, raking his nails down the length of my back.

Something electric danced around us, and I broke the kiss, scenting the air. My skin tingled, my balls so fucking heavy.

"What's wrong?" Cyrus asked, his voice slightly slurred.

I grabbed his arm, dragging him in the direction of the honey scent. It was the same scent that had been mocking me for days now. And I was powerless to fight it any longer.

My beast was in control now.

# CHAPTER NINETEEN

the forest

Sana

---

Frustration churned in my gut as I marched past Cyrus. My wolf bellowed, desperate for me to turn around and fix things with Tallis. She wanted me to stay, to be with them, to claim both wolves as my own.

It made me want to scream until my throat bled.

With Cyrus's constant loving care, I felt better now than I ever had in my entire life. I was shifting faster and becoming stronger. But my beast was still a complete asshole, fucking determined to go against every damn thing I wanted.

The wind shifted, blowing the thick scent of pollen and earth into my face. Something foreign coated the back of my throat, and I turned toward the smell. The hairs along my arms stood up with a sense of awareness. Leaves and grass swayed with the breeze, rustling in the otherwise quiet forest. My wolf bared her teeth, sensing something in the trees. The odd thing was, I could feel it too.

Something painfully warm twisted deep inside me, and I backed up, away from the smell.

The urge to run beat hard in my chest. *I needed to get the fuck out of here.*

I turned and ran, not stopping until I reached the cave.

A painful wave of heat rolled up my spine, and I stumbled, praying there wasn't someone behind me. I just needed to get inside the cave. There were too many harsh smells, and they all stuck to the inside my nose, making me dizzy.

I grunted, pulling myself over the lip of the cave. Cool air moved over my face, chilling the sweat along my hairline. I curled into myself, trying to ease the ache deep in my gut. I was hot. Too hot. But cold at the same time. Cold sweat bloomed along my sides and back, and I felt like I might be sick.

Practically crawling, I inched across my bed of moss and leaves. A few discarded clothes littered the floor, and I grabbed the nearest shirt, wiping the sweat off my face. It smelled deeply of Cyrus's earthy, clean scent. A bit of Tallis's woodsy aroma lingered around the collar and sleeves. I buried my face in the fabric, inhaling deeply.

*It smelled so good.*

My mouth watered, and I wrapped my lips around the sleeve, sucking hard. The instinctual need to find both wolves pulled hard within me. My beast snarled and roared, urging me to find them *now*.

A sharp pain stabbed through me, running from my abdomen to my groin. I choked and gasped for air, trying to breathe through it, but it was impossible. My heart was beating way too fast.

Unable to take the twisting heat inside me, I pressed my knees to my chest, panting hard and rocking back and forth. "Fuck," I snarled, a whine slipping from between my clenched teeth.

Fierce contractions ripped at my womb, stabbing at my pussy and making me gasp. It was an agony I had never felt before. I was empty and open and needed to fuck something hard and fast.

I needed Cyrus.

I needed...

The deeply sweet scent of freshly split white oak and rushing spring water made me turn.

Tallis loomed over me, his massive size forcing me to tip my head all the way back to see his face. His fists were curled tight and his hair a wild mane around his chiseled face. He growled low in his throat, his eyes glowing that beautiful crimson as he stared me down.

He looked every bit the powerful alpha he was. Unhinged and crazed.

A renewed energy flowed through me, and I stood, ripping my shirt away and flinging it into the distance. Tallis's eyes pulsed red, and he pushed his wet tongue forward, licking his bottom lip.

A twisting cramp ripped through me, and my sex opened, but I remained completely still, despite the grunt that pushed from my throat. Tallis's eyes moved down my body, watching as slick poured out of me, thick and sticky. I moaned with relief as the flood of hot liquid coated my thighs, puddling at my feet.

Then I pounced.

Tallis caught me just as I wrapped my legs tight around his middle, holding his face with my clawed hands. My wet pussy slipped over his smooth abs, and I rolled my hips, coating him in my slick. My clit was so sensitive and engorged, I let out a hiss as it dragged.

"On your back," Tallis snarled, digging his fingers into my hips. But the need to dominate him was just too strong, making my nipples pebble hard against his chest.

"No!" I roared, channeling my fingers through his soft hair. I gripped the roots, then pulled hard. He hissed, squeezing my flesh so hard, it was sure to leave bruises. "You aren't the alpha today," I snarled.

His eyes flashed crimson. "The fuck I'm—"

I jerked his hair again, ripping as hard as I could. He stumbled, his face scrunching up with pain and pleasure. His cock pushed out the top of his pants, pressing against the seam of my ass. "*I'm* the alpha," I whispered, my wolf sitting proud and sure. This was her cave. Her pack. Her alpha. Tallis was *mine*.

Tallis bared his fangs, the tips pushing into his bottom lip. "If you think I'm just going to—"

"I think you're going to do whatever the fuck I want." Striking fast, I bit his bottom lip hard. My fangs slipped into the tip of his tongue, and I sucked at his tangy, metallic blood. It was sweet and woodsy, flooding my veins with his riled aggression. I could *taste* how pissed he was.

Turning us, Tallis slammed me hard into the wall, making me grunt, but I refused to let him go. His aggression only amped me up even more. If he wanted a fight for the upper hand, I'd give him a fucking fight.

He crashed his mouth to mine, kissing me wild and deep. And I met each one of his powerful movements, forcing his head to the side then breaking the kiss before he was ready.

"Sana!" He gripped my upper arms, and I locked my ankles around his back, keeping myself in place. He struggled for a moment, trying to pull my fingers from his hair, but I held firm, needing him to submit.

"Beg me," I whispered.

He froze, every hard muscle in his big body straining with absolute rage. He was fucking gorgeous like this.

He released my arms; then, in one breathtaking jerk of his arms, he brought both palms down on my bare ass hard. My back arched from the force of it, and slick flowed from my pussy, dripping over his abs and down the front of his pants.

"Sana," he whispered, his voice dangerously tight. His nostrils flared, getting his fill of my arousal trickling down his stomach.

I smirked, then leaned forward, ghosting my mouth just over his. "Beg me," I repeated, my breath fanning warm over his face "Beg me to fuck you."

The corner of his lips twitched as a deep chuckle left his throat. I could feel the fight leave his shoulders as something far darker took its place. "Please, sweet alpha." He squeezed my thighs, groping as much flesh as he could hold. "Crawl off me so I can force my cock so far down your throat, you won't be able to breathe."

I moaned, unable to help myself, and the fire in his eyes doubled.

His big hands moved over the curve of my ass, squeezing my freshly spanked flesh. It stung, so raw. "I'm going to fuck that mouth so hard and fast, you'll be *begging me* to stop."

Cyrus's soft whimper made both of us jerk our heads around.

The omega stood next to the entrance, his dark eyes blown wide, not really focusing on anything. He looked drunk, flushed and glistening with a thin layer of sweat. He was wrung out on alpha pheromones and shivering with far too much need.

A female alpha in heat was demanding, insatiable, and even violent. But omegas—male or female—were soft and submissive, unable to take what they needed, built only to accept what their mates gave them. And, right now, Cyrus was a leaf caught in a storm. The torrential mix of my heat and Tallis's growing rut had the poor omega so strung out, he could barely speak.

I slipped off Tallis's big body, landing softly on the balls of my feet.

"Omega," I purred. Cyrus closed his eyes, a shudder working through him. Just the sight of his soft, tan skin made my mouth water.

Somewhere behind me, Tallis's belt jingled, followed by the rustle of clothes. I half expected the alpha to attack me as I prowled toward his mate, but I honestly didn't give a shit. I'd fight the fucker if I had to.

"What do you need, my sweet Cyrus?" I whispered, reaching to cup his cheek.

Tallis flung his hand out, capturing my wrist. I instantly snarled at the alpha, but I didn't move to attack him. Not with Cyrus so close.

"P-please," Cyrus whispered. His voice was so strained, and his abs clenched hard.

The small cave flooded with his delicious scent of sweet slick. It wasn't like mine. It was pure sugar, and it made my fangs tingle.

"Please!" Cyrus gasped as a full body shudder racked his frame. He stumbled, catching himself on the wall.

Tallis instantly reacted, picking up his mate and carrying him to his nest. I rushed after them, wanting to crawl in with them, but I didn't have Cyrus's consent. I hesitated at the edge, torn between the need to cater to the omega and the inability to disrespect Cyrus so deeply by entering his nest without permission.

"Cyrus," I licked my lips, my womb clenching hard, "may I come into your nest?" His head rolled, not really hearing me. Panic started to build up inside me. I needed to touch him. Feel him. Taste him.

"It's okay," Tallis whispered, pulling at Cyrus's belt, then slipping off his pants.

I stared at his perfect body, unable to help myself.

Cyrus's cock was so hard, the skin an angry red and leaking freely. A string of precum stretched from the crown to the soft grooves just at his belly button. Tallis swiped his finger through the sticky fluid, then to my absolute shock, he held his finger out, offering it to me. I gripped his hand before he could change his mind and pushed it deep into my mouth.

The omega's natural flavor burst across my tongue, and I hummed, licking every inch of Tallis's hand, trying to gather every drop. The alpha growled in approval as he palmed Cyrus's balls, working the omega up into a frenzy. Cyrus's heat built, his scent so fucking thick, it made the air taste sweet.

I inched a little closer, my knees pushing at the edge of his nest as my eyes darted between Cyrus and Tallis. I was so fucking worked up, desperate to claw my own skin off just to get to them, but I couldn't. Not without deeply offending Cyrus.

Desperate for relief, I slipped my fingers into my cunt, watching Tallis palm and jerk Cyrus's cock. I *needed* both of them inside me. My wolf demanded it. It was a shameful, greedy desire. One that my previous heats had never prepared me for, but I no longer cared. I wanted to be stuffed in every filthy way possible.

"This ass is so ready for me." Tallis pushed his fingers deep into Cyrus, making his back arch. Slowly, Tallis turned his head, smiling at the frustration and rage pouring off me. I wanted to rip his fucking head off. "His slick tastes even better, doll," he mocked, removing his drenched fingers. They glistened with the sticky fluid, shimmering so pretty in the dim light. "I bet you want a taste real fucking bad."

Screaming desire beat down hard on me, and I bared my teeth, ready to swipe wildly at the alpha and drag his sadistic ass out of that fucking nest if I had to. "Don't you fucking—"

"Sana." Cyrus's voice was hushed, slurred, his eyes trying like hell to focus on my face.

"I'm here! I'm here," I said quickly, my voice just as manic as the desire pumping in my veins. "May I come into your nest?"

He raised his hand, weaving slightly in the air, beckoning me forward. I immediately rushed at Tallis, shoving him away from the omega, and I swore the fucker smiled. Then I carefully straddled Cyrus, conscious of his heightened state of arousal. His abs flexed beneath me as my slick dripped over his hips, mixing with his own sweet fluids.

"My sweet Cyrus." I cupped his cheeks, leaning down and placing a soft kiss on his lips.

He looked up at me, his eyes finally really seeing me. He smiled sweetly, caressing my sides with trembling fingers. Taking a moment to admire his angular nose and full lips, I pressed another gentle kiss to his lips. He opened for me, letting me slip my tongue into his mouth and claim it, kissing him hard and deep.

I nipped at his lips and tongue, tasting every inch of his

sweet mouth as he moaned. Slipping his hands up my side, he palmed my breasts, caressing and feeling me. His gentle touch had my wolf spinning with a possessive desire to mark every sweet inch of his skin with my fangs.

A hard slap landed on my ass, and I moaned loudly in Cyrus's mouth.

Then another slap.

Then another.

I broke the kiss, then glared over my shoulder at Tallis. His dark eyes narrowed. "Fuck him already," he ordered.

His command washed over me, and my wolf was happy to obey. *For now.*

Gripping my ass, Tallis moved me up, then fisted the base of Cyrus cock, pushing the tip just at my entrance. I leaned up, ready to sink down, but before I could, Tallis shoved my hips down, burying Cyrus's perfect cock deep inside me.

All the breath whooshed out of me at the deep connection as Cyrus keened, pushing his hips up and gasping loudly.

Moving just next to me, Tallis leaned down, then both shocked and delighted me as his tongue slipped over my clit. My whole body shuddered with pleasure, and I gripped the back of his head, holding his mouth to my sex. Their combined scents swirled around me with potent pheromones. My nostrils flared as I pulled in as much of it as I could. I pushed my ass down hard, grinding into Cyrus's hips while Tallis's long tongue teased my sensitive nub. *It felt incredible.*

Heat coiled in my stomach, and my skin flashed hot. All too quickly my orgasm rippled, then burst, spreading outward into every pore. Tipping my head back, I moaned and shook, continuing to ride Cyrus's perfect cock.

Then, without any warning, Tallis grabbed a handful of my hair, jerked my head to one side, and shoved his fangs deep into my neck.

Marking me.

Calming me.

Taking me for his own.

# CHAPTER TWENTY

## *the nest*

Cyrus

---

MY HEARTBEAT JACKED UP, AND MY VISION BLURRED. TALLIS'S beast was dragging his connection with Sana into my head, making me dizzy and nauseated at the same time.

He claimed her. He fucking claimed her without asking. *Fuck.*

I tried to stay present in the moment, to think of what I needed to do, but my body stole all my attention, and I bucked my hips up, trying like hell to find relief in Sana's sweet heat. Her pussy fluttered around me, her body continuing to climax even while she struggled to remain conscious.

My stomach clenched hard, and more slick pushed from my hole, soaking my nest.

"Tallis," I mumbled. "I need..." My words slipped into a string of pained grunts as another wave of my heat hit hard. I was covered in sweat and slick, desperate to get off.

Sana twitched against my chest, her hands smoothing down my chest and abs. Moving slowly, she placed her hands on either side of my head, then tried to sit up. Then she was gone.

Tallis ripped her off me, slamming her onto her back just next to me. Her eyes widened with shock, but her pupils were still blown out, black consuming all color. She was still lost to the fog a mating bite brought, unable to really think or move.

"Fuck her," Tallis snarled, grabbing my arm and jerking me up.

I gasped at the force of his strength. It was hard and demanding, but he still managed to somehow be gentle as he forced me between Sana's legs. Unable to stop myself, I pushed my hips forward, sinking into her wet heat. Her cunt squeezed me, stealing my breath for a moment.

Sana's hand immediately flew to my shoulders, holding me to her. She moaned and snarled, demanding I go faster.

Sana clawed at my back, her eyes blown wide and her mouth parted with silent pleasure. I fell into her, rolling my hips and kissing her sweet lips. She flashed her pointed fangs, her lips puffy and red. Pushing into her harder and faster, I dipped my thumb into her mouth, pleased when she turned her head, sucking it. Her soft tongue brushed against the pad of my thumb, and my cock swelled, ready to come.

Sensing my end quickly approaching, Tallis growled in my ear, "Not yet."

"I'm not going to last," I whined, Sana's cunt tightening, her own orgasm building fast. "Oh, fuck, alpha."

Tallis's thick fingers pushed into my ass, quickly stretching and preparing me. Then his thick cock slipped easily inside me, and the tension in my shoulders evaporated. *This* was what I needed. The euphoric sensation of my ass being filled at the same time as my cock buried to the hilt made all thought slip away.

"Harder!" Sana growled, reaching past me to fist Tallis's hair.

Tallis growled loudly then unleashed himself on me. He fucked me wild, pushing my cock deep into Sana with each snap of his hips. His knot quickly expanded, and Sana's pussy gushed. She screamed out her orgasm at the same time as Tallis. The wave of pheromones that burst off both alphas ripped through me, but just before I could come, Tallis pulled his engorged cock out of me, forcing a desperate scream from my throat. Dazed, I didn't have time to register what was happening. I was on my back with Sana on top of me, her back to my chest.

Tallis settled in front of us. His eyes were crazed, the crimson color within them pulsing and deepening, going almost fully black. He jerked Sana's knees up, gripped the base of my cock, then he shoved me deep into her ass. It was the tightest thing I had ever felt, and I was sure she'd never been touched there before. I expected her to scream or fight, but her heat was too strong, and she fell back against my chest, pulling at her nipples.

"Have you ever had two cocks in you, pretty doll?" Tallis snarled, flashing long, pointed teeth.

Sana whimpered, trying like hell to bounce up and down on my length.

I was used to catering to Tallis's rut. He was forceful and unforgiving in the pleasure he forced from my body, but the way he moved and commanded Sana was like nothing I had ever seen before. He was a completely different beast. And it was thrilling.

Tallis's skillful tongue slipped over my balls and up my

shaft while Sana continued to roll her hips. He kept moving up, and she keened, throwing her head back. I could only guess he was sucking her clit. The loud sound of kissing and sucking filled the cave as the beautiful she-wolf writhed on top of me.

"Fuck me!" Sana snarled, grabbing a handful of Tallis's hair and forcing his mouth off her.

He sat up and fisted his cock. I gripped Sana's hips, holding her still for him. She thrashed and writhed, trying to move. My balls tightened as my climax quickly built, tingling at the base of my spine. Then I gasped as Tallis pushed forward, breaching her wet center.

Sana's mouth dropped open in a silent scream. The she-alpha had only ever been with a beta before, and I was sure the stretch was shocking to her.

Tallis's thick shaft squeezed in, tightening the feel of Sana's ass around me. The bulbous crown of his cock pushed so fucking tight against my length, sliding deeper and deeper, until he was fully seated. His balls pressed against mine, and Sana shuddered.

"You're in my fucking guts," she snarled, her claws pushing so hard into Tallis's shoulders, blood dripped down his biceps.

A wicked smirk consumed his face. Then he moved.

Slick poured out of Sana's cunt, coating Tallis's hips and dripping down my balls. It was jerky at first, difficult to find a rhythm. I gripped Sana's knees, holding her open for my mate as he moved her hips, forcing her to fuck both of us.

"What a filthy, wet little doll," Tallis growled. "Look at you stuffed and fucked."

She nodded and babbled, exposing her mating bite to both of us as Tallis pounded into her. Wanting to know what it tasted like, I closed my lips around Sana's mating bite and sucked. My eyes rolled into the back of my head at the flavor that consumed me.

My orgasm barreled through me, and I turned my head, rubbing Sana's blood on my cheek. Tallis roared at the sight, fucking into the she-alpha harder.

She was limp pinned between us, her curvy body jerking like a rag doll. The back of her head hit my shoulder, giving me the perfect view of her jiggling tits. They were so big and her nipples so puffy.

Tallis growled and snarled like an animal as his knot began to take hold. In one fierce thrust, he shoved his cock into Sana's tight pussy, sealing the three of us in a vise-like grip. It was almost painful against my sensitive shaft, and I whimpered, riding the relenting waves of pleasure my mates brought me.

Slowly, my body finally stopped screaming with sensation, and I felt limp against my nest. Sana sagged against my chest, both us looking up into Tallis's dark but loving eyes. My two alphas.

## CHAPTER TWENTY-ONE
# *three days later*

Sana

---

STRADDLING TALLIS'S HIPS AS HE SLEPT, I LET OUT A CONTENTED sigh. His firm chest was warm against my cheek, his hand on my hip. His consciousness drifted through my mind, our bond still forming. I wasn't sure how long a mating bond was supposed to take to form, but I was always under the impression it was instantaneous. Maybe I was wrong. Or maybe it was because Tallis was already mated. It didn't really matter either way. I could still feel faint traces of him along the edges of my mind, and it was still better than anything I had ever imagined.

He was exhausted, but happy. Even while he slept, his love and affection for Cyrus blended with his intense feelings for me. *He wanted me.*

A more rational alpha would have been enraged to be claimed in the middle of her heat. Especially considering Tallis never expressed interest in me other than being an absolute dick, but it felt right. While he never shut the fuck up, it was so clear now that he was just shit at expressing himself, but I could feel him in our bond.

I let out a contented sigh, still unable to believe it.

These two wolves were mine now. I belonged to them, and they belonged to me. I wasn't alone anymore. I clasped my hands under my chin, trying to keep the flood of emotions contained within me.

Cyrus snored softly, tucked tight against Tallis's side. His long fingers twitched as he slept. He was having a good dream. I'm not sure how I knew, but he was thinking of something that made him feel warm and soft.

My sweet omega.

Moving slowly, I placed my palm on Cyrus's chest, slipping my hand down to the cut V grooved at his hips. His soft cock was still swollen—not with arousal but from continued, unrelenting use. Tallis and I drained him thoroughly, then demanded even more. He never once faltered or complained.

He was amazing. They both were.

"Don't wake him," Tallis whispered. "He's always drained after my rut. He needs to sleep." There was a hint of alpha command in his tone, and, while I thought of challenging him, I decided against it. He was right, Cyrus needed rest, so I slowly pulled my hand back.

I had experienced many heats in my twenty-three years on this earth. I had even been serviced during a few by that sweet beta in the stables, but for the most part, I handled them on my own. Since my cycle was so unpredictable, the pain was always hard to bear, whether I was alone or not, but this time it was like a dream. I had never felt so cared for. So safe and...*loved?*

"Are you okay?" Tallis asked, his hand tightening on my

hip. He pushed some comfort through our bond. I smiled, figuring he confused my emotions for sadness.

"I'm okay." I sat up, looking down at my mate. A rush of their combined fluids dripped out of me, puddling on Tallis's lap. It was disgusting and comforting at the same time.

"Look at that mess pouring out of you," Tallis growled as he stared at the puddle on his stomach. "You look good bursting with cum." He smoothed his hands down and over my calves, squeezing my tight muscles hard.

"That feels good." I tipped my head back, resting my hands on his firm chest. I swore his tits were bigger than mine.

Gentle fingers traced the mating bite just beneath my ear, circling the tender flesh. "This looks good on you," he said, his deep voice sending shivers through me. "I mark my mates well." There was something so soft in his eyes as he watched the motion of his fingers trace it over and over again. It tickled.

I caressed the lines of his perfect abs, following the groves to each freckle and mark. A dark scar rested at the juncture of his shoulder and neck, and I reached up to touch it. It was slightly curved and appeared to be from a burn. "What's this from?" I caressed the rough skin.

Tallis jerked, slapping his hand over it. "It's nothing," he said quickly. "I can barely remember." His emotions bounced around the inside of my head, his feelings unsettled and quickly changing. It was hard to focus on what was actually going on inside him.

I put my hands on my hips, not liking the intense unease pouring off him. "You're a shit conversationalist."

He pulled a face. "But you've also told me I talk too much. Which is it, doll?"

"Oh, you say plenty." I crossed my arms, pushing up my breasts. His eyes immediately fell to them. "You just don't say anything that matters."

He squeezed one of my breasts, palming my flesh. "Like what?" he asked, distracted. Like he didn't give a shit.

"Like why you left your village." He released me, and his expression went surprisingly hard. "Or where you got this scar."

I couldn't tell if he was angry or annoyed. Or maybe scared? But then, as if flipping a switch, he forced a smile and squeezed my ass. "There are some things not worth talking about." I opened my mouth, but he cut me off. "*I'm* the alpha in this relationship, and if I don't want to—"

"Not anymore," I said loudly, loving the way his eyes widened at the realization. "*I'm* the alpha in this relationship."

Tallis chuckled deep in his chest. It was dark and mocking. Flashing his teeth, he gripped my thighs and pulled me closer. "Listen here, doll. When alphas mate alphas, there's always a dominant one, and that's me. But if you need a reminder, I can always bend you over and fu—"

"I don't think so," I shot, slapping one of his pecs so hard, my palm stung. His beast moved through his eyes, and I shoved back the urge to laugh at his growing frustration. It was infinitely easier to work him up now that I could feel him inside my head.

"Sana." His tone was a warning, power and strength dripping in every decibel.

"If you two don't stop bickering," Cyrus mumbled, his face still pressed against Tallis's arm, "then this relationship won't have any alphas."

A sliver of Cyrus's consciousness drifted through my bond with Tallis. It was cloudy, like the shadow of a feeling, but I could still feel him. Even though the omega looked annoyed and sleepy, he was euphoric to have both his alphas by his side.

I smiled at him, loving that I could share his happiness.

"We were hard on you," Cyrus said sweetly, touching a few deep bruises sprinkled across my hips and sides. There were also bite marks along my inner thighs and the bottom swells of my breasts. They were tender, but they felt good. Too good.

"Thank you." I leaned down, pressing a quick kiss to my omega's lips.

He smiled, cupping my cheek as I pulled away. "What for?"

"I don't know." I shrugged, feeling a little overwhelmed by the emotions dancing around and through me. "For taking care of me during my heat."

Tallis pushed his big hands up my thighs, squeezing my flesh. "That's what mates are for."

"Cyrus and I are mates?" I asked, needing to make sure. "Even though we aren't bonded?"

Cyrus brushed a finger over my mating bite. "Yes, my sweet alpha. And once I have some of my strength back, I will insist on you marking me too."

"We can both claim you?" My eyes widened. "It won't drive you crazy to have so many in your head?"

Cyrus laughed softly, shaking his head. "While I don't know a ton about triads, we did have a few in my village. From what I understand, it can be uncomfortable at first— the connection burrowing a little deeper the second time— but it's worth it."

Tallis grabbed a handful of my breast and squeezed hard. "I haven't decided if it's worth it yet, but you do have much better tits than Cyrus. His ass is better though." The mouthy alpha sent a teasing pulse through our bond, making me smile.

"I need out of this cave," Cyrus groaned, standing on shaky legs. "It reeks of cum, slick, and sweat in here."

I inhaled deeply, loving the thick aroma left by our intense lovemaking. I could scent every layer of my two men. It was delicious and earthy. Sweet and smoky. Sexy and wonderful. My nose was sharper than it ever had been before.

"Up." Tallis popped the side of my thigh. "I need to stretch."

Cyrus reached for my hand, making sure I didn't fall over. My legs wobbled, and my sex ached. It felt as if I had been horseback riding for weeks on end. Muscles I didn't know I had hurt.

Arching my back, I groaned, "I'd kill to have someone draw me a bath right now."

"*Draw you a bath*?" Tallis asked as if the word was a foreign language.

"Yes." I couldn't believe he didn't know what it meant, but he didn't seem to be joking. "When someone prepares a bath for you."

"Forgive him." Cyrus picked up the water canister, and removed the stopper. "He's from Myphic. They live rough and ugly out there."

"You're telling me," Tallis spoke slowly, a shitty smirk already lifting one side of his mouth. I crossed my arms, ready to hear whatever rubbish was about to fall out of his mouth. "You don't even run your own bath water?" He let out a jerky laugh. "What kind of pampered, bullsh—"

"Yeah, I get it," I said loudly, meeting his ridiculous expression head on. " I'm pampered and spoiled and all that other bullshit, but we can't all be you. Now tell me," I paused, enjoying his weary expression, "were you forced to cut your own umbilical cord or did you fight the midwife for the honor?"

The big alpha tipped his head back, laughing long and hard. The sound tingled my spine, making my nipples pebble. "You know," he said, raking his nails up and down his chest as he stretched, "my mother was a real bitch of a wolf. She always tried to curse me, praying I'd mate someone just as annoying and stubborn as she was. I'd think she'd fucking love you."

I snorted. "I hope she beat you as a pup."

"Someone feed me," Cyrus demanded, taking my hand and walking toward the entrance. "Then we can discuss getting your sister out of Casin."

I paused, looking between both my mates. I hadn't let myself think about what Tallis mating me meant for saving Emmy, but a small part of me thought I might never get her back. "Really? You'll help me?"

Tallis squared his shoulders, his big body consuming the cave. "We can't leave our new little sister in danger, can we?"

My heart swelled with so much love and affection, it hurt. Cyrus kissed my cheek, circling his arms around my waist. I settled my chin on his shoulder, letting him love me for a moment. Tears burned the backs of my eyes, and I cleared my throat roughly to keep my emotions in check.

"I need to use the washroom." I pulled away from my omega, determined not to cry in front of them. "I'll meet you both at the stream."

"Wait a second," Tallis said. "We'll all come. Just give me a minute."

"I know that I've peed in front of you before," I shook my head, wishing I could block out the memory, "but I really don't need an audience. I just need a moment to myself."

"Be quick." Cyrus squeezed my hand, worry making his brows pull together.

"I *am* an alpha," I reminded the omega. "A well-trained one." I winked at Tallis.

"Go on." Tallis shook his head, waving me off. "Try not to use all that training all at once."

I rolled my eyes, then set off.

Every muscle in my body throbbed and screamed as I climbed down the side of the rockface. The warm breeze whipped around me, brushing over my exposed skin and making me very aware of several bite marks on the backs of my thighs that I hadn't seen yet.

My mind wandered as I walked through the dense forest, stepping carefully over the twisting roots and thick brush. My leg felt almost normal, even as everything else ached. Looking over my shiny scar, I noticed the very dark bruises on both my knees. I let myself remember how I got them—Cyrus's cock hitting the back of my throat while Tallis took me from behind. I clenched my thighs together, cursing myself for not staying with my mates.

The ground slowly shifted from uneven, jagged rocks to hilly dirt covered in moss, and a patch of those bitter white flowers caught my eye. They swayed with the hot summer breeze, looking so damn innocent. A few loose petals and wisps of blue pollen caught the breeze and whipped into my face and hair. The stench was ten times stronger than it was a few days ago. It was sour, almost acidic, as it burned the back of my throat.

Picking a petal out of my hair, I crushed it between my fingers, then threw it on the ground. Tallis had to be wrong. I simply couldn't believe my parents poisoned me, but at the same time, it couldn't have been an accident. After all, if someone had fed these flowers to me by accident, then Emmy and Davon would have gotten sick as well. And they never had the same health issues I did. Especially Davon. He was a mountain of a wolf, so sure in his abilities, no one ever challenged him.

Except for our father.

I turned away from the flowers, then froze. Fear ripped through me, followed by blinding rage. I couldn't see him, but I could smell him. Tamen's muted scent of moss and cedar hit me hard, and I turned my head, shocked at how strong it was.

"I've been looking everywhere for you."

I spun to his voice, then glared at the wolf stalking toward me. I thought briefly of trying to cover my bare chest, but I refused to let him know it bothered me to be seen like this.

His brown eyes moved down the full length of my naked body. His lips twisted in disgust at the sight of so many bites and bruises. "From the looks of it, it seems I'm not the only one who's found you."

"I suggest you leave." I crossed my arms, trying not to let my fear display. "My pack will be here soon and you don't want—"

Tamen roared with laughter, my mother's favorite guard, carrying on her disdain of me even in her absence.

*I fucking hated him.*

"Sana, you might have been a whore for a few rogues, but savage wolves don't make for a pack." He looked so satisfied. "Your mother will be *very* pleased to have you home safe."

The muted scent of two other alphas tingled the inside of my nose. Tamen wasn't alone, and it was stupid of me to assume he was. If they got anywhere near the cave, they'd easily find Tallis and Cyrus. The whole area was still thick with pheromones and reeked of sex. To keep them safe, I needed to get these wolves out of here.

I clicked my tongue and shook my head. "So, Hund Valley didn't rip her throat out for my actions? They didn't put my father's head on a spike?" His eyes narrowed, trying and failing not to react. "What a shame. I had such high hopes for Hund Valley. They were rumored to be vicious and proud, but I guess not everything we hear is true."

"Get it out of your system now, Sana," Tamen sneered. "Luna Morana has been through hell, and she doesn't need your attitude to—"

"To what?" I snapped. "To make her feel worse? To make her *sad*?" I mocked. He opened his mouth, but I growled, cutting him off. "If I am a burden to my mother, then I am *hers* to discipline. *Not yours*! Now, you will fix that pathetic look on your face, address me as 'My Lady,' and escort me home. Any other commentary you might have on the way I look or how I've conducted myself since leaving home can be kept to yourself."

His jaw clenched, his fists curling tight. Moving very slowly, he took a small step to the side and held out his hand, motioning for me to take the lead. "This way..." he pressed his lips together before finally gritting out, "My Lady."

# CHAPTER TWENTY-TWO
## *the stream*

Tallis

---

CYRUS STEPPED INTO THE COLD STREAM. HIS MOVEMENTS WERE slow, but he seemed better than usual after my rut. Sharing my attention with Sana was clearly good for him. I held out my hand, pulling him toward me and deeper into the stream. The chilly water rushed around my hips, making goosebumps flash across my chest and back.

"It feels good," Cyrus whispered, his teeth chattering a bit.

I set to work cleaning my mate, washing dried slick and cum off his abs and thighs, and even out of his hair. I searched through our bond, trying to get a feel for his emotions, but my mind was still fuzzy. It was difficult adjusting to having two mates push their way into my head. There was so much noise, I couldn't tell who felt what or why.

"How are you?" Cyrus asked, searching my face with his gorgeous dark eyes. "It's hard to feel you right now."

"My balls are thoroughly drained, and my thighs feel like I climbed a fucking mountain." I nodded in approval, then winked at my mate. "I like it."

Narrowing his eyes, Cyrus glared right through my bull-shit. "Tallis."

I hated it when he looked at me like that. It was like he could see straight to my soul. He had the power to rip me apart and put me back together with only a glance.

"Talk to me," he whispered, cupping my cheek. "You're distant. What's going on?"

I swallowed hard, feeling exposed. Cyrus knew me better than anyone else on earth. He was my mate, lover, and best friend. And I couldn't help but feel that I had betrayed him. "How do you feel...about me..."

"Claiming Sana?"

I nodded, hating how ashamed I felt.

"I'm okay," he said. "But it's driving me crazy that I don't know what's going on inside that ridiculous head of yours."

"I feel like shit," I said honestly. "And I feel like shit because I'm so fucking happy."

"You make zero sense." Cyrus snorted, smoothing his hands down my chest. He rubbed at a crusty bit of dried slick, washing it away.

"*You* are my mate," I said, placing my hands on either side of his face. "You begged me to consider Sana, and I said no. Then I turned around and fucking mated her without talking to either one of you. The fact that she didn't wake up wanting to scratch my eyes out shocks me."

Cyrus gave me a kind smile, placing a quick kiss on my lips. "My wolf has felt a pull to Sana since the moment I saw her, and so has yours. You haven't betrayed me or our bond. You've made us stronger."

I couldn't help but smile at his kind words.

"I'm just shocked you actually did it," he said. "Between your shitty attitude and Sana's unrelenting fire, I was sure you'd end up killing each other long before realizing how much you wanted each other."

I chuckled in agreement. "She's just so much fun to fight with."

"Am I not fun?" he feigned offense.

"No," I said flatly. "You're calm and even-tempered, and when you actually get mad enough to yell, it's usually because I've really fucked up." His eyes widened at my confession. "But Sana snips and snarls. She's easy to rile up, and I fucking love it."

Cyrus brushed his fingers over my neck and smiled. "It's going to be weird seeing a mating bite on you. I wish I could leave a permanent mark on both of you."

"Me too." I hugged him, pressing him tight to my chest. I wanted to bend him over and take him slow and soft to prove my love, but we were both still so sore, and showing my affections to both my mates could wait until we were no longer dehydrated and hungry.

"Is Sana happy?" Cyrus asked. His dark eyes filled with worry. My sweet omega, always troubled about something. "I can feel only a teeny bit of her through you. Is she happy?"

"Well, right now, all I can feel is you and the fears swirling around in that head." I channeled my fingers through his thick dark hair. "Our bond is still forming, but from what I can tell, she's very happy. A small part of me was worried when I woke up this morning that she'd be really fucking angry that I claimed her, but she adores you too much to reject me."

"She adores *you* just as much as me." He pushed a finger into my chest. "And if you can't see that, then you don't deserve either one of us."

I laughed, quickly kissing his cheek. "I don't deserve you either way."

He took a long breath, looking at me as if I were ridiculous. His gaze drifted down my face, settling on my shoulder. His fingers brushed my scar, and my smile instantly fell. "We need to tell her."

"I know." I stared off into the distance, looking for Sana. "I will. Just not yet."

"Why not? She's our mate."

"Because," I swallowed thickly, trying not to allow the rush of memories and emotions to consume me, "I already hate myself for what I did. I don't want her to—"

"You did nothing wrong," Cyrus said forcefully. Our bond blazed with his anger. He never accepted my role in why we left our village. I loved him for that, but it didn't change what I did. "What happened was an accident, and Sana will understand." His voice dropped as he whispered, "You aren't a rogue, Tallis. You're an honorable alpha."

I nodded, struggling to meet his eyes. "I promise I'll tell her, just not today. We're freshly bonded. Let me enjoy this new connection for a bit."

He let out a long sigh before finally nodding. "I just don't want it to be a secret. We're mates, and secrets are how triads fall apart."

"I promise," I said quickly, still struggling to believe I allowed a third into our relationship. My wolf mocked me, knowing damn well it was never my choice. Cyrus and Sana picked me. We were destined.

"Where is Sana?" Cyrus asked, turning toward the shore. "She should be here by now."

I looked for her through our bond. Cyrus's loud emotions twisted with my own fears, muffling her presence, and it took me a moment to focus squarely on my she-alpha. There was a beat of fear in her, but more than that, she was pissed. Really fucking pissed.

"Come on," I said, pulling Cyrus out of the water. I reached for the satchel, grabbing a pair of pants for both of us.

"Where are we going?" Cyrus asked, taking the clothes and pulling them on. He struggled for a moment, the tight fabric resisting the pull over his wet skin.

"I'm not sure," I said, concentrating hard on my new mate. "All I know is we need to find Sana."

Cyrus nodded, his expression going hard. He understood my fear and the sense of unease growing inside me, but instead of panicking, my fierce mate pulled on the satchel, cracked his knuckles, then said, "Lead the way."

---

My heart plummeted into my gut as I realized that Sana's sweet scent was leading us back to the village. *And she wasn't alone.* The musk of a few other alphas twisted with her woodsy aroma, but I only recognized one. It was the same damn alpha that had been tracking our part of the forest for weeks now. *The fucker just wouldn't give up.* We should have left the area, then come back after a few months for Sana's sister.

I was so stupid to think they'd give up on finding the pack alpha's daughter so easily.

"What do you think?" Cyrus whispered, staring at the village gates.

Dusk was quickly approaching, and the night guard apparently consisted of not one but four alphas standing at the ready. They wore only dark slacks, their chests easily visible in the dimming, setting sunlight. It made sense. Out here, all kinds of monsters could beat on their door at any moment. Taking the time to remove a shirt to shift into your wolf could be the difference between life and death.

"I don't think they'll stop us if we enter," Cyrus whispered.

"It's not them who worry me," I whispered.

"Then what is it?"

"If they have this many guards on a locked iron gate, then how many are patrolling the packhouse?"

His eyes widened, understanding our problem. "How will we get in to get our mate?"

"Exactly."

Cyrus shifted uncomfortably next to me. He was scared shitless for our she-alpha. He tried to hide his fear from our bond, but I knew him too well. "We have to try," he whispered, deep lines etched between his brows. "I can't just sit here all night, waiting."

"Come," I said, taking his hand. "Let's head to the tavern. I've got an idea."

# CHAPTER TWENTY-THREE
## *the cellar*

Sana

---

I STARED AT THE STONE WALLS, MARVELING AT THE DETAIL I COULD see in the dark. In the past, when my parents locked me in the cellar, I struggled to make out anything, but my alpha senses were stronger than they had ever been before. Even with only a sliver of the Moon peeking through a tiny window near the ceiling, I could clearly make out every line and divot in the gray rock and the twisting grain on the barrels around me. The smooth wood was velvety in appearance except for the few dark stains splattered across one side. It was dried blood. *Rainer's blood.*

The familiar scent of mold, oak, and whiskey swirled around me, reminding me of that horrible night. It was barely a month ago. The hook where Rainer's hands were bound dangled above me, and my feet rested where his blood had puddled on the floor. The dusty ground was slightly darker there, the blood not fully coming up.

The cellar door creaked open, and Tamen's sharp scent flooded the room before his feet touched the last step. I turned my head, ready to glare him down. I wanted to rip him to shreds and watch his life puddle beneath his broken body, but I knew better than to challenge a stronger wolf, and Tamen was both stronger and meaner than me. *There was a reason my mother adored him.*

I just had to be patient. Tallis's lessons repeated in my mind: *A restless hunter goes hungry. A patient one feasts for days.* Today, I was a patient hunter. I'd get Emmy, then I'd get the fuck out of here.

Tamen came around the corner, coming to a stop just in front of me. A mirrored sheen danced off his eyes in the dim light. "Luna Morana has requested an audience with you."

"Fine," I said, loving the way his jaw tightened at my clipped tone.

"The Luna would like you to clean up before being brought to her chambers. It would—"

"I'll go to her chambers, but I'm not putting on a show."

He let out an annoyed sigh, gnashing his teeth together. "You are so lucky your mother is such a patient woman. She has—"

"Does my father know you're fucking his mate?" I asked loudly, reveling in the look of shock that flitted across his face. He reined it in quickly, but not before I could see and enjoy it.

"I would never!" he barked, balling up his fists as if ready for a fight.

I stood, dusting off my still bare ass. "Just keep your mouth shut and escort me to my mother. She's spent her whole life disappointed in me, and I would be doing her a great disservice by cleaning up and stealing her opportunity to rip into me yet again."

Tamen shook his head, disgust making his lip curl. "The way you make her suffer is inexcusable. The sight of you will surely—"

I smirked, picturing Tallis's teasing expression and how it always burned through me. "I cannot wait to watch you die."

Tamen's wicked smile returned, and he crossed his arms over his burly chest. "Are you going to kill me?" He snickered. "A weak, little wolf like you only has one real purpose, and from the looks of you," he dragged his gaze up and down my naked body, "you're good at it."

I smiled sweetly, trying to look as unaffected as possible. "Oh, Tamen." His jaw ticked, his arms tightening a bit. "You have happily catered to every single one of my mother's evil whims. You reveled in my punishments. You even killed my sweet Rainer. But worse than any of those crimes, you simply bore me, and I'm done with you." I smiled wider, then shoved past him, making my way quickly up the stairs.

He was on my heels, his breath pushing out in restrained growls as I made my way through the empty kitchen. My eyes glided across the room, looking for Emmy, but she was nowhere to be seen. She was either in her room or the library.

The few guards in the main hall raised their brows as I walked by without a stitch of clothing on. Most immediately turned their backs, refusing to make eye contact should my mother appear and see the lust in their eyes. The few who didn't turn, Tamen barked at, forcing them from the house.

My breasts bounced as I took the stairs two by two, making the puncture marks sting and my heart squeeze. Surely by now, Tallis and Cyrus realized I was gone. Were they looking for me? Would they come to the village? Would my father kill them?

I prayed my new mates packed up and headed toward the sea, leaving me and my fucked-up family behind them. I knew it wasn't likely, but I needed to think of them living safe and free, and not sneaking into this hell hole, straight toward their deaths.

All too quickly, my mother's bedroom door loomed large at the end of the hall. It was an intimidating sight. The way the light cut under the door and the shadows that moved underneath felt ominous, hearkening back to my days as a pup, waiting for my punishment. *Nothing good ever came to me in that room.*

Max, our family guard, stood at attention just next to the door. He smiled at me, the scar across his cheek lifting at the motion. I furrowed my brow, not understanding why he was here. He normally guarded mine and Emmy's hall. That meant Andrus was watching over my sister, and I snarled at the idea. I hated the thought of him being anywhere near her.

Not waiting to be announced, I pounded my fist on the door, then flung it open. Sitting at her desk, Mother jerked her head around as the door banged against the wall. Rage already marred her pointed features. Her eyes focused on my face then pulled down my body. She grimaced, then stared at her very organized desk. A few neat stacks of paper sat in front of her. The quill in her hand was poised to write.

Slowly, her face melted from anger to something much different. It was a look I had never seen from her before. Slowly, she placed the quill back in its case, then stood and rounded her desk. Her dark blonde hair flowed behind her, frizzy at the ends. She looked ready for bed. Her purple dressing gown was secured tight around her middle. Her face was bare of any makeup, and she wore no jewelry. I couldn't remember the last time I saw her in a natural state.

"Sana," she sighed softly, reaching for my hands.

I took a quick step back, unable to find my words. This was not the reaction I had expected.

She squeezed my hands as she looked me over again. Sadness pulled at the corners of her eyes, and a twinge squeezed my heart. I wished her reaction was true, but I knew it wasn't. It was a show for the maids putting away her clothes and turning down her bed.

She cupped my face then placed a small kiss on my forehead, making me flinch. It set my teeth on edge. It was like waiting for a landslide. The cracks were there, the scent of dust in the air, I was just waiting for the ground to shift and her rage to bury me.

"What have they done to you?" she whispered, looking at the bite marks on my chest. She slipped a strand of my hair through her bony hand. "The things you must have endured. Tamen!" She spun to the guard waiting in the doorway.

His dark eyes widened, and he leaned eagerly toward her, waiting for his orders. He was definitely fucking my mother. No one looked that enamored by a command....except maybe an omega.

"Get Mallin and the healer," she said. "I want every inch of my daughter inspected and the rogues who did this to her tracked down and killed." Her eyes pulsed red, and her hand tightened around mine, her nails digging into my palm.

Tamen acknowledged his order then turned on his heel.

"Everyone else out," she said, keeping her back to the staff. "I want to speak to my daughter in private."

The maids scurried out. Not a single one met my eyes. They knew what was coming just as well as I did. Max pulled the door shut, and my mother's hand landed on my cheek with a sharp crack.

I was embarrassed at how much it shocked me. *I knew it was coming.*

"How dare you," she snarled, keeping her voice low so no one would overhear.

"I missed you too," I said loudly, forcing a pointed smile as my cheek burned.

She growled high in her throat then marched to her wardrobe. She pulled out a long blue nightshirt and threw it at me. I swatted it away. I had no interest in covering myself up. I would never cover up my true feelings or intentions ever again.

"It's my fault really." She glared at the garment, then at me. "Your father wanted to up your discipline. Force you to submit, but I wouldn't let him."

I crossed my arms, pushing my breasts up so she was forced to see the bruises Tallis's fingers left on me. She snarled then stalked slowly back to her desk. Her eyes bore into mine as she slowly lowered herself into her chair, resting her hands on the smooth, dark wood.

My fangs pushed forward as my beast readied herself for whatever my mother had planned next.

"This is my fault." Her voice was soft and controlled. Too soft. "I told your father that forcing an alpha into submission too early causes too many problems. It was something your mate was meant to do." She let out a long sigh. "And you ended up wild anyway. All my hard work gone to waste."

I kept my tone flat, trying not to give my spiraling emotions away, "You must be so disappointed." Not a single muscle in her face moved, but her eyes flashed red, and I smiled.

"I'd usually wait for your father to return, but—"

"Where is he?" I asked, a little surprised he was gone. My father didn't like leaving the comforts of home. He rarely left the packhouse anymore, forcing Davon to do all the real work around the village.

A slow, evil smile split her face. She reveled in the tense silence she commanded. It made the hairs on the back of my neck stand up. I wanted to rip the smirk right off her face. I wanted to beat her senseless for every awful thing she ever did to me, Davon, and Emmy. I wanted to see her blood paint the walls.

A quick knock made me flinch, and the door creaked as the healer and Mallin entered the room. Both bowed to my mother, then me.

"Healer Johns," Mother stood, gesturing to me, "I need to know that my daughter is healthy. It's clear she's been..." her eyes fell to my breasts again, "...handled by rogues, and I have no intention of allowing that kind of trash to enter our bloodline. I want a thorough check-up and something to help her sleep."

Mallin stepped forward, holding up a cup of tea.

Relief softened my mother's features, and she whispered a quick *"perfect,"* moving quickly to take the cup. I wished she had stayed at her desk. The barrier between her and me had been reassuring even if it was flimsy.

Mother turned to me, holding the blue teacup out. The familiar scent of the overly sweet tea filled my lungs, then it went bitter, burning the back of my throat. All the air flew out of me like a punch to the gut. *It smelled exactly like those fucking white flowers.*

"Lady Sana," Johns whispered, his tone always calm

and soothing as he slowly approached me. I tore my eyes away from the tea. "I'm so sorry about what's happened to you." His gaze moved over my mating bite, deep sorrow etched around his eyes. This was how true sadness was meant to look, and I was receiving it from the staff. "If it's okay with you," he whispered, "I'd like to do an exam and see what injuries you might have. Your leg." He paused, glancing at my scarred flesh. "Did you break it?"

Mother's eyes snapped to the scars along my shin, then they slowly moved up my body as if looking for any other sign of real injury. Anyone else would have thought the gesture caring—a mother looking for signs of pain on her daughter's body—but not this she-wolf. All she saw was damaged property that would be harder to sell.

"Healer Johns," I said softly, "would it be possible to check me over in the morning? I'm too exhausted, and my wolf is already distressed." She wasn't. My beast was ready to run. She was ready to fucking fight.

"Oh course, My Lady." Johns bowed low, then turned to my mother, waiting for her to command or dismiss him. After a tense moment, my mother finally nodded at the beta, allowing him to take his leave. Mallin stayed rooted to her spot, but her eyes followed Johns as if wishing she could follow.

"Drink your tea." Mother held out the teacup again. I glared at it.

"You first," I said, my jaw tense as I waited. I needed her to drink it to prove me wrong. I needed to know that she never meant to poison me.

"Me first?" Her brow twisted with confusion. "Stop being ridiculous and drink your tea. You always feel better after a cup." She lifted it a little higher.

The brown liquid looked the same as always. Tiny flecks

of withered leaves and cream-colored petals settled at the bottom. It looked so innocent, but the bitter tang in the air all but confirmed what it was. And it gutted me.

"I'm not thirsty." I was thankful when my voice didn't crack.

Mother's face went hard, and the sinewy muscles in her neck pulled tight. "Why can't you ever be easy on me?" she snapped. "You fight with me over the most ridiculous things. Now. Drink your fucking tea."

"No." My voice was so small, and tears burned my eyes. Tallis was right. She did this to me on purpose. "No," I repeated, my voice having no strength.

A flit of realization danced across my mother's face, and she turned to Mallin. "Please have Max double the guards along the borders and the packhouse. I don't want the rogues who hurt my daughter thinking they can steal her back."

"Yes, Luna." Mallin bowed, backing out of the room.

Mother watched her maid, not speaking again until the door was firmly shut behind her. She swallowed thickly, then bore her dark eyes into mine. "What the fuck did you let happen to you out there? Who did this to you?"

"No one," I snapped, trying to keep the rage, grief, and betrayal from pouring out of me. It pushed hard at my chest, making me want to fight and scream and cry at the same time.

"No one?" she snorted.

"No one!" I yelled as loud as my voice would allow.

I didn't have the strength for her games anymore. I just wanted to find Emmy and get the fuck out of here. As stupid as it probably was, I still felt like I could escape. Especially since I held no purpose for my parents anymore.

Hund Valley would never accept me now. Not after embarrassing them so thoroughly.

"So you're telling me you did this to yourself," she gestured to my body, "that you put bite marks between your thighs? That thing..." She jabbed a finger at my mating bite then snarled, unable to finish her thought.

"What does it fucking matter who did it? I'm here now. You've won."

"It fucking matters," she growled, taking several steps toward me. I flinched, expecting her to hit me again, and the simple reaction put a satisfied glint in her eye. "After everything we've done for you. The life I've allowed you to have, this is how you repay me? Mated to savages?" She shook her head. "I should have snuffed you out at birth," she seethed.

Her venom caught me off guard. She was a horrible woman, but she had never outright wished me dead. At least not out loud.

"Now," she held out the cup again, "drink your tea and take your punishment. We'll discuss this further when your father gets home."

Rage exploded in my chest, and I swatted at her hand. The delicate porcelain shattered against the wall, brown liquid dripping down the white paint and soaking into the carpet. "How could you!" I yelled. "How could you poison me? Do you have any idea what you've done to my wolf? To my mind?" My voice cracked as my fists shook and tears fell. "I just wanted to be a normal alpha! I wanted to fight and run and be of some use, but you poisoned me! Why? Why—"

A hard hand landed on my cheek, and without thinking, I swiped my clawed hand through the air, landing a sharp slap on my mother's face. Her eyes went wide, and she stumbled back. A thin line of blood bloomed on one cheek.

Her hand jerked to her face, ghosting over the mark. "How dare you," she snarled, baring her fangs.

"How dare *I*?" I growled high in my throat. "You have poisoned me every single fucking day since I presented as an alpha. What the fuck did I do to earn such a horrid fate? Why the fuck would you risk killing me?"

"Stop being so overly dramatic," she snapped. "It was not every day, and you damn well know it. But you forced my hand. You were out of control. Picking fights and talking back—"

"I was acting the way all alphas do when they're young!"

"You were acting like your fucking mother!" Her chest heaved, and her eyes flashed with so much hatred.

A wave of shock washed over me, followed quickly by nothing. I was numb. I tried to speak, but nothing came out. I just stood there with my mouth hanging open.

After a moment, Mother fixed her expression and squared her shoulders. "Your birth mother was a whore and rogue. Your father felt the need to save you from that kind of life and brought you home with him."

"Is he..." I swallowed hard, my brain struggling to keep up. "Is he...my..."

"He is *definitely* your father." She crossed her arms, tipping her chin up. She looked far too stiff to be discussing something that should be painful. "He'd never bring home a wild mutt just to be kind." She shook her head as if I asked the most ridiculous question. "Your presence was wholly unnecessary, but I was kind and let you be raised by a family within the village. You were very well cared for." She gave me a pointed look as if I should be grateful for such kindness.

"Then the orcs pushed at our borders," she continued, "and Hund Valley came to our aid. Half the village was destroyed, and our numbers were depleted. We had nothing of value to offer them for their kindness, but your father decided to offer you. I had to admit it wasn't a horrible idea. Alpha Rollen had a son about your age, so it made sense. But there was no way he'd accept a bastard of a rogue bitch, so we moved you into the packhouse and insisted you were mine. We gifted you with a life you would have never had otherwise."

I forced myself to breathe, still unable to move.

"I couldn't risk you turning into a wildling." She kept talking as if the silence unsettled her. "There were flashes of her within you. You were so aggressive—"

"Davon is aggressive," I gritted out, my voice coming back at full force. "You and father and all fucking alphas are aggressive. I was a normal pup. I did nothing to deserve what you did to me!"

She narrowed her eyes, and her voice dropped, "What *I* did was give you a chance. You would have died outside the borders, and I was well within my rights to have you disposed of. Raising your mate's bastard offspring is just not done, Sana. But *I* did it! *I* let you live!"

"You tried to kill me." I flung my hand out to the broken teacup. "You poured poison down my throat for ten years, and you expect me to thank you?"

"There was never enough camas in there to kill you. Just to calm your temper and ease you to sleep. I was very careful."

"You knew," I whispered. I already knew that, but hearing her admit it was far more gutting than I imagined.

"My wolf was disjointed, and my senses were out of control." Rage pulsed through me, making it difficult to see straight. "I couldn't shift properly or smell things or," I choked on my words, doubling over with a pained scream. I had never felt so out of control. My wolf pushed and pulled within me, wanting to kill the woman standing in front of me. And, fuck, I wanted to let her.

"Pull yourself together." I could hear the disgust in her voice. "This is not how a wolf of your status acts. A status *I* gave you."

"Mother..." I paused, panting hard. "Morana." Her cold eyes narrowed at her name. "You didn't give me shit."

She laughed, and her high-pitched cackle pounded at the back of my skull.

It was all too much. Too much rage. Too much hate.

"Now," she said, her voice as sharp as her glare, "I'm going to have another cup of tea brought for you, and, unless you want your whole body black and blue to match those disgusting bites, you *will* drink."

# CHAPTER TWENTY-FOUR

## *the tavern*

Tallis

"Drink," I said, taking a sip of my pint.

Cyrus snapped out of his thoughts, jerking slightly. He pressed his lips to the foam settled at the top of his ale, but he didn't actually drink. His fear thrummed through our bond, and I sent back long soothing pulses to ease him. But, as hard as I tried to hide it from him, I was also scared shit-less. There were too many unknowns.

We didn't know the lay of the village, we didn't know where Sana was being kept, and we didn't know how to get into the packhouse.

I just wished like hell I could get a solid feel for her. She was still pissed, her emotions swinging from angry to downright murderous, but that was all I could sense. Nothing else. No physical pain or sadness or distress. It was like there was a stopper in our bond, and only the strongest of her emotions could seep through.

"Tallis," Cyrus hissed, giving a slight jerk of his head to the table next to us. A squat alpha with dark brown hair and weirdly blue eyes stared at my mate as if trying to figure out what kind of species he was. I had thoroughly marked Cyrus before entering the village. I had hoped my scent, coupled with his unusual height, would keep anyone from noticing he was an omega. The last thing we needed was unwanted attention.

"Do you have a fucking problem?" I barked at the asshole. His wide-set eyes shifted to me, and I pushed my fangs forward, making my challenge very clear. He downed his ale, then grabbed a passing barmaid, lavishing her with attention.

Cyrus wrapped both his hands around his stein, pulling it closer to his chest. "How much longer do you think they'll be?" he whispered, glancing once again at the pair of betas at the end of the bar. "Are you sure—"

"I'm sure," I said softly, radiating as much calm as I could. Our bond flooded with his unease, and I took another drink. The bitter, cold liquid spread across my tongue and slid down my throat. It tasted good, but I was too tense to enjoy it.

"Don't you think a guard's uniform—"

"No," I cut him off, scanning the room to make sure no one heard. "Guards live together, dine together, drink together. I'd be found out before we made it anywhere near the packhouse."

"But can't—"

"No," I said firmly. "We have a plan, and we aren't changing it."

"Stop interrupting me!" he snapped.

The noise in the bar dipped at his outburst, then immediately rose again. No one gave us a second look once they realized no blood would be shed.

Cyrus was normally so collected in a crisis. He had the perfect temperament as a healer. But he loved Sana—he hadn't said it, but I felt it—and the thought of anything happening to her had him terrified.

"It's going to be okay, Cy." I placed my hand over his, caressing him with my thumb. "Sana is okay. I can feel it."

It was a lie. I couldn't pull anything specific from her through our bond. I could feel that she was alive and intensely pissed, but other than that, I had nothing. The subtleties I felt with Cyrus had yet to form between Sana and me. I could only assume it had something to do with her not being bound to our omega, but honestly I had no fucking clue.

"I'm just scared someone will recognize you," Cyrus dropped his voice. "Do you think our old home would send notices to the other villages? Since they weren't able to properly brand you? Would that happen?"

Pushing out a slow breath, I forced myself to take another drink. I didn't have an answer for him. I just prayed it wouldn't be an issue.

"There," I whispered, giving a pointed look just past my mate. Cyrus turned, following my gaze to the end of the bar.

One of the betas we had spent the last hour watching slowly stood. His rounded cheeks were fire red, and his black hair stuck to the sweat on his forehead. He stumbled a bit as he moved off his stool, making the other beta snort and laugh. His ale sloshed down the front of his service uniform, turning the dark green fabric almost black. They were both completely shitfaced.

The red-faced beta slapped a few coins on the bar, then made his way toward the door. *It was about fucking time.*

"Remember what to do?" I whispered to my mate.

Cyrus nodded. "Then I'll meet you behind the tavern."

"And if you can't find what you need?"

"I won't do anything stupid, and will meet you behind the tavern," he repeated the plan back to me. A small part of me wanted to crack a joke about what it actually took to get me in a fucking tavern for the first time in over a year, but I didn't have it in me.

"Go," I whispered, taking another slow gulp of my ale.

Cyrus cut swiftly around the table, following the drunk beta. His stride was far too urgent, weaving through the crowd. He looked like a fox on the hunt. I pinched the bridge of my nose, praying he'd settle once outside.

I took my time finishing my pint, then polished off Cyrus's too. It wasn't the stiff drink I wanted, but it would have to do. Securing the satchel across my chest, I slid out of my seat and made my way through the crowded room. I held the strap firmly in place, smoothing it repeatedly to make sure it hid the scar on my shoulder.

The air outside was surprisingly cool compared to the bolstering heat inside the tavern. The hot summer weather would have felt stifling any other night, but right now, the sweat on my brow welcomed the breeze.

Forcing myself to walk slowly, I made my way into the town square, leaving the noisy tavern behind me. The village was mostly empty. A few alphas were on patrol, and the occasional beta closed up their shop, but other than that, it was quiet.

I moved toward a dark cluster of shops, waiting until the sound of footsteps and hushed voices vanished. Cutting a quick glance over my shoulder, I took note of the empty road, then rushed down an alleyway. It would take Cyrus a little while to get what he needed, but I didn't want him waiting on me.

Circling back, I finally made my way to the back of the tavern. A dim lantern sat on the single step at the back door. There were a few crates filled with empty glass bottles, and the ground next to the door was muddy with soapy water.

The tavern door flung open, and I froze. A young beta stepped outside and hurled the contents of a bucket onto the ground. Dingy water splattered, hitting the beta's bare feet. He turned to go back inside, then froze as his eyes met mine. I could practically smell the fear radiating off him.

Needing to show him I meant no harm, I took a few steps back and leaned against a tree. His expression eased a bit, but his eyes still clung to me as if I might attack at any moment.

"You okay?" I asked, crossing my arms. I had hoped it would make me look more relaxed, but the way his eyes moved over my chest told me it didn't have the effect I was hoping for.

"Tallis," Cyrus called out in a harsh whisper.

The young beta snapped his head to my mate, then back at me. His eyes narrowed, and I prayed he'd just go back inside.

Cyrus jogged up to me, a relieved smile on his face. He was wearing a beta's dark green service uniform and had a few folded garments tucked under one arm. He patted his chest and smiled wide. "They were exactly where you said they'd be. The laundry behind the Beta Den was—"

I grabbed my mate and crashed my mouth to his, shutting him up. Cyrus tensed for a moment then relaxed in my arms, my omega submitting to his alpha. I broke the kiss and turned to the young beta.

"You got a fucking problem?" I barked.

He jerked, gripping the empty bucket as if it were a shield. "No, Alpha," he whispered.

"Then fucking go," I snapped. "Unless you want to watch?" I grabbed Cyrus's ass, ignoring the muted groan of annoyance that left his lips.

The young beta shook his head furiously, then disappeared back into the tavern. The door swung shut, taking all the chatter inside with it.

"You could have handled that better," Cyrus said flatly.

"He was acting like I was going to attack him. I was just standing here, and he froze like a doe caught in the brambles."

"You are an enormous alpha he doesn't recognize, hiding in the shadows behind the tavern." Cyrus raised his brows. "I wonder how many drunks have been kicked out of there, then tried to force their way back in through the back door."

I released him, not willing to admit his point.

Cyrus shook his head, then opened the satchel, stuffing the extra clothing inside. "I'm confident these will fit Sana, but the pants might be a tiny bit too short." He glanced at the door. "Let's go in case he returns with some muscle to chase you away."

We moved quickly along the back of the stores and through the square. I prayed Casin had a similar layout to our old village, so we'd be able to find the packhouse easily.

"Tallis," Cyrus whispered. "What does this mean?" He motioned to three dark stripes on one sleeve.

I shook my head, not sure. "It doesn't matter. Right now, we just need to look like we belong. And it's pretty dark tonight." I glanced up at the cloudy night's sky. "I doubt anyone will notice or care at this hour."

A large house came into view, and I released a tense breath. The wide path that led to the door was flanked by well-trimmed rose bushes, and what appeared to be a large garden sat to the side.

"This has to be it, right?" Cyrus whispered, looking over the two-story building.

While it was much bigger than the other houses within the village, it wasn't the compound most packs had. Servants, higher-ranked guards, and advisors usually lived in the packhouse, as well as the family, but this place appeared too small for that. A twist of fear squeezed my chest as I scanned the area, worried they might be keeping Sana somewhere else. A guest house or perhaps the stockades?

"I expected it to be bigger," Cyrus said, pulling the satchel off my shoulder and tucking it beneath a lush rose bush. A few pink petals floated to the ground before being carried away with the wind.

"This is a very small village," I reminded him. It was why we settled in these mountains. We thought there wouldn't be any guards outside the borders but failed to take into account the mountain creatures that required them to frequently patrol the area.

Keeping low, we crept within the shadows the trees provided, making our way around the back of the pack-house. The garden was mostly bushes, forcing us into the open moonlight. I felt so exposed, and my wolf snarled for putting our omega in danger.

"There are a lot of guards stationed at the doors," Cyrus whispered, peeking over a bush.

"It's standard. Nothing to worry about." But he was

right. There were two guards for every door, but they didn't move to patrol the area. They just stood there.

I frequently forgot how peaceful our old village was compared to others. We didn't have elves, orcs, griffins, or bloodsuckers to deal with. Even rogues rarely came our way, preferring the mountains over the flat lands that surrounded our old home.

"We just need to find the kitchens. The cleaning staff might still be coming and going. It'll be the best place for you to enter." I pulled Cyrus deeper into the garden, a little surprised to find it empty. With as many guards as were manning the doors, surely they had alphas making the rounds.

"There," I whispered, pointing to a large wooden door at the end of the building. A small brick was wedged inside the doorway, keeping it ajar. "Once you find Sana—"

"What do you two want with Lady Sana?" a deep voice cut through the silence behind me.

I immediately spun, placing myself between the guard and my mate. I recognized the alpha immediately. It was the scarred fucker from the market. The asshole that touched Cyrus.

"Hey, Max!" A she-alpha rushed up behind him, her uniform pulling tight across her muscular arms. "If that's Racen, tell him to fuck off already. His mate is going to kill him if he doesn't get his shit together." Her friendly smile slipped as she approached, and her muscles tensed at the sight of me.

"Karis," the guard, Max, said, keeping his eyes squarely on my face. "Let the Luna know the wolves who took Sana came back for her."

"Took Sana?" Cyrus snarled, trying to step around me. I

held my arm out, not letting him get any closer. "We didn't
—" A bag slipped over his head, jerking him backward.

I roared and reached for my mate, but before I could
shift into my wolf, something was pulled over my face, and
a fist connected hard with my gut. My wolf bellowed within
me, trying like hell to push forward, but the thick stench of
wolfsbane flooded my lungs, keeping my beast trapped
within me.

# CHAPTER TWENTY-FIVE

## morana's chambers

Sana

---

I EDGED AROUND THE ROOM, TRYING LIKE HELL TO FIGURE OUT how to get out of here. Morana stood between me and the door with a satisfied look on her face. I glanced behind me at the balcony door, realizing it might be my only way out.

"It's locked," she said, sitting on the edge of her enormous bed. "But if you're that desperate to break free, then please, by all means, jump to your death."

"I'm an alpha," I snarled. "I can handle that height easily."

"Can you?" She raised her brows, smoothing down the front of her silky purple robe.

I glared at her, refusing to answer. Tallis had jumped a much greater distance out of the cave, but I had no idea what my leg could handle.

"While I'm pleased with your confidence," she gave me a pointed smirk, "I don't think someone who has been...

*poisoned*...their whole lives—weakening their mind, body, and wolf—as you put it," she mocked my words, "should be risking something so stupid." My eyes flashed red, and the corner of her mouth lifted ever so slightly. "This is where you belong, Sana. Just accept it."

Adrenaline pounded hard in my veins as I spun, looking for something I could use as a weapon, but there was nothing. Just her desk, stacks of paper, and a mountain of fucking throw pillows. Rage burst out of me, and I grabbed a shiny pink vase, flinging it across the room. It hit the wall, and the pale lavender roses exploded. Shards of shimmering glass covered the carpet, followed by floating purple petals.

I turned, ready to scream my rage at the she-wolf, but her expression stopped me cold.

She looked...*happy*?

"And this is why we gave you the tea," she said pointedly, dragging her gaze from me to the water still dripping down the walls. She let out a long sigh, then spoke as if bored with the whole conversation. "You know, over the years, your father has broken more than one servant's heart with his charm. I hated exiling them from the village, but you don't fuck the pack alpha and expect to keep your job. But siring a child with a harlot, then forcing me to raise her..." She pursed her lips as if a sour taste flooded her mouth. "My charity is almost painful sometimes."

My beast growled low within me, and I bared my fangs.

"You might think I'm heartless," she picked a loose thread off her robe, letting it float to the floor, "but the arrangement with Hund Valley was better than you deserved. Any other Luna would have cast you out or killed you on the spot. I let you live, even raised you as my own.

And now..." she glowered at my bare chest, "you're just a rogue's whore."

"Does it bother you?" I asked, putting my hands on my hips, proudly displaying every mark on my body. "Knowing rogues have used me?"

Her jaw ticked, and I smiled.

"I'm ruined," I said in an overly sweet tone. "I've been thoroughly fucked and bred." Her eyes flashed, and I smoothed my hands over my stomach. "I might even have one of their bastards growing inside me right now."

She was across the room in a flash, gripping my hair and jerking my head to the side. "This means nothing." She poked my mating bite hard, making me wince. My muted bond with Tallis squeezed, and our connection grew for a moment. He could feel me, but that was all I knew.

She released my hair, shoving me back. "The only use you've ever had is to bind us to another pack, and that's what you'll fucking do!"

I laughed, resisting the urge to rub at my scalp. "There are many things I don't know, but I am sure Hund Valley has far too much pride to accept me now. I'm marked, used, and mated. It would humiliate both of you to force me on them."

She crossed her arms, an evil glint sparkling in her eyes. "Not Hund Valley," she said. "Hala."

"Hala?" I snorted. "What the hell makes you think Hala will want me?"

"Hala already agreed to a mating with our offspring. Emmy was meant to mate Andrus. He's the pack alpha's nephew. It really was an easy arrangement to agree to since they were both so fond of one another."

"Emmy was *meant* to mate Andrus?" I asked. Dread slipped down my spine, settling hard in my gut. I had a million questions, but only one that mattered. "Where is Emmy?"

A slow smile consumed her face. "In Hund Valley."

A cold panic hit me like a fucking wave. "Emmy is underage," I whispered, not wanting to believe she'd make the young omega mate the Hund Valley wolf. "She's a pup! How the fuck could you do that to her?"

Morana ignored me, continuing to speak as if planning a garden party. "In the morning, I'll write to Hala and let them know we're interested in an arrangement soon. If you are with pup, we can't wait until you're fat. A bonding will need to be sealed quickly. Your brother will be relieved. We were close to sealing an arrangement with one of the pack alpha's daughters, but I think this will be better."

"No one will touch me. I'm mated." I pushed my hair over my shoulder, proudly displaying my still raw mark.

She narrowed her hard eyes at me. "There are ways to handle that."

"What the fuck are you going to do?" I shot. "Rip it off?"

Her brown eyes went dark, and a chill settled in the air between us. *That's exactly what she'd do.*

I wanted to destroy her, rip her throat out and feed her pathetic body to the orcs, but shock held me in place. "You are a monster," I whispered.

"You will do as you're told, Sana," she said in a dangerous whisper. "I have no use for a wildling who refuses to strengthen our village. You will be sweet, agreeable, and you *will* drink your tea."

I swallowed hard, refusing to meet her eyes. I had spent my whole life fighting this woman's hatred. And I wasn't sure how much I had left in me. Maybe leaving for Hala was best. It wasn't like I was going to ever see Tallis and Cyrus again.

A loud knock rapped on the door, and it pushed open. "Luna Morana," Mallin whispered, "Alpha Tamen is here, and he says they've captured the rogues who took Sana."

My wolf snarled and growled deep within me. They shouldn't have come here. *She'll kill them.*

"Lead us to them," I said, turning to the maid. Her mouth hung open as she cut a nervous glance behind me.

"I don't think so," Morana chuckled, coming up beside me. "There is no way—"

"Yes, you will," I said, giving her a pointed look. "You want my obedience? My submission? You want me to mate some asshole in Hala? You already know, *Mother*," I growled her name—a name that didn't belong to her, "that I can make your life an absolute nightmare even with that fucking tea sitting in my gut. Give me a meeting, and I'll give you what you want."

She flashed her teeth as she spoke, "You expect me to bring you to the very wolves who kidnapped you?"

I snarled at her ridiculous lie. "The wolves who *kidnapped* me?" I repeated.

She nodded once, making it clear. I had to agree to this lie in order to see them.

*"If* you let me say goodbye and let them go unharmed," I met her glare with one of my own, "then I'll mate whoever you want. But I want your word they won't be hurt."

She snorted as if what I said was both confusing and ridiculous.

"You owe me," I whispered.

"I owe you nothing." Her voice was filled with so much venom.

"You owe Rainer!"

Her lips pursed as she thought it through. She was going to agree—we both already knew that—then she was going to have them killed. But I knew this was too tempting for her. She'd get to hand me one moment of happiness before stealing it away forever. This was the kind of violence my parents lived for.

"Fine," she said, nodding at Mallin. "You can see them. Then you can say goodbye."

# CHAPTER TWENTY-SIX
## a dark room

Cyrus

---

I SHIFTED SLIGHTLY, MY KNEES DIGGING INTO THE HARD STONE floor. Tallis grunted next to me as he continued to try to free himself. Our hands were both bound behind our backs, and Tallis still had the burlap sack over his head.

"Be careful not to hurt yourself," I whispered to my mate. There was something sharp along the edges of my bindings that kept pushing into my wrists, pinching my skin. And based on the thick stench of blood in the air, Tallis had them too. "Are they getting any looser?"

Tallis growled low in his chest, continuing to struggle. "They're elvish," he grunted. "I can't break them."

I grimaced, my hope faltering. The thin metal was forged with mercury, which prevented an alpha from shifting. The poison weakened them as well, stealing some of their strength. Not that you'd know it from the way Tallis growled next to me. He seemed determined to rip his hands off if he had to.

Unable to watch my mate struggle any longer, I turned my attention to the dimly lit room. The walls were the same gray stone as the floors, and the ceiling was very high, almost like a temple, and made of dark wood. Spokes holding lanterns were positioned near the heavy wooden doors and at each end of the room. But there were no windows, furniture, or anything else in the space that gave away what it might be used for. It seemed to have no real purpose.

"What can you smell?" I whispered, narrowing my eyes at the darkest corners of the room. Something like a tapestry hung from the far wall, but it was too dim to tell what was on it. "Anything useful?"

Tallis inhaled deeply. "There are two alphas in here with us." I nodded, glaring at the guards near the door. "I can also smell mold, dirt, oak, rust, and..." he inhaled again, "blood. But it's not just wolf. It's something else. Maybe orc."

A chill ran down my spine despite how stifling the air was around me. "What do we do?"

"Stop talking," the female guard snapped at me. She was tall and muscular with thick brown hair that she wore in a high ponytail. The scars that ran down both her forearms made me wary to challenge her.

"Karis? Right?" I hoped to get her to at least take the bag off Tallis's head. "Can you—"

"You speak again, omega, and I'll be forced to gag both of you," she shot. I shivered at her command, my wolf growing more nervous.

"It's okay," Tallis whispered, leaning toward me. He

pushed a soft tug of assurance through our bond, and I took a calming breath. I wished I could see his face.

The guard next to Karis leaned against the door jam, hooking his thumbs into his belt. He was much younger, with black hair that fell into his eyes. He seemed almost disinterested, yawning several times before Karis finally popped him in the gut. He pushed himself away from the door, rubbing his middle.

"What was that for?" he whined.

"You need to stay alert," she hissed, turning her attention back to us. "These wolves hurt Lady Sana, and now they're back for her. Do your fucking job and watch them."

His eyes went wide, and he looked at me as if really seeing me for the first time. "That *omega* took Lady Sana?" he asked, disbelief making his mouth hang open.

"Yes," she said, crossing her arms and glaring at me. "So stay on your toes. If we fuck this up, Luna Morana will have our heads."

"The alpha I get," he said, looking at my still struggling mate. "I had no idea omegas had that kind of savagery in them."

"All wolves have savagery," Karis snorted. "Even omegas can be fierce when cornered."

"Omegas are best when they're cornered," the young guard smirked.

"Really?" Karis glared, and the young alpha's expression fell. "Stop acting like the rest of the assholes who live in the den."

"Sorry," he mumbled.

Footsteps echoed on the other side of the door, and the young guard jumped to attention. He fumbled to pull open the door, the heavy wood creaking loudly, echoing off the walls. Karis smiled, watching him struggle.

"What's happening?" Tallis whispered.

"I don't know. Someone's coming."

The door pulled open, and a tall female alpha stepped into the room. The lanterns cast a golden light over her features. She was older, with soft wrinkles around her eyes and down the front of her neck. She wore a long purple dressing gown, and her dark blonde hair was pulled into a bun. She walked toward us, her movements stiff but somehow still graceful. The rage in her eyes was clear even though they didn't burn red, but her beast was still there. Just out of view.

The intensity on her face made me look down, and I shivered.

Another figure entered the room, and I glanced up. It was Tamen, followed quickly by Max, the scarred guard Tallis had punched in the market. *That felt like a lifetime ago.*

Max studied my face, but he didn't look angry. Pity? No, it was something more. He nodded at Tamen, then turned to the young guard and whispered something in his ear. The youngling beat his fist once against his chest, then rushed out of the room.

"Who the fuck is there?" Tallis roared, snorting and jerking his head back and forth. The bag stayed firmly in place.

"I will not tolerate that kind of language from a rogue," the older she-alpha snarled. Her voice was exactly what I expected. Firm, posh, and it contained an edge of authority that made me want to curl into myself and cry.

"Where is Sana?" I asked, struggling to look her in the eye. She was just so...dominant.

"You don't get to ask me about my daughter after what you did to her!" she snapped.

I widened my eyes, really looking at the mighty she-alpha. After all the stories Sana had told me about her parents, this woman was not what I envisioned. She wasn't the evil monster I had pictured. She looked...normal. Scary but still normal.

"I did nothing to Sana," I said, my wolf's hackles raised. "*You* poisoned her. You—"

A meaty fist landed hard in my gut and I doubled over, choking onto the gritty floor. My eyes burned, and tears clung to my lashes.

Tallis roared and jerked hard. There was the sound of a scuffle followed quickly by overlapping voices demanding my mate to calm the fuck down.

"Cyrus! Tallis!"

I looked up at the sound of Sana's panicked voice.

Max held Sana by her slender arm, keeping her from touching us. She wore a blue nightshirt that fell just past her knees, and her hair was just as wild as ever. She struggled against the brute, trying desperately to reach us.

"Leave him alone!" Sana snarled at Karis—the female guard loomed next to me, her fist tight and ready to use again.

"My Lady," Max said softly to Sana. "Please calm down. You'll hurt yourself."

Sana growled high in her throat, then swung a clawed hand out, catching the guard across the face. He released her, immediately covering his right eye. She didn't wait for his reaction, racing to Tallis.

"Are you okay?" she asked me as she ripped the bag off Tallis's head. He looked feral. Despite the wolfsbane, his fangs were fully distended, pushing into his lip, and his eyes were crimson. He locked onto Sana's face, and his breathing slowed.

"Sana," he growled, relief pouring through our bond. "Are you okay? Did they hurt you?"

"Did *we* hurt her?" Sana's mother snapped, stepping a little closer. Her features were pointed, not soft like Sana's, and her build was lean and tall. Outside of the blonde hair, they looked nothing alike. It was clear Sana took after her father.

Sana's mother, the Luna, snarled at my mate as she approached. "How dare you say something so, so—"

"True?" Tallis growled, the rumble bouncing off the walls. He opened his mouth to continue yelling at the woman, but Sana cupped his cheeks, quieting him. Our bond burned with his rage and conflict. He wanted to comfort me and Sana, but more than that, he wanted to kill the she-wolf looming just behind our mate.

"It's okay," Sana whispered. "I'm okay." A red mark sat high on her cheekbone. It looked as if someone had hit her. She brushed her hand down my chest, and I could feel the tremor in her fingers. I nodded at my mate, hoping it soothed her a bit.

"Mother," she turned to the stiff woman, "might I have a word with my pack?"

"Your *pack*?" The Luna laughed, her eyes going wide. After a few deliberate breaths, she forced her fists to uncurl, then turned to an older, dark-haired beta behind her. "Mallin," her tone held a false sense of distress, "they've brainwashed her. They stole my baby, then brainwashed her."

The beta stepped up to the ridiculous woman, taking her hands. "It's okay, Luna," she whispered. "Sana's home now. It's all okay."

The Luna nodded, pressing her fingertips to her lips. "I know," she whispered.

"Mother," Sana repeated, standing up. Her respectful tone was odd given how much snark she usually gave Tallis. "Please. A moment alone."

The room stilled as everyone stared at the Luna. Sana's fingertip brushed over her mating bite, a silent conversation clearly passing between the two women. Then the Luna gave a curt nod. "Fine. But their chains stay on."

"Luna Morana." Max's eyes widened as he took several steps toward the she-alpha. "I don't think—"

"I didn't ask for your opinion," she snapped.

With great force, he bowed his head and took a step back. It was clear he didn't want to leave Sana with us, but it wasn't like we could escape. This room was our prison, and more than likely, it was to be our tomb.

# CHAPTER TWENTY-SEVEN

## the stone room

Sana

I waited patiently for the guards, Mallin, and then my mother to leave. Max walked so damn slow, not taking his eyes off me until he had to as he pulled the wooden door shut at a glacial pace. It clicked into place, and two sets of big feet cut the shadows just under the door, staying close. I knew I didn't have much time. Morana was counting down the seconds until she could order Tallis and Cyrus's heads removed from their shoulders. She'd probably demand they be displayed in the town square. I pushed the thought away and moved around to Cyrus's back.

"Are you hurt?" I whispered to my omega as quietly as I could.

"No," he said, mimicking my tone.

Tallis leaned back a bit to see what I was doing. "Do you have a key?"

"No," I bit my bottom lip, concentrating on the bindings, "but these don't require keys."

I could sense the look Cyrus and Tallis exchanged while I raised Cyrus's hands the best I could without hurting him. He leaned far forward so I could better see his bindings.

"You either let the prisoner struggle until their hands are cut off, or..." I moved slowly, slipping my hand between a clasp and Cyrus's skin, "Someone has to manually release it, cutting themselves in the process."

"That's stupid," Cyrus said at the same time Tallis said, "That's smart."

"Think about it," Tallis whispered to our mate while I carefully worked my hand in place. "You have to be willing to be caught to let someone go. With this elvish metal, it'll take a few days for an alpha to heal from a cut caused by them. Which means—"

"If a prisoner disappears, they just have to check the guards' hands to see who let him go," Cyrus finished for him. "That is smart."

"Okay," I said to Cyrus, "don't move a muscle."

His body stilled as I found the flat pin. I knew the mechanics and had seen this done once before. Max insisted Emmy and I know how to operate the chains in case the packhouse was stormed. My father refused to allow him to teach us, insisting the packhouse was a fortress, but thankfully Max disobeyed him. The three of us sat in the garden, going over how they worked. Emmy giggled wildly the whole time, elated at the idea of doing something so forbidden.

Poor Max did everything he could to get her to focus, and after a full hour, he gave up, making sure I had a good enough understanding for the both of us.

Lining the two tiny spikes up with my palm, I pushed.

The barbs burned as they slipped into my flesh, grinding against bone, then releasing the clasp. I took a deep breath, then squeezed my hand tight, making the bindings fall away.

"You're bleeding," Tallis said, his voice a bit too loud. Cyrus immediately hushed him as he slipped both shackles off, resting them softly on the ground.

"Tallis," Cyrus groaned as he shimmed next to me to look at the alpha's wrists. "What the fuck?" The razor-like links were embedded deep into his flesh.

"You've got to be fucking kidding me," I mumbled. "All that talk about patience and planning, and this is the shit you pull."

Tallis turned his head, looking at us over his shoulder. "Both my mates are in trouble. Cyrus is tied up, and you're stuck with assholes who have poisoned and abused you. There is no patience when those you love are in trouble."

Pure joy burst from my chest. I wanted to tell him I loved him too. That I loved both of them from the moment I saw them, and they were my saviors in so many ways, but I couldn't find the words, so instead I slapped his cheek. "Turn around," I ordered. "We don't have time for this."

He winked, then did as he was told.

"Show me what to do," Cyrus said, inching closer.

I shook my head, refusing to let him. "No, I—"

"Sana," he cut me off. "You are injured. It might be small, but if you can just rely on me to help—"

"Fine," I said, stopping his lecture. I glanced nervously at the door, wondering how long Morana would give me. "We don't have much time. Give me your hand."

It was a nightmare. Tallis had worked the metal so deep into his skin that by the time we got Cyrus's hand in place, it was already shredded.

"What's this room for?" Tallis asked, trying like hell to stay still as I carefully helped Cyrus line up with the two spikes.

"It's for holding and questioning the monsters that make it within the borders of the village. Orcs and mountain men." I bit my bottom lip, wincing as a sharp point slipped into Cyrus's palm. He didn't make a sound, just helped remove it, then pushed his hand in further.

"Your security is shit," Tallis snarled. His fingers twitched, his patience wearing thin.

"Our numbers are too few," I said. "We do the best we can with what we've got. You can't save a sinking ship with a ladle, but you've got to fucking try."

Cyrus stifled a grunt and squeezed his fist tight, releasing Tallis from his bindings. Tallis immediately grabbed Cyrus's hand, lapping at the wounds along his fingers and wrists.

"Now what?" Cyrus asked.

"Now we fight our way out," I said, marching to one of long metal poles holding a lantern.

"We still need to get your sister," Tallis said, looking over Cyrus's hands one more time.

I pressed my lips together, trying to find my words. I couldn't say she was forced to mate the Hund Valley wolf without bursting into tears. My sweet innocent sister was sold and her innocence stolen all because I didn't have the strength to push back against my father.

"She's not here," Cyrus whispered. "Is she?"

I shook my head, concentrating on the metal pole in my hand. I could feel both their eyes on me as I removed the lantern and unscrewed the base. The metal rod resembled the sticks Tallis taught me to wield in the forest.

"Try not to kill the maid," I said, rolling my shoulders

and popping my neck. "She's a good beta." They both nodded, but I knew none of us could promise it. I turned to Tallis. "Can you rip the hook off the end of this pole?"

He glanced at it, confusion pulling his brows together. He mumbled a quick "yes," then pulled at the hook, making the metal groan, then snap.

I looked over the jagged, pointed curve. Then I grabbed his hand and positioned it right at my neck. "Now, you just have to get your hostage out of here."

# CHAPTER TWENTY-EIGHT

## sometimes we fight

Tallis

---

WE WAITED FOR WHAT FELT LIKE FOREVER. I COULDN'T BELIEVE they were giving Sana so much time with us. Perhaps they were assembling an army behind the doors. Or maybe they were locking us in and letting the three of us starve to death.

It wasn't like Sana's mother wouldn't risk killing her. She'd been slowly killing her for years. Maybe this was her endgame: a weak death, filled with begging and longing for water. Not the warrior's death an alpha deserved.

Sana's body stiffened against mine, and I looked up at the door. Feet danced in the light beneath it, and hushed voices drifted toward us. Whatever was being said out there, it was causing a flurry of activity.

Both heavy doors pulled wide open at the same time, and I tensed.

Surprise washed over me at seeing the exact same

guards as before. The female and young male, Max, and Tamen. Not exactly the fleet I had imagined. But I was thankful to see the maid was gone.

Sana's mother marched into the dark room, a look of amusement on her face. "Really?" She laughed at her daughter, eyeing the metal pressed against her throat. "Are we pretending to be a captive?"

I fisted Sana's hair and jerked her head back, pressing the sharp end of the hook into her skin. "Who's pretending?" I growled.

The she-alpha's eyes flickered to me, then back at her daughter. She let out a long huff of annoyance. "Come here right now," she demanded. "I don't have the time or the patience for this shit."

"I'm not going anywhere," Sana said softly. Her back pressed closer to my chest, and I steadied myself, ready to snatch her and Cyrus up and run if needed. "You have no idea how crazy he is," she continued. "I suggest you let them go."

The older she-alpha's eyes narrowed, then she turned her attention to a piece of weathered paper in her hands. "I know how fond you are of Emmy, Sana." She smoothed the edge of the paper between her thumb and forefinger. "I can't imagine what these rogues told you to earn your trust, but I don't blame you for believing them. I'm just happy we got you back before they could kill you."

"They aren't rogues," Sana hissed.

Max sneered at me, and dread twisted in my gut. They knew. They had to.

Cyrus adjusted his hold on the long metal pole in his hand and crouched, ready to fight.

"Careful there, omega," Max growled at my mate. Cyrus shivered at his commanding tone, and I flooded our bond with all the strength I could muster. "This won't end well for either one of you. Don't make me call on the rest of my guards. Don't make this harder than it has to be."

"There are only a handful of you," I said, pushing my fangs forward. The small transformation hurt, making me dizzy. "It won't be hard at all."

"I have confidence that you can handle this, Max," Sana's mother said. "These rogues have hurt my daughter, and she's confused. I don't want the whole pack to know what she's been forced to endure." She took a few steps toward us. I growled, but her eyes stayed focused on Sana. My fierce mate didn't tremble or whimper; she stayed firm, her body poised and ready against mine.

"As an alpha, I know you feel a pull to protect omegas." The she-alpha's eyes cut to Cyrus. "You protected Emmy all the time. From her father, other alphas, even her own wild imagination."

"From you!" Sana roared. "I protected her from you! You hated her and hurt her. Anyone willing to treat an omega in such a way doesn't deserve to live."

The she-alpha's eyes glowed red as they met mine, and she smiled wide. "I agree," she whispered pointedly, holding out the paper.

I swallowed hard, the rock in my gut doubling, tripling, until I could barely breathe. Cyrus inched a little closer to me, sending me swift assurances of his love. *I know he loves me, but would Sana?*

"What is that?" Sana jerked her chin at the paper, refusing to touch it.

"It's a notice," Max said. "I had a run-in with these two in the market about a month back. After they ran out of the village, I checked the posts. They're wanted in Hala. This alpha killed an omega. Then he kidnapped his mate and ran."

It felt as if Sana's body dropped a full ten degrees. I wished like hell I could see her face.

"Lies!" she yelled, jerking forward a bit. I dropped the hook, scared I'd accidentally cut her. "You lie!" A vicious roar ripped from her throat, and her wolf flowed out of her —a beautiful and skilled transition. I tried to follow suit, but the poison from the bindings had seeped deep into my cuts. My wolf raged at me, furious he wouldn't taste blood.

Movement caught my eyes, and I turned as the young male guard shifted into his wolf. He jumped toward me, and I swung my fist as hard as I could, hitting him right in the snout. The youngling didn't even yip. His beast simply fell to the ground, knocked out cold.

Rolling my shoulders, I turned to Max. He pulled off his shirt and tossed away his dagger, getting into position.

Both of us were ready to spill blood.

# CHAPTER TWENTY-NINE

*the fight*

Sana

---

I relished the look of shock on Morana's face as I shifted into my wolf. In all honesty, it shocked the shit out of me too.

I prowled a little closer to my shocked mother, my paws moving silently over the gritty stone floor. Tamen took a step in front of Morana, acting as a barrier. It took a moment for the look of shock to wear off her face, but when it did, it was replaced by a murderous rage.

"I cannot fucking believe you'd pick these animals over your family!" Morana snapped. "After all I've done for you!"

My wolf form lunged, but Tamen blocked me, shoving me hard. I rolled away then scurried back, ready to try again. Tamen angled his body forward, ready to attack me if needed. But I knew he wouldn't. Not without Morana's orders.

The sound of fists hitting wet flesh and heavy grunts echoed around the hollow room, but I didn't turn to look at my mates. I only had eyes for my prey. I lunged again, Tamen's big hands swatting me once more. But this time, I was ready and managed to land on my paws.

A flit of surprise crossed Tamen's face before he corrected it. "Stop this now, Lady Sana," he said, holding his arms out to shield my still-seething mother. She looked so fucking angry as I stalked, waiting patiently to make my move. "I know you're upset." He took a step to the side, blocking my view of Morana's face. "You've been through so much, but you don't want to hurt your mother."

My wolf howled and snarled, and I pounced. Tamen failed to get his arms up in time, and I managed to nick Morana's forearm. The guard shoved me even harder this time, and I flew across the room, hitting the cold stone with a pained yip.

"Shift back, doll," Tallis yelled at me from the other side of the room. He ducked, dodging Max's fist. "Keep your head and fight in the form you need to win!"

Max swung again, but Tallis was ready, landing a mighty blow to the side of the guard's face. Max's head snapped back, and he fell, unconscious, a deep gash in his forehead. Karis sat not far from him with a long pole shoved through her gut. She coughed and wheezed, her hands trembling as she tried to hold the pole still.

Cyrus limped toward me, breathing hard. He was covered in sweat and a splattering of blood. "Let's go," he panted, picking up a dagger off the ground. I recognized the engraved hilt. It was Max's.

I slowly pulled my human form forward and stood.

"No!" Morana yelled, shoving Tamen out of the way.

Apparently, he had a bit more sense than the old woman because he gripped her arm, keeping her from getting too close. "You don't get to leave," she growled. "You belong to me. You owe me your life!"

"No!" I panted hard, rage making my voice shake. "*You* owe me *your* life. This is your death day, but *I* have decided to let you live. And each moment of your pathetic life from this moment forward belongs to me."

Her brow wrinkled as she continued to struggle against Tamen's hold, but it was clear from the way his fingers softly circled around her wrist that she wasn't really fighting him. It was all a show.

"Let it go, Mother. No one is coming to save you," I said, my voice low and angry. "You did nothing when Rainer was ripped from me, you let Emmy's innocence be destroyed by a stranger, and you have poisoned and tortured me my entire life. And you have done all of it with a smile on your face. You deserve to die," I said. My chin quivered and I gritted my teeth to stop it. She did deserve to die, but I couldn't do it. As much as I hated her, my treacherous heart still loved her for some reason.

"Your guard is down," I said, motioning to the limp bodies around us. "Stand down, and I'll let you live."

Tamen's eyes glowed red, his gaze shifting from me to my mates, then to the three guards behind me. Seeming to come to a painful decision that made his face contort with rage, he huffed, then pressed his lips to Morana's ear. It was intimate, and I didn't miss the way she leaned into him as he spoke.

"Please, my Luna," he said in a gruff whisper. "Let this burden go." Her expression remained hard for a moment, then to my shock, she smoothed her hand down his chest.

"It will be okay," he whispered, looking deep into her eyes. "Trust me."

Her throat bobbed as she swallowed hard. She tipped her head back and opened her mouth, pausing briefly as if struggling to find her words. "Sana," she said, her voice as hard and pointed as ever. "Leave. But don't expect to get far. We found you once, and we will find you again."

Tamen let out a long breath of relief, then slipped his hand down the Luna's arm, their fingertips lingering as they touched. The look that passed between them was so tender. I always believed Morana incapable of love or affection, but here she was, giving her softer emotions to the fucker who killed my best friend.

And it was more than I could bear.

I ripped the dagger out of Cyrus's hand and hurdled it across the room. The long silver blade flew swift and sure, slipping into Tamen's chest like embers through honey.

Tamen stumbled slightly, looking down at the blade protruding from his breastbone. There was a moment of confusion, and no one moved. Disoriented, Tamen's eyes darted around the room as if looking for help. His panicked stare met mine, disbelief pouring off him.

Morana screamed, and I moved.

I rushed Tamen, all other sound and movement fading away as his large eyes widened with so much fear.

Out of the corner of my eye, Morana swiped out a clawed hand, but Tallis grabbed her, pulling her out of my periphery. Her screams became muffled, turning into muted grunts and growls.

I stopped just in front of Tamen, his hands hovering over the handle. "For Rainer," I whispered. Then I ripped the blade from his chest and brought it back down over and over and over again.

Slick, sticky blood coated my hands and face, the copper scent flooding my lungs and seeping into my mouth.

All I could hear was my own frantic heartbeat and the soft squish of the blade as it repeatedly pushed into Tamen's chest, neck, and stomach. Blood sloshed from his wounds, and the blade slipped for a moment. I stopped, unable to hold on to my weapon steady any longer.

Panting hard, I realized I was sitting on Tamen's lifeless body. I didn't remember him falling to the ground or crawling on top of him.

Fear burst from my chest and I turned, frantically looking for my mates.

*Please, let them be okay.*

Tallis stood not far off, watching me carefully while Cyrus hid his face behind our massive alpha. Morana sat at their feet, her mouth hung open with shock. Tears streaked her face, slipping down her neck and soaking into the soft purple fabric of her dressing gown. I had never once seen her cry. I honestly didn't think she was capable.

"Time to go," Tallis whispered softly, pulling me to my feet. Cyrus stayed at his back, our omega's face pale and his body shaking slightly from the overwhelming onslaught of so much violence.

Moving slowly, Morana crawled toward me, her eyes locked onto Tamen's lifeless body. She gulped deep breaths of air, sobbing so hard, she couldn't form words. She would have beaten me senseless if I ever showed that kind of emotion.

Tallis's warm hands circled my waist, and I was lifted.

With shaking hands, Cyrus forced the dagger from my tightly clenched fist then draped something soft over my shoulders. I rested my head on Tallis's shoulder as he rushed toward the hallway. I stared at my mother's slim form sobbing over Tamen's corpse. She was cold and cruel, and after all the torment she inflicted, she finally felt something.

This was the justice I had craved my whole life, *and I hated the bitter taste it left in my mouth.*

Tallis whispered softly against my temple, assuring me I was safe as he ran through the packhouse. I had a vague memory of Cyrus grabbing something out of the bushes, then we raced through the village. Before I knew it, we were out the gates and gone.

No one stopped us. There was no alarm, no rush of warriors, no cause for concern. So much blood had been spilt at the packhouse, and not a single guard was aware.

This was the house my father built. Coated in blood and lacking any protection.

---

It wasn't until dawn broke that I realized how far we were from Casin.

"Where are we going?" I asked, looking around the unfamiliar forest. I had hoped we'd return to our cave. I knew we couldn't, but my heart still squeezed at the thought of losing the tiny home where I met my mates.

"We're looking for somewhere to clean up," Cyrus said, his voice rough with exhaustion. He looked so pale.

Tallis jerked his head toward a puddle. "I think that might be the best we can get."

Cyrus groaned, moving toward it. He sat next to the murky water, swishing his hands though it and cleaning off the dried blood. Then he turned his attention to me. Tallis kept me pressed to his chest, not releasing me even when I tried to lean forward.

I hadn't even realized I had a cut above one eye until Cyrus started cleaning it. He ripped off a small section of my blue nightdress. The sleeves and neck of the soft cotton material were torn from when I had shifted, but it still covered me for the most part.

Pressing gently, Cyrus dabbed at my temple. It stung, but I was too tired to protest. Once he was done with my cut, he turned his attention to Tallis, cleaning the alpha's wrists and checking over his nose. It had a sizable bump and was bleeding.

"Will Karis live?" I asked, thinking about the carnage we had left behind. I didn't regret killing Tamen, but the others didn't deserve to die. They were only doing their job.

"The female alpha?" Cyrus asked, rinsing the cloth in the cloudy water. "I don't know. Alphas are resilient, though. She might."

"Unfortunately, that scarred fucker will live." Tallis rubbed his shoulder. "Put up one hell of a fight though."

"Max," I said. "His name is Max. He was one of mine and Emmy's main guards. He was always nice to me."

"Well, he's a fucking asshole."

"So are you," I snorted, unable to help myself. I needed a distraction from my rising guilt and grief, and teasing Tallis always made me feel better.

Tallis's mouth fell open in feigned shock, my goofy alpha giving me exactly what I needed. "How dare you," he gasped.

"It's true," Cyrus smiled, pulling what looked like some Casin service uniforms out of the satchel. "You are an ass, but I wouldn't have you any other way." He leaned in, kissing the alpha's cheek, then kissing mine. It was sweet and soft, and after the violence we just endured, it was almost enough to make me cry.

"I'm sorry about what that woman said about you," I whispered, unable to say my mother's name. For as long as I lived, I would never say her name again. She didn't deserve to live in my memories. "What she accused you of was...horrible. And I'm sorry."

Cyrus's soft smile fell, and Tallis roughly cleared his throat before shifting me to sit on the ground next to him.

A smile lifted one side of my mouth, waiting for the joke. "I don't believe it." I almost laughed. "There's no way you'd kill an omega."

"He didn't," Cyrus said. But the grave look on his face ripped the smile off mine.

Tallis dropped his gaze, staring at his hands, and my chest squeezed with fear and disbelief. "It was an accident," the alpha whispered.

"Bullshit!" I balked. The way he talked about beta rights and saving Emmy and how protective he was with Cyrus. There was no way he'd hurt someone weaker than him. "I don't believe you," I said, watching his expression carefully.

"There was a fire," he said softly, shame pulling his gaze to his big hands. The intense need to sit down washed over me, but I was already sitting.

"There was a fancy dining hall in Hala where all the celebrations were held," Tallis said softly. I wanted to see his eyes, but he kept his head down, refusing to look at me. "There was a mating ceremony that night, and half the village was there. I don't know how the fire started, but before we knew it, the blaze was out of control. I ran all over the building, rounding the pack up and getting them out. But, upstairs..."

Cyrus bowed his head, and Tallis immediately reached for his hand, squeezing it. "I overheard a voice calling for help up the stairs. By the time I found the omega, smoke was everywhere and had started to pour in from under the door. I couldn't risk opening the door, so I dragged her to the nearest balcony. I tried to hold on to her…" his fists tightened, and the thick corded muscles in his arms pulled tight, "but my hands were covered in soot and sweat."

Slowly, his hands uncurled, and when he finally looked up at me, his eyes were glassy with tears. "I dropped her," he whispered. "There was nothing I could do. She just… fell."

"How could they blame you for that?" I touched the side of his neck. His heart was beating so fast beneath my fingertips. "It was an accident." I turned to Cyrus. "Did no one see?"

He shook his head. "She was one of four omegas who died in the fire. A nearby guard did see her fall, but it was so dark and smoky. When he saw Tallis jumping down next to her…" He sighed hard. "It was chaos." He smoothed his hand over the burn mark on Tallis's shoulder. "They declared him a rogue before the sun even came up. The village was destroyed by the lives lost, and there was no one to blame, so in their grief, they blamed Tallis for what they could. I think it was easier for them since he wasn't raised there."

I traced the dark scar on Tallis's shoulder, noticing for the first time the clean circular shape.

"It almost killed him that our pack thought he'd do that," Cyrus said, caressing Tallis's shoulder. Our big, strong alpha nodded and pressed his lips into a tight line, trying his damnedest not to cry. "In his grief, he decided to accept his punishment and be branded a rogue, but I wouldn't let him. I told him I'd die without him."

"They tried to brand me." Tallis brushed his fingers over mine. "That fucking poker barely touched my skin when I broke free and ran. I don't know what came over me, but accepting that mark made me feel like I had done something wrong."

"He wasn't going to take me with him, but I chased after him." Cyrus smiled, looking at Tallis with so much love. "We ran through the village, out the gates, and over the mountains."

"You should have stayed in Hala," Tallis said gruffly. "Your family—"

"There is no life in Hala without you," Cyrus said, his face filled with not a trace of regret.

"Your mother is right." Tallis turned to me. "I'm a rogue. I might not have a full mark, but I'm still too lowly to be allowed around civilized wolves. I don't blame you if you hate me. You should. I failed to save so many."

"I'm part rogue." I shrugged. "My...that woman...didn't birth me. She barely raised me. My real mother was a rogue my father bedded...assuming that story is even true. But there's no way to really know. And I failed Emmy. I abandoned the omega I was tasked with protecting, and she was forced to mate the Hund Valley alpha who was meant for me. So we're both loathsome." I smiled, relieved when he smiled back. "Only Cyrus has any real worth."

Tallis smiled wide at our mate. "Yes. But we knew that."

Cyrus forced a tight smile, his nerves clearly frayed. "You're both very lucky that I'm so patient and loving, and willing to bless you with my presence. Now," he rubbed hard at the back of his neck, "we should probably eat before we start our trek to Hund Valley."

"There's no point in going to Hund Valley," I said, my shoulders slumping forward. It was all I could do not to burst into tears. "I'm too late. Emmy is mated to the pack alpha's son. If she's created a bond with him, stealing her away could kill her. Omegas are so sensitive, and Emmy is even more so. I just can't risk it."

"You don't even want to see her? Make sure she's okay?" Cyrus tucked a strand of my hair behind my ear.

"Of course." My voice was rough with emotion. "But I couldn't ask you to—"

Tallis gripped the back of my neck, pulling me to him. It was possessive and felt fucking amazing. "You are mine, Sana," he growled. "You belong to me and to Cyrus. And I'll be damned if we don't get a chance to greet our new sister."

I simply nodded, letting him be the alpha of our little pack today. Tomorrow, he would follow my lead.

"Come." Tallis stood, pulling me up with him. "We need to find somewhere where I can fuck you both," he growled, and I jerked at his words.

"You can't be serious?" After everything that happened, the last thing I wanted was to have sex.

Tallis gave Cyrus a quick glance before leaning into my ear. "Our omega needs to be close to his alphas right now. He's barely holding it together."

He was right. Cyrus ducked his head, his eyes dark and his hands trembling as he twisted them tight. I was so caught up in my own feelings, I didn't even notice how much my mate was suffering. The violence he was just forced to witness would have sent any other omega into full-on distress.

"Yes," I smiled sweetly at Cyrus, cupping his cheek, "let's find somewhere to tend to our mate."

Resting his hand over mine, Cyrus squeezed softly. "And the sooner you claim me, the quicker our bond will seal," he said. "Right now, Tallis is a bit fuzzy because his mates aren't linked as well. We'll all be more connected and safer if we're mated."

I pushed out a quick laugh. Even covered in blood and sitting on the edge of his mind, our sweet omega was still just as calm and logical as ever.

"Come," Tallis said, helping me and Cyrus to our feet. "I need to get off."

I rolled my eyes as I eagerly followed him, ready to be claimed by my men.

# CHAPTER THIRTY

## *claiming her triad*

Sana

---

"Let me see those gorgeous tits," Tallis growled, grabbing a fistful of my nightdress and jerking me to him.

"You are such a romantic." Cyrus laughed, arranging a few branches to better block out the rest of the world. The overgrown thicket wasn't the best place to complete our bonding, but the grass was lush, and it smelled strongly of lavender and my mates. It was perfect.

I pulled the nightgown over my head, and the fabric caught on my breasts, making them bounce as it pulled free. Tallis groaned at the sight, and Cyrus licked his lips. Both wolves looked like they wanted to devour me, and it had my body thrumming with anticipation.

"Come." I reached for Cyrus, pushing his face between my breasts. He squeezed the sides as he inhaled me deeply.

"You're so beautiful," Cyrus whispered, capturing my nipple between his lips. He sucked and flicked, his hot mouth contrasting wildly with the cool morning air. The sky was still gray as the sun drifted higher and higher, not quite reaching the tops of the trees just yet.

"Squeeze her tits," Tallis ordered, taking a step back.

Cyrus obeyed, palming both my breasts as he lavished them with attention. His lips and tongue were so soft, followed by the intense sensation of his teeth nipping my flesh. Tallis's heated stare stayed on me as he undid his belt. His pants pooled at his feet, his thick cock jutting out at me. Cyrus nipped the tender flesh just under my nipple, and I gasped.

"That feel good, doll?" Tallis growled, wrapping his big hand around his shaft. He jerked himself, moving from base to tip.

"Yes," I moaned as Cyrus did it again, squeezing and pulling my tight nipples. A warm trickle of slick rolled down the inside of my thigh, and Tallis's eyes glowed red, a bead of precum pushing from the tip of his shaft.

"Pull his cock out," the alpha ordered.

I bristled at first, but the eager way Cyrus stood urged me to give my omega what he wanted. I fumbled with his buckle, then jerked his pants down, gripping his hard length. Moving my hand up and down, I stroked him, squeezing the shaft and pressing my thumb into the wet slit at the top.

"How does that feel, Cy?" Tallis squeezed his own cock, pushing more of that delicious liquid from the tip. It rolled down his shaft and over his fingers. I wanted to lick it up. "Does she jerk you right?"

"She's perfect," Cyrus moaned, pressing his lips to the column of my throat. His devilish fingers kept pulling at my puffy nipples while he nipped just beneath my ear down to my shoulder.

Tallis grabbed the hem of Cyrus's shirt and pulled it over his head, exposing our omega's firm chest. The sight of so much muscle and power between the two men in front of me was almost as overwhelming as their intoxicating aromas.

"Sana?" Cyrus whispered, his hands smoothing down to cup my ass. He looked so sweet and soft, almost unsure as I waited to hear what he wanted. "Can I..." He swallowed hard, glancing at Tallis briefly.

"What do you need, mate?" I asked, eager to give him whatever he desired.

"Can I eat your pussy?" He bit his bottom lip, and my eyes widened with delight. "I've never...done that before."

"Of course," I purred, moving onto the soft ground and spreading my legs wide. The hungry look in both my mates' eyes had me already eager to come. Cyrus licked his lips, but before he could fall into me, Tallis reached down between my legs and slapped my pussy hard. I jerked and yipped, the sensation jolting straight through me.

"What the fuck?" I snarled.

"That's for scaring the shit out of me." Tallis smirked, landing another sharp pop on my clit. "Never stray farther than ten feet from me ever again."

I growled high in my throat, torn between tending to Cyrus and clawing Tallis's eyes out. "Do it again, asshole."

Tallis laughed deep in his chest, the sound skating across my sensitive skin. "First, I want to see Cyrus make you cum." He leaned into the omega's ear. "Make her come all over your face so I can lick it off."

Cyrus kneeled, grabbing one of my knees while Tallis grabbed the other. The long, hard swipe of my omega's tongue had my head falling back, and I released a wild moan.

"That's it." Tallis smiled, watching Cyrus work. "Flick her clit. Now suck it. A little harder. Do it again."

Cyrus obeyed, following Tallis's precise instructions. It took a moment, but Cyrus soon found his rhythm, slipping his tongue up and around my swollen nub before sucking and flicking and driving me absolutely wild.

Tallis growled, then to my absolute delight, pressed his face next to Cyrus. Their tongues worked in tandem, teasing me until my thighs tensed and my claws distended. *I was so fucking close.*

Cyrus's gentle fingers spread my lower lips open, allowing both their tongues to hit my clit dead-on. I thrashed and jerked, the sensation so fucking intense. Tallis placed his strong arm over my stomach, holding me in place. Then two thick fingers entered my pussy, and I bucked my hips up as my orgasm slammed into me. Unrelenting pleasure rushed back and forth, and stars filled my vision. I felt like I was falling, everything falling away except the feel of my two mates feasting on me.

It took several minutes before I came down, and when I did, I was gifted the beautiful sight of my two sexy mates kissing.

Their strong jaws moved against each other, Cyrus' fingers digging into Tallis's waist while Tallis gripped Cyrus's hair painfully tight. They were both so strong and sexy. *And they were mine.*

"Lie down," Tallis commanded, squeezing Cyrus's ass. "I want to see her ride you."

I moved quickly to straddle Cyrus, eager to have both my boys inside me. *I wanted this so bad.* To be mated and bound to my loves.

Cyrus gripped my hips, pulling me down onto his perfect cock. His crown breached me, then I sank down, sucking him deep inside me. The stretch was lovely, rubbing every inch of my still-sensitive flesh. Tallis moved behind me, the heat from his body warming my back. Placing his hands over Cyrus's, they both rocked my hips, pushing Cyrus's cock deeper and deeper inside me.

"How does he feel?" Tallis growled in my ear.

With half-hooded eyes, I glanced at him over my shoulder. "I could use a little more."

A devilish smile pulled at his lips, and he pressed a quick kiss to my shoulder. "Are you sure you're ready for us, doll?" He smiled against my skin.

"Stop stalling and fuck me already," I snarled, then gasped as Cyrus thrust his hips up hard. I had to fling my hands onto his firm chest to keep from falling over.

My omega placed his hand behind my head and pulled me to him. He took my mouth, kissing me into a dizzy mess, while Tallis rubbed his cock along my thighs and ass, leaving a trail of precum while coating himself in my slick.

After a few blissful moments of Cyrus's dizzying kiss, Tallis squeezed my ass, spreading me painfully wide. The fat crown of his cock pressed beside Cyrus's, trying to force its way into my already full cunt.

Fear slipped down my spine, and I cupped Cyrus's face, trying to distract myself with the feel of his tongue in my mouth. Tallis's cock slowly eased in. The stretch burned, and my nails pushed into Cyrus's neck.

"Tallis," he barked. "Easy, alpha."

Tallis stilled for a moment, slipping his hand down my back. He caressed me, channeling his fingers through my hair and squeezing my breasts, not pushing forward until I relaxed again.

"Okay," I whispered, lying flush with Cyrus's chest to give Tallis better access.

I could feel Tallis's hand on his cock as his crown breached my opening. The immediate stab of two cocks inside me made my breath hitch and my fists clench.

"Easy," Tallis growled, purring soft and slow for me. "Let me in. That's it. Nice and slow."

I carefully pushed back against them, forcing both the alpha and omega deeper. They were both so slippery with my slick, they moved easily despite the tight fit. Then I jerked my hips back again, forcing Tallis to enter me fully. Both wolves moaned in pleasure, then stilled, letting me adjust.

I had never felt so full before.

It was tight, near painful, but blissful at the same time.

It felt so right.

Tallis let out a deep growl, flexing his hips against my ass. Both cocks slipped even deeper, and I cried out, their combined girth hitting parts of me I didn't even know existed. It burned for a moment, but was still so exciting as my orgasm started to build.

*I wanted to come so fucking bad.*

Cyrus pushed my hips up, and Tallis thrust forward, both my mates taking me hard and deep. "Fuck, Cy," Tallis snarled against my shoulder. "Your cock feels so good pressed up against mine."

"Don't stop," Cyrus whimpered, digging his fingers into my flesh so hard, it was sure to bruise. "Fuck her, alpha."

My entire body trembled uncontrollably as my climax ripped through me. One cock pulsed within me. Hot, wet heat flooded my insides as Tallis's knot started to expand. Cyrus cursed loudly, and my beast roared to life, my tight cunt milking both of them at the same time.

Pleasure flowed so intense, it spiraled and burst, making my whole body shake. My fangs pushed out, and I moved on pure instinct. I bit hard into Cyrus's neck, right over Tallis's mating bite. Then a hard hand jerked my hair, pushing my head to the side as fangs pushed deep into my shoulder.

My heart pounded wildly in my chest. My fangs in Cyrus, and Tallis's fangs in me. We were finally one.

---

Everything hurt. My legs, neck, and pussy. Fuck. Even my temples pounded as I tried to sit up.

"Easy, alpha," Cyrus whispered, wrapping an arm around my shoulders and holding me to his back.

It was dark out, the Moon high in the night's sky. Reaching out, I slipped my hand down Tallis's chest. I could feel only a shadow of the alpha through our bond. My connection with Cyrus stole most of my attention. The omega's consciousness danced beautifully in the forefront of my mind. He was so happy.

"How do you feel?" Cyrus cupped my pussy, slipping gentle fingers through my folds. It wasn't a touch that demanded arousal, but soft and soothing. "We took you pretty hard."

"Blissful," I whispered. My voice was rough and slurred as if I had drunk far too much whiskey. "But my head hurts a bit."

"That's normal." He kissed my shoulder. "A triad bond is a lot for our bodies to take, but once it takes hold, it's everything."

"Tallis is just as fuzzy as before." I looked over the alpha's relaxed features as he slept. "Did I do it wrong? Is it because I haven't claimed him yet?"

"No need to worry." Cyrus smiled against my shoulder.

"It just takes a minute. Tallis mated you first, and now I'm shoving him back inside your mind to make room for me. Once our connection is fully bloomed, your mind will open to Tallis too. You don't have to bite him to seal the bond."

"I will, though," I said, letting a bit of alpha slip into my voice. "I want my mark on him too."

Cyrus smiled sweetly, caressing my collarbone. "And it will be beautiful when you do." He kissed my cheek. "Go to sleep, my sweet Sana. Let your mind rest."

I let out a contented sigh, pressing my forehead to Tallis's chest. My mind wandered as my connection with Cyrus engulfed me. The soft feel of Tallis danced at the edge of my mind, his presence slowly growing. His unbridled bliss made me smile before sleep finally took me.

# CHAPTER THIRTY-ONE
## on the way to hund valley

Cyrus

---

"I don't know, doll," Tallis grumbled to Sana. His voice held as much tension as his shoulders. I nodded at my mate, agreeing with him. We had stumbled upon the Casin encampment early this morning, and Sana insisted on watching them. I didn't understand why; it just felt dangerous to be this close.

Burly guards moved around the little tents and dotted fires. Several had daggers strapped to their hips or spears in their hands, and the smattering of scars just showed how willing they were to use them. This wasn't a timid pack; that was for sure.

Sana stared intensely at one wolf in particular. He was young, maybe a few years older than her. He had dark brown hair and brown eyes, but his nose and the shape of his face was similar to Sana's.

"Who is that?" I asked.

"My brother," she whispered, not taking her eyes off him. "I don't see my father yet, but he's here somewhere."

I squeezed her hand, my nerves flaring. "I don't feel good about this. I really think we should go."

Tallis nodded in agreement, but our bond with Sana flared with anger and grief, and she stood. "I need to speak with my brother," she said firmly, letting her natural authority bleed into her words. "I need to warn Davon about what awaits him at home. Then we'll go."

"I thought you hated your brother," Tallis growled, his eyes flashing red as he glared at the alpha in the distance.

"I do," she sighed. "And I'm pretty sure he hates me too. But we shared a lot of pain in that house. Something like that binds you. He's still my kin."

Tallis smoothed his hand through my hair and down my back, trying to ease my anxiety, but it didn't help. "Sana," I whispered, trying to be understanding. "What do you hope to gain here? Why talk to him at all?"

"If anyone can convince my parents to give up on hunting us, it's him," she said simply. "My mother will die trying to find you two. Davon can help us."

"This is too dangerous," I whispered, twisting my hands together. "Your father is somewhere in there. What if he tries to snatch you up? Refuses to let you go?"

"I have a plan," she whispered, cupping my cheek. "Trust me, mate."

She turned, glaring into the camp. I followed her gaze, landing on a slightly older, black-haired alpha. He was a bit older than Tallis and walked with purpose. The guards around him moved out of his way, and the service betas bowed their heads. Whoever he was, he was important.

Sana dropped my hand and moved. Tallis and I immediately followed. Staying low to the ground, we edged around the brush, circling the camp. The balls of my feet landed softly on the lush grass, and the breeze moved in our favor, keeping our scents hidden from the dangerous wolves around us.

She followed the black-haired alpha, tracking him carefully as he walked into the forest. The sounds from the camp fell away as we moved deeper. Tallis shook his head at me, and I settled next to a tree. Sana kissed my cheek lightly, then pulled my dagger from the sheath on my hip. I pushed all my love and strength to her through our bond, but in truth, I just wanted to get the fuck out of here.

Leaving me a safe distance behind, my two mates stalked carefully toward the black-haired alpha. He braced his forearm on a tree and began pissing onto the roots. Sana steadied herself, holding the dagger tight, then she rushed up behind the alpha and pressed the blade to his throat. The alpha's whole body went tight, but to his credit, he finished peeing.

Standing on her tiptoes, Sana growled low in his ear, "Kade."

His head turned slightly, some of the tension in his shoulders falling away. "Lady Sana?"

"Don't do anything stupid," Tallis warned. I inched closer to hear better, standing just behind the tree next to them.

Kade adjusted his pants, then slowly turned. He slowly raised his hands in surrender, not a trace of fear on his face. "We've been so worried about you." The genuine concern in his eyes caught me off guard.

"Were you concerned when you gutted Rainer?" Sana spat, pressing the blade into his throat. It slipped over his stubble, leaving a thin red mark. A tiny drop of blood seeped out, but Kade didn't even flinch.

"I don't regret following the orders of my pack alpha," he said simply.

"How can you say that?" Sana asked in disbelief. Tallis placed a splayed hand on her back, steadying her. "You killed one of the only pure things in my life. Rainer and Emmy were all I had."

He lowered his hands, placing one on her shoulder. Tallis pushed past her and gripped his throat, shoving Kade into the tree. "Don't fucking touch her," he growled softly.

I stood, angling my body, ready to attack if needed.

Kade's eyes glowed red at Tallis's challenge, and his fangs slipped, peeking out from under his top lip. "My men outnumber you, wolf. I'd be careful if I were you."

"You don't get to do that." Sana dropped the dagger and gripped the front of his shirt, balling the crisp material up in her fists. "You don't get to kill my best friend, then threaten my mate."

Kade's eyes softened, brown irises taking hold once again. "My Lady," he said stiffly. "I have known you since you were just a pup. And while I would never hurt you, I don't have the luxury of questioning my pack alpha's orders. If I did, Casin would fall to ruin. We are built and live on order. And I will keep it. However I am commanded."

Sana bared her fangs at the alpha. "It must be so lovely to brush away all your sins and blame them on duty."

"It's not," he said in a harsh tone. "It's fucking hell, My Lady. But we all suffer in our own way." Something like sorrow filled his eyes, and Sana's grip on his shirt loosened. Our bond flooded with her anger and confusion. A bit of grief twisted hard inside her as she released the alpha.

She was so tired of fighting.

"I want to see my brother," she said.

Kade smoothed his shirt down, adjusting his belt. "I'll escort you." He eyed Tallis, then me. "I'm assuming your guards will be coming too."

"Yes," I said quickly, not giving Sana an option. Tallis growled.

"No need," Sana said. "Just bring Davon to me. I have no interest in seeing my father."

Kade's expression fell. The lines around his eyes softened as he looked back at the camp, then once again at Sana. "Your father isn't with us. Davon is leading us home." There was something off in his tone. His posture was just so tight.

"I don't have time for this shit, Kade," Sana snipped, "I just want a word with Davon."

The big alpha bit the inside of his cheek. He looked over her face as if struggling to summon the courage for what he was about to say. "Your father is dead."

Sana stumbled back as if his words physically pushed her. I was instantly at her side, holding her up as Tallis gripped her hand tight. "What?" she whispered.

"I'm so sorry, My Lady." The soft tenor of his voice confirmed it.

Sana jerked then ran. Tallis and I rushed after her as she raced toward the camp. She broke the tree line before Tallis could grab her.

A throng of Casin guards sat on the outskirts of the camp, sharpening their weapons. Two of them immediately stood as their eyes focused on Sana. The others remained seated with their mouths open, shocked as if seeing a ghost.

A flood of intense anger pounded hard in my temples, and I stumbled.

"Sana," Tallis whispered harshly, grabbing my hand to

keep me from falling. "You need to calm down, doll. You're hurting Cyrus."

My mates' scents intensified as they moved close. "Are you okay?" Sana whispered, squeezing the back of my neck in a possessive and comforting way. It was the same way Tallis touched me when I was frustrated or upset.

"I'm good," I said, taking several deep breaths. "Our bond is still new. I'll get the hang of it."

"Come," Sana whispered, taking my hand. Her anger was still there, but her worry for me edged out all other feelings.

She led me through the crowd, Tallis at our back. The camp was deathly silent as we moved, everyone staring at Sana with absolute shock. I half-expected someone to attack, rip me and Tallis away from her, kill us for being so near their leader's daughter. But they remained still, watching Sana march straight to the brown-haired alpha who shared her nose.

"Davon!" she yelled, her fingers tightening around mine.

The alpha spun, his eyes going wide as they landed on Sana's face. "Unbelievable." He whispered so softly, I almost didn't hear him. He looked past me—I'm sure at Tallis—then his narrowed eyes landed on me. The dominance that radiated off him was almost too much, making me want to bow my head. Tallis moved directly behind me, his warm presence keeping me steady.

"I found your sister in the woods, Alpha Davon." Kade bowed to Sana's brother, the simple gesture cementing what he had already told us.

"It's true then," Sana asked, her tone almost light. "Father is dead?"

Davon gave her a curt nod.

"How?"

"Heart attack," he said in a matter-of-fact tone. The casual way the two spoke of their kin and his death made me grimace. I shuddered to think of the horrors they must have survived as pups to feel nothing for their father's death.

"Interesting," Sana said. "I was convinced he didn't have a heart."

A smirk slowly spread across Davon's face, and he crossed his arms. "You actually smell like an alpha. How did you manage that?"

Sana crossed her arms, mimicking his stance. "Your mother has been poisoning me."

"Is she *my* mother?" he asked with an amused lilt in his voice.

Sana laughed. "From now on, she's all yours."

Davon barked out a mighty chuckle, taking some of the tension out of the conversation.

I half-expected her to tell him the awful truth about her parentage, but the easy feeling rolling off her told me she wasn't going to. *I guess some secrets aren't worth sharing.*

"These are my mates," Sana said, motioning to me, then Tallis. Davon nodded quickly but didn't extend his hand or greet us properly. "I just wanted to see you before moving on. Let you know that I have no intention of going back to Casin. So if Mother wants to continue looking for me—"

"Say no more." Davon held up his hand. "While I don't agree with how you chose to abandon your duties, it seems everything has somehow worked out."

Awareness made my skin tingle, and I glanced at the guards around us. It seemed that every wolf in the camp was glaring at Tallis, ready to attack the second the order was given. I leaned into him, wanting to shield him from their tense glares. It was stupid, but I still tried.

"There will be no fight here." Davon gave a wave of his hand, making his men stand down. "I think we can all agree enough have died."

Kade nodded quickly, and several others followed suit. But a few older guards snarled and growled as they stalked off. I released a long breath of relief, then glanced up at Tallis. He looked a little disappointed at losing the opportunity for a fight.

"Would you like to see your father, My Lady?" Kade asked. I didn't miss the way Davon's body tensed.

"He's here?" she asked, a little shocked.

"He passed away in Hund Valley while visiting your sister, Luna Emmy."

Sana pressed her hand to her chest and whispered, "*Luna* Emmy? Our tiny baby sister is a Luna?"

Davon gave her an exasperated look. "You should see her," he said. "She's fierce."

"Is she really?" Shock laced Sana's tone. "Our fragile little Emmy? The omega who cried in the kitchens and hid behind doors?"

"The very same," Davon said. "Come." He held out his hand, motioning for Sana to walk ahead of him. "I'll take you to our father, then you can be on your way."

I stayed right on their heels. I half expected a guard to pull us back or block our way, but I was thankful when no one did. Sana was my mate, and I'd be damned if I let her out of my sight. The intense emotions pouring off Tallis told me he felt the same.

A large wooden wagon sat near the edge of the woods, covered in dried grass and herbs. The thick spread of flowers that draped over the body did nothing to hide the scent of rot drifting toward us. A tight circle of guards surrounded the entire area, giving us narrowed curious looks. The numerous alphas smelled thick with anger and grief, and my feet slowed as we approached, not sure if I could handle so many dominant odors.

"I've got you," Tallis whispered, encircling his big hand around my upper arm. His hold was soft but reassuring.

Two guards bowed low to Sana's brother, then parted, letting us through. Sana hooked her foot into a spoke of a wheel then pulled herself up, peering down at the wrapped figure.

"His face, hands, and feet have already been bound in linen and wax," Davon said. "I'm sorry you can't see his face."

"This feels fake," she whispered, brushing her fingertips over a bundle of lavender. A flutter of sadness pushed through our bond, and Tallis and I both squeezed our connection, letting her know we were right here.

"I need to see if it's him," Sana said to her brother. "I need to know for a fact he's there."

Davon turned to his guard, ordering the whole circle to take several steps away from them. His eyes fell to Tallis, and both alphas tensed, an unspoken challenge passing between them.

Sana flung her hand out, smacking her brother in the stomach. "Stop glaring at my mates," she snapped. "They're your kin now, and they aren't going anywhere."

Davon snarled at Tallis, then turned his back to us. He moved slowly, removing the grass and flowers out of the way, then pulling a linen shroud off the body's torso. I craned my neck, trying to see. Just visible over the flowers was a fancy blue vest with a paisley pattern made of gold thread.

"He loved that damn vest," Sana snorted.

"Yes." Davon nodded. "It seemed like a good choice."

"I used to sneak into his closet as a pup and pop the buttons off."

An unintentional laugh pushed from Davon's throat, and he coughed quickly to hide it.

"Can I see his scar?" she asked.

Gold buttons were unfastened, and Davon exposed his father's chest. An old, long scar ran over the dead alpha's breastbone. It had an unusual pattern, healing in a splintered fashion that twisted and turned like the roots of a tree. Sana brushed her fingertips over it, and I stumbled back. She was bursting with so much grief and rage.

"It's okay," Tallis whispered, hugging me to his side. But I wasn't sure if he was talking to me or Sana.

Sana's fingers hesitated over the edge of his open vest, then she slowly pulled it open. Her hand jerked back, and Davon moved quickly to pull his father's vest closed. Sana abruptly turned and hopped down from the wheel, her whole body tight. She rushed toward me, pulling me away from Tallis and enveloping me in a crushing hug.

"Are you okay?" I whispered, circling my arms around her middle.

She didn't answer, simply breaking the hug and pulling in a sharp breath to steady herself.

"Come," Davon said, placing his hand on Sana's elbow. He pulled her toward a large, ornate tent. I rushed after them, unable to figure out the growing fear bubbling inside her and the rage twisting inside Tallis. *Had he seen something I couldn't?*

The inside of the tent was comfortable and lush. A thick pallet covered the center, stacked high with furs, quilts, and pillows. I hadn't seen something so soft and inviting in over a year, and the urge to burrow into it pulled hard inside my chest.

"Heart attack?" Sana whispered harshly to her brother, her tone as sharp as her fangs.

Davon glared at Tallis. "I'd like to have this conversation *without* an audience."

"Too fucking bad," Sana snarled. "They aren't going anywhere. Now what the hell happened?"

Davon flashed his teeth, leaning into Sana's space. "Keep your fucking voice down."

She didn't back down from his anger, stepping a bit closer. I edged behind Tallis's big body and reached for the hilt of my dagger.

"*You* chose to run away, Sana," Davon snarled.

She tipped her head back and narrowed her eyes, not backing down.

"*You* abandoned your family and your duty and those who remained had to fix it. *I* was left to fix all of it. Our father's spiraling mind. Our mother's thick rage. Our relations with Hund Valley. *I fixed it.* You don't get to look at me with any kind of accusation in your eyes when you dumped all of it in my lap."

Sana's fists curled tight, and her voice dropped to barely a whisper, "Did you stab him or—"

"You don't get to ask any more questions," Davon said in a firm tone. "I made the choices I had to. Mother, Father, Emmy. We are all paying for your freedom."

"Am I truly free?" Sana asked. "Are you going to send guards to track me all throughout Havre?"

"I don't have the fucking time, men, or energy for that," Davon snapped before turning and plopping into a plush chair. He leaned against the high back, his long legs stretching out over the ornate carpet.

Sana pressed her lips together. "Mother might disagree with you on that. I'm sure she'll have plenty of energy to track me down."

Confusion pulled Davon's brows together. "Why?"

"I killed Tamen."

Her brother's eyes widened with shock before melting into amusement. A big grin split his face, and he leaned forward. "Does Mother know it was you?"

"Oh yeah." She nodded, pulling a face. "She was there."

Davon laughed loud, the barking noise making me flinch. "Well, I guess it's a good thing you won't be returning to Casin. That old woman loved her toys, and I do believe Tamen was her favorite."

An amused look passed between them, something familial and affectionate. The kind of bond only siblings had.

"Well," Sana sighed, "I'm sorry about Father. It must have been shocking to find such a powerful alpha had succumbed to a heart attack of all things," she said, giving in to her brother's lie. "And I'm sorry I won't be able to help you with the burial services back home, but it's time I moved on."

Some of the tension left Davon's shoulders, and he bowed his head quickly. "Thank you."

Sana reached for my hand, squeezing it softly. "I'm sure there will be many questions when you return home."

Davon narrowed his eyes at the tent's entrance. "I'm ready to answer to anyone with the balls to question me."

Sana nodded, then pulled me with her as she marched toward the exit. Tallis pulled at the tent flap as Davon called out, stopping her. "Where will you go?" She narrowed her eyes, refusing to answer. "I have no intention of tracking you," he said. "I just want to make sure you're safe."

"I am safe." She gave Tallis a knowing smile. He returned it, looking down at her with fierce pride. "But if you must know, I'm going to see Emmy. Because while you may hesitate to anger Hund Valley, I don't give a shit. If she looks anything less than blissful, I plan to burn the whole fucking village down to get her out of there."

# CHAPTER THIRTY-TWO

## *hund valley*

Sana

THE SIZE OF HUND VALLEY WAS ALMOST SHOCKING. IT MORE closely resembled a city rather than a were-village. My old home was a collection of redwood cabins built on dirt roads with border walls that were visible from all sides. The city before me was strikingly different, and as much as I hated to admit it, it was intimidating.

The streets were paved with cobblestone, and most of the storefronts were either a pale oak or painted white. The guards at the front gate carefully checked over our necks for any indication we were rogues. Tallis gripped the strap of the satchel hard, not breathing until they gave him the okay to enter. Cyrus and I had convinced the alpha to cut his hair short, and he shaved as close as he could with Cyrus's dagger before approaching the village, just in case any wanted notices had been sent this far west.

"So what's the plan?" Tallis asked, scratching nervously at his shorn hair. Cyrus grabbed his hand, squeezing it affectionately. I could feel the big alpha ease at the omega's touch.

I narrowed my eyes just past the market. "I plan to walk up to the packhouse door and knock."

Tallis whipped his head around to me. "That's it?"

"I'm here to visit my sister, not storm the castle and steal the queen." A twinge of fear twisted in my gut. What would I do if she wasn't as happy as Davon claimed? Could I get her out of here? Would she even want to go?

Cyrus grabbed my hand as well, rubbing his thumb in gentle circles. "She's okay here. I can feel it."

"What makes you say that?" I asked, needing some of his certainty.

"Look around, doll." His eyes swept over the storefronts and cabins in the distance. "The omegas here don't hide."

I glanced around, really noticing the pack this time. Two young omegas arranged flowers in a shop while an alpha watched them with a loving gaze. Another omega giggled wildly as she left a bakery with her mate. He pressed a quick kiss to her neck, making her complexion darken around her cheeks. And a gaggle of elder omegas sat in a park, knitting and chatting loudly.

It was so odd to see them all exposed and out in the open.

"Are the alphas not scared their mates will be stolen?" I whispered in disbelief.

"Guards," Tallis whispered, his tone tense. And he was right. There were guards everywhere. Alphas and betas. They strolled leisurely, checking over the village, their eyes lingering protectively over the omegas as they went. It all seemed so safe. And it set me on edge.

"It's not a trick," Cyrus whispered in my ear. "Sometimes happiness is just that. It's not a mask to hide pain."

I nodded, but I still wasn't about to let my guard down. "I hope Emmy loves it here," I whispered, watching a couple of pups battle with two long flower stems. "She deserves a bit of happiness."

We moved quickly through the village. Past the shops and market, through the town square, cutting between several gardens filled with bundles of lavender and bright white and yellow lilies.

"Now that's a packhouse," Cyrus said in awe, taking in the enormous building in front of us. I had to agree.

"Half their pack could live in there," Tallis snorted.

"What business do you have here?" An incredibly tall alpha marched toward us with tense shoulders and a very straight back. He had long black hair, and his eyes appeared to glow purple before fading back to a soft dark color.

Tallis stood tall, a pleased smirk lifting one side of his mouth at seeing he was ever so slightly taller.

"I have business with Luna Emmy," I said, smoothing my hand down the front of my shirt. I wished I was wearing something other than a Casin service uniform, but ultimately it didn't matter. Emmy would just be happy to see me...*I hoped.*

"Is the Luna expecting you?" The guard narrowed his eyes.

"She's not," I said, hoping he wouldn't send me away. "Please tell her..." I swallowed hard, fear pounding hard in my chest.

"Her sister is here to see her," Cyrus said for me. "Lady Sana of Casin."

The purple-eyed guard stared hard at my face before finally speaking. "Stay here." He waved to a guard walking along the side of the packhouse. The guard's head snapped to, and he ran toward us. "Watch them. If they move even an inch, don't hesitate to attack."

The young alpha cocked a smile and crossed his arms, assessing us. He looked a little excited at the prospect of a brawl. Tallis's expression mimicked the youngling's, as the two just silently stared at one another.

We waited quietly, the minutes feeling like hours. My nerves were too shot for conversation, so I just looked at the rows upon rows of windows. Could Emmy be in one of those rooms right now?

"What do you want with my mate?" A tan alpha with shaggy dark hair walked briskly toward us. Rin looked the same as he did that day in the garden. *The last time I saw Emmy.* And now he was her mate.

*Her mate...*it was still so hard to believe.

I forced my mouth to lift into a smile. "I wish to see my sister."

"It's a little late to pretend to care about her well-being, isn't it?" Rin snarled, and Tallis stiffened next to me.

The alpha's words cut through me, and I clenched my jaw. Over the last several weeks, I had prepared myself to accept that she might not want to see me. But now, standing just outside the packhouse, the desperate need to see her sweet face was almost painful. I just needed to *see* her. Just once. Even from a distance.

"Your mother said you died the morning we were to be mated," Rin snarled, crossing his arms over his thick chest. Tallis immediately did the same, puffing out his chest to appear bigger. He didn't have to try hard. "Care to tell me what the fuck really happened?"

I narrowed my eyes, wondering if he spoke to Emmy the same way. "Is my sister here or not?"

"Leave," he commanded, nodding at the purple-eyed alpha.

Cyrus held up his hands as the guard took a step toward me. "Please," he bowed his head in a respectful manner, "Alpha Rin, we just—"

"Leave!" Rin's eyes glowed red, and his fangs lengthened. Cyrus trembled, and I pulled his arm, forcing him behind me.

"Is this how you treat omegas?" I snarled. "Where the fuck is my sister?"

Rin's upper lip curled upward, displaying his fangs. "She is none of your concern."

"Sana!"

I spun around at the sound of Emmy's voice, and my heart burst with so much regret and fear and love. The small omega raced toward me. Her short legs pumped wildly, kicking up the hem of her dress with a brilliant smile consuming her pretty face. She flung her arms out, hitting me full on and forcing both of us onto the ground.

Tears burst out of her, crying freely as she snuggled deep into my neck. I couldn't help but laugh. She was mated—a Luna—but she was still my sensitive baby sister.

"Sana," she mumbled against my throat. "You came! You're actually here. You came!"

"I never meant for this to happen." I sat up, hugging her even tighter. Her chestnut brown hair smelled so sweet, like spun honey. It was far more intense than I remembered. "I went back for you, sweetheart. I went back to save you, but you were already gone."

"Really?" Emmy leaned back, her big brown eyes brimming with so much happiness. "You didn't...leave me...on purpose?"

"Never!" I cupped her cheeks. "You were underage, I

never even considered that they'd force you into a mating. I mean, what kind of wolf mates a pup?" I glared at Rin. He snarled but didn't rip Emmy from my arms. It surprised me.

"Rin's not like that," Emmy said, looking over her shoulder at her mate. There was so much affection in her sparkling brown eyes, and Rin's tense expression softened. It was hard to imagine him caring for her properly, but she seemed so relaxed in his presence. Emmy was always so nervous around alphas. It was odd.

"Rin," Emmy stood, pulling me toward her mate, "this is my sister, Sana. Sana, this is my mate, Rin."

He gave me a curt nod, not moving to shake my hand. I ignored him, looking down at Emmy. She seemed somehow smaller since the last time I saw her.

"This is Tallis and Cyrus. My mates." I motioned to both of them, and I couldn't help but puff out my chest with a bit of pride. They were both so strong and beautiful. I didn't deserve them.

Surprise flashed across Emmy's face before she blinked and exchanged a shy glance with Cyrus. Then, as if a silent understanding passed between them, they hugged. Cyrus stooped a bit, while Emmy stood on her tiptoes. Cyrus smiled wide, squeezing her around the middle. I eyed Rin, ready to defend my omega if he saw their connection as an offense, but I was surprised to see him watching my sister with a gentle smile.

"I'm so happy to meet you both." Emmy squeezed Tallis's waist. Rin growled, but she ignored him, squeezing Tallis even harder. My mate stood stiff, patting the top of her shoulder with uncertainty. I had to press my lips together to keep from laughing.

Emmy turned to me with so much joy, then her smile faded, a shadow drifting over her lovely features.

"What's wrong?" Rin was instantly at her side. His hand ghosted over her back, not quite touching her.

"Sana," Emmy whispered. "Father..." she swallowed hard, "he passed away."

It took everything in me not to smile. Emmy's relationship with the old man wasn't any better than mine, but she was soft and sweet, and my joy would more than likely cut her.

"I know." I took her hands in mine. "We crossed paths with Davon. I saw him."

"Are you okay?" she asked, her big eyes searching mine. It was so odd to have her caring for me. That was my job.

Giving Rin a cautious glance, I leaned down and whispered in her ear, "Is he good to you? Does he hurt you?"

She stood on her toes, speaking softly, "He's the best thing that's ever happened to me."

I hugged her tight as my heart burst with relief and happiness. Emmy was a shit liar, and her scent was still light and sweet, confirming just how happy she was. Rin balled up his fists as if wanting to snatch her way from me, but he kept his distance, letting us hold one another. Most alphas didn't give a shit what their omegas wanted, but he seemed to be moving carefully, not wanting to upset her.

Perhaps Emmy wasn't so helpless here after all.

"You must stay." Emmy tipped her chin up to look in my face. Tears dripped off her chin, and her nose was red and shiny.

"I don't think your mate would be very happy having me break bread at his table."

She turned to Rin, seeking his approval. His hard glare stayed on me for a moment before shifting his gaze to Emmy. She smiled wide at him, her soft energy making the air sweet. "Please, alpha. It would make me so happy."

For a brief moment he seemed to hold his breath, as if weighing the options of having someone like me at his dinner table versus disappointing his mate. Finally, he let out a long sigh, his exterior cracking. "Fine," he said, nodding at the purple-eyed alpha. The guard marched off into the packhouse, probably to let the kitchens know.

"Emmy," I whispered, not sure if I should accept her invitation or not. I felt like such a failure. I fucked everything up for everyone, but managed to do enough right that I couldn't even redeem myself. While I didn't exactly deserve death, I definitely didn't deserve her hospitality or kindness.

As if sensing my rejection of her offer, Emmy's eyes dimmed a bit. "Please, Sana. I've missed you so much. And," she smiled at Cyrus. "I want to get to know your omega. Please, stay for a bit." Her big eyes held mine, begging me.

"Of course we'll stay," Cyrus spoke up, his face bright with joy. "And I don't want to hear anything from you two." He eyed me, then Tallis. Tallis's jaw was so tight, I could practically hear his teeth grind together. "Once we leave, it'll be days before we have an offer of a hot meal, and I'm not wasting it."

Emmy beamed, practically bouncing on her toes. She hugged Cyrus hard around the middle, then hooked her arm through his, moving up the walkway to the packhouse. "You must tell me how you met my sister and how you fell in love," she said, looking at my omega with so much sisterly affection. Rin smiled at her expression, walking directly behind them.

Tallis and I shared a soft look as our mate walked excitedly with Emmy.

I didn't know what our future held, which was so

exciting and new. But today I would dine with all the most precious people in my world.

And tomorrow, I would take my mates to see the ocean.

---

Need more **Sana**, **Cyrus**, and **Tallis**? Sign up for my newsletter at kittlynn.com to get access to a sexy *epilogue* of Sana putting her mark on Tallis.

# *need more?*

Want to find out what happens when Davon meets his future-mate, Calla, and finds her not to be the proper omega he expected. Preorder their story, Davon's Salvation.

**Also By Kitt Lynn**

_also by kitt lynn_

### The Hund Valley Series

An Alpha's Promise

Fated

Feral

Tethered

### The Blushing Moon Trilogy

Until The Moon Ends

The Blue Path

Broken Stars

### The Casin Village Series

Sana's Escape

Davon's Salvation

Demi's Guardian

### The Broken Omega Series

The Last Rose

Violet Flames

Threats of Jasmine

### The Madra Series

A Winter Gift

Spring Blossoms

Ruined Summer

**Novellas**

A Cure for Loneliness

Kiss Me For Christmas

## THANK YOU FOR READING!

It means so much to me that you read my little book. I hope you enjoyed this story as much as I enjoyed writing it. If you did, it would be so lovely if you could write a short review on your favorite book website. Reviews are so important for authors and even just a single line can make a big difference. Thank you so much!

# *about the author*

Kitt lives in Oklahoma with her husband and stacks on stacks on stacks of fantasy books. She writes not-so-exciting technical things in her "real" job but lives for the evenings when she can visit her paper friends in their magical worlds.

She is obsessed with fantasy, fairylands, love stories, and horror in general. If you dig these things then you might enjoy her books. You can find pictures of her sweet puppies, her coffee obsession, and the ridiculous things she says to keep herself motivated on her Instagram @kittlynnauthor.

Join my free newsletter to enter giveaways and receive exclusive content! Please visit
kittlynn.com